THE PRESCOTT DIARIES

DIONA L. REEVES

CHAPTER 1

Headlights bobbed against the slick mountain roadway as Jacqueline Darcy sped along.

Five. That was the death count for Prescott's roadways this year. The record was eight. With New Year's a little more than a week away, there was no chance it would hold. Drunk drivers took to these winding roads like they were part of the racing circuit, only to realize too late their vulnerability.

Jaq's radio crackled as a piano rendition gave way to a choir-driven Christmas carol. The lead singer belted the first bar, her melodic voice overtaking the instruments and filling the car with hope and love.

Jaq snapped the dial to the left. There was nothing cheery about being out here on the frozen roadway this time of night.

She rounded the s-shaped curves, her car hugging the center white line. Prescott natives knew how to maneuver this roadway, even in the snow and ice. City people, not so much.

Just last week, two vehicles collided on a similar stretch, neither driver heeding the weather warnings. The first, in a cherry-red sports something-or-other, walked away. But only after introducing his hood to a large Sugar Maple. The other hadn't fared much better, his shell of metal and glass unrecognizable by the time Jaq arrived.

Thankfully, her job that day was to document just the car bodies. No obituaries to write, no follow-up with loved ones distressed beyond consolation. Both drivers were fortunate to return to their normal lives, even if they did not appreciate this fact at the time.

A deer stood near the edge of the roadway, and Jaq eased off the gas. The animal's eyes flickered in her headlights before it bolted for the thicket of pines.

She dug her fingernails into the steering wheel, not caring that they left pits in the faux leather. This was all Dahlia's fault. Thirty minutes ago, Jaq was at her cousin's, eating pizza and watching her favorite movie. All was well with the world. And then her phone buzzed. Over and over, not even the cinematic tones reverberating through Samantha's stereo system enough to mask its rattling on the coffee table.

Jaq stepped into the hallway as the movie's soundtrack hit a crescendo and the lead character descended from the skies.

"Miss Darcy! O.M.G."

"Dahlia..."

"I lost my pass! I don't know how. It was in my bag... Yesterday. And now it's gone. Ethan's gonna kill me!"

Jaq stifled a laugh. Their boss would have to be sober for that to happen. Two days before Christmas? Doubtful. "Dahlia, it's okay. We can get you another one after—"

"It can't wait, Miss Darcy. I'm at a scene downtown, and the cops won't let me through."

Jaq gritted her teeth. She never should have agreed to cover for Ethan over the holiday break. Not with Dahlia the only other reporter working. "Tell me where you are," she said. So much for her night off.

"I'm at The Cornelia. You know where that is, right?"

The Cornelia was where Cara Worthington lived.

With her ex-boyfriend Ben.

Jaq clenched her fists and said she'd be there as soon as possible.

Dahlia squealed her thanks, and Jaq ended the call before she could change her mind.

"Would it have killed you to hit pause?" she asked as she re-entered the living room, significantly more irritated than before.

Sam shrugged and reached for the remote. "We can go back."

"Don't bother." Jaq scanned the space. A half-eaten bag of popcorn sat propped against the couch. Two pizza boxes and a handful of empty cans littered the coffee table.

"Dahlia?" Sam asked.

"Yeah." Jaq retrieved her keys from beneath a grease-soaked paper towel. "You know, it takes a special kind of person to lose their press pass."

Sam leaned forward just enough to set her beer can on the table. "Just ignore her," she said and stretched her arms high into the air. "When's Ethan back again?"

"Sometime next week." Jaq yanked her coat off the back of Sam's recliner. "You seen my boots anywhere?"

Sam watched Jaq stumble over a throw pillow that had fallen to the floor. She yawned and leaned against the couch arm before muttering something about the fireplace.

Jaq glared at her cousin. "You really are a jerk."

Sam grinned. "And you are way too uptight. I'm telling you, let Ethan deal with this crap when he gets back. It's bad enough you're stuck covering for him over Christmas."

"Don't tempt me." Jaq surveyed the mess. "You good?"

Sam nodded and ramped up the stereo, leaving Jaq to face the icy night on her own.

She continued along the lonely highway, seeking the telltale gloss of black ice. She should be at Sam's right now, all warm and toasty as they switched from one movie to the next. Not fighting to keep her car off the embankment as she headed downtown to deal with who-knows-what.

But she had agreed to take charge while her boss was on vacation, and that meant dealing with work even when it ruined her plans.

The road shimmered twenty feet ahead, frozen liquid hiding in plain sight. Jaq downshifted as she braced for another curve.

It was going to be a long night.

CHAPTER 2

ನಾನಾ

The buildings of downtown Prescott lit up the sky as Jaq made her final descent. The stoplight at the bottom of the hill switched from yellow to red, and Jaq eased off the gas, resisting the urge to slam the brake pedal to the floorboard.

Her car skidded forward anyway, and she jerked the steering wheel to control the skid. Finally, she came to a stop, her arms on fire and her knuckles locked around the steering wheel as her car idled in the intersection. If anyone attempted a left turn off Murphy right now, her car would fare no better than the ones she photographed last week.

Jaq pumped the gas and slammed the shifter in reverse. Her tires spun, refusing to gain traction. "Dammit!" She pounded her fists against the steering wheel. She had no business being out here. Not on a night like this.

As if on cue, thick flakes floated in the sky, glimmering against the beam of headlights.

Jaq gripped the wheel once more and gradually accelerated, her back tires slipping as she propelled forward. The tail-end of her car kicked to the right, and she narrowly missed a truck abandoned on the shoulder. She wrenched the wheel straight and finally made it through the intersection.

She straightened the nose of her car and crept forward in low gear. As she neared downtown, the slush gave way to a filmy brine, the road still slippery but not so perilous. The salt trucks had done their job downtown, at least.

Jaq eased into second gear and picked up speed. She passed office buildings and newly built townhomes, their silvery lights filling her windshield. Christmas wreaths hung from lampposts, thin layers of snow coating their crimson bows. A banner from last weekend's Christmas parade flapped in the breeze, welcoming her to downtown Prescott.

The landscape evolved with each passing year, but the recent changes outweighed anything she ever envisioned for her town. Small, dated high-rises had given way to condos and luxury apartments. Historical buildings morphed from near dilapidation to pristine elegance. All courtesy of Lawrence Worthington and his family's conglomerate.

Jaq's head pounded as she slowed for the next light. The Worthingtons were a cancer, taking root and gobbling up everything good. She didn't care how much their business invested in Prescott, or its claims of bringing "the nightlife to the mountains." Just because Great Grandmother Cornelia grew up on land that formed the riverfront did *not* make them the founding family. Prescott was a collaborative effort, a group of pioneers unafraid to venture from the resources and populace that formed most Georgia cities.

Yet, many of the locals—people she always assumed held similar values—shifted their priorities when the Worthington family returned. People she once respected, like Calvin Miller, owner of Derringer's Sporting Goods, and Sandra Watkins from Treats Galore, no longer spent their energy on serving the locals. They were too busy chasing photo ops with Cara or Lawrence to further their social media presence.

When the real estate branch of Lawrence's company snatched up acres of prime real estate north of the city, no one in town questioned the motives. No one except Jaq.

She frowned. Others might chalk up the Worthington acquisitions to a love of Prescott, but benevolence and altruism were nothing more than talking points coined by media consultants. Lawrence Worthington took what he wanted, with no regard for who he trampled on.

Like his purchase of a dilapidated hotel in the heart of downtown. It had nothing to do with saving Prescott or even expanding the family business. Appointing Cara to renovate it was nothing more than a father's attempt to keep his youngest child out of rehab.

Jaq gripped the steering wheel again, her emotions as white-hot as the poker she used to stir embers in her fireplace. Of all the places to spread their influence and wealth, the Worthingtons had chosen her peaceful town. And nothing had been the same since their arrival.

If only they had stayed in New York! Prescott might be on the verge of extinction, but she could have salvaged the family homestead. Maybe even salvaged her relationship with Ben.

The light changed, and Jaq slammed her foot into the gas pedal, not caring if her car drifted. Why couldn't it be Cara's face she stomped? That woman was the root of so much wrong in her world.

Her pace slowed as she neared downtown. Police cars and news vans lined both sides of the street. Jaq waited for a van to finish parking, and scooted through, her passenger-side mirror barely missing the driver as he climbed out. He hollered in her direction and waved his fist, but she ignored him and drove on.

A group of reporters huddled on the sidewalk, their fur-lined parkas zipped to their chins. Cameramen stood nearby, clutching their gear in gloved hands as they waited for their signal to record. They looked more prepared for a trip to the Arctic Circle than an assignment in the North Georgia mountains.

Up ahead was The Cornelia, aptly named after the Worthington matriarch. A reporter from Channel Eleven stood before the large, glowing welcome sign, speaking into the camera as Jaq drove by, looking every bit as frozen as her colleagues.

A Sheriff's deputy stepped out of the shadows and waved his flashlight in her direction.

Jaq came to a stop and put the car in park.

Red and blue strobe lights spun just beyond the man's head. He was heavyset, in his mid- to late-fifties, if thinning gray hair combed to hide the signs of baldness was any indicator of age. He was new to the area—handpicked from somewhere down south to join her uncle at the Sheriff's Office—but Jaq had spoken to him last week at the accident scene. A quick glance at the breast of his uniform confirmed his name was Jenkins.

Jaq rolled down the window and flashed her press pass.

"Miss Darcy," he said, shifting the flashlight away from her face and leaning against her door. "I figured you'd get here eventually."

"Definitely not how I wanted to spend my evening." Jaq tucked the pass in her coat pocket. A few flakes trickled through the cracked window and landed on her leggings. She flicked them away before they could soak through the fabric.

"It's a cold one, that's for sure." He cast his light toward the sky. "Shoot, I can't remember a time it got this cold so early..."

The weather in the North Georgia mountains was a mixed bag this time of year, but it was not the time for a debate. Jaq nodded in the hotel's direction. "What can you tell me?"

Jenkins smacked on a wad of gum as he spoke. "You know Morales, don't you?"

Jaq nodded. Morales had worked with her uncle for years.

"Park there," Jenkins said, swinging his flashlight beyond her hood, toward an opening several cars ahead. "Then go find Morales. He should be able to help."

He stepped aside, and Jaq wedged her car between a pickup truck and a news van. She grabbed her camera bag from the backseat and climbed out.

Jenkins wasn't kidding about the cold. Frigid air slapped Jaq's cheeks and her lungs burned as she struggled to catch her breath. She crossed the street, her steps deliberate. Every reporter in town was at the scene. And Veronica Daniels, with *The Beacon*, would love nothing more than to see her competition splayed across the sidewalk.

Jaq sidestepped a patch of ice. The reporter in front of the sign had retreated, and she stopped there to assess her surroundings. Gazing at the six-story hotel, she hated to admit it, but Cara's impeccable taste had breathed life into a dying structure. Modern, white-washed brick with a hint of black trim served as the perfect replacement for a once-faded exterior. Lights gleamed from the entryway, a mixture of high-end fixtures and glass more reminiscent of Atlanta than a getaway retreat.

A miniature city with a mountain view. A place to visit for the holidays or enjoy the lakefront in the summer. That's what the Worthington brand promised, its marketing campaigns filling the papers and the airwaves.

Jaq felt the familiar flush of anger. The Cornelia was a monstrosity detracting from the natural beauty of Prescott. The Worthington public relations team could spin it all they wanted, but the renovations did nothing but promote a packaged experience to the upper echelon while Prescott's residents—and the small-town vibe she'd grown up with—deteriorated in its wake.

Rumors were already circling about Cara's next project, a bistro down the street from the hotel. No wonder Ben bought into it all. For someone looking to make a name for himself, Cara was the perfect blend of celebrity and wealth.

Jaq's skin bristled beneath the thick layers of her coat, and she forced herself to focus on the surroundings. Now was not the time to dwell on her feelings of betrayal and loss.

She noted the crowd of reporters gathered nearby, like bees swarming a hive. Dahlia hadn't provided much in the way of details, but one thing was clear. Whatever happened here must involve Cara. Only she could draw a crowd like this at one o'clock in the morning on the coldest night of the year.

Jaq pulled her coat snug and tucked her head down to avoid the wind. She shoved her hands in her pockets, and her camera bag beat against her shoulder as she headed for the entrance.

Maybe now Ben would see Cara for what she really was... Trouble, parading around in thousand-dollar boots.

CHAPTER 3

ನುನ್ನು

The symphony of lights outside The Cornelia grew brighter. Uniformed deputies stood behind yellow crime tape, a wall against the throng of reporters vying for information.

"Can't you tell us anything?" a high-pitched voice demanded.

Jaq recognized its owner before she placed her in the crowd. Six feet tall and dressed in heavy, fur-lined boots and a red trench coat, Veronica was impossible to miss.

"Have you identified the victim?" another reporter shouted. His head bobbed behind Veronica's towering figure, his features animated as he tried to speak above the din. "Is it Cara Worthington?"

The deputies turned their backs to the crowd, refusing to entertain the media's questions.

Jaq pulled her camera bag closer to her chest, like it was a shield. Hiding behind a lens kept her out of the fray, but is also served another purpose: giving the victims time to recuperate. Others might run with whatever information they retrieved, but Jaq's mindset was "question everything." It meant longer turnaround times, but she refused to print anything that wasn't vetted.

Prescott might be small, but its residents deserved the truth.

Jaq slipped the hood of her coat over her head and squeezed by. Gathering information at the scene was not her concern tonight, but it *was* Dahlia's. Where was she?

Jaq squinted as she tried to make out individual faces beneath the winter garb. No Dahlia. She scanned the line of vehicles parked along the street but did not see her there either.

Jaq walked alongside the yellow tape to the alleyway behind the hotel. It was dim and quiet, the commotion confined to the main entrance. She squinted as her eyes adjusted. Dumpsters stood side-by-side to her left, with several cars in makeshift parking spots beyond them.

There was a rustling in the shadows, and Jaq jerked her head around as a hand grazed her arm.

"Oh, geez, Miss Darcy. I'm so sorry. I didn't mean to make you jump."

Jaq took a step backward, her boots slipping on the wet pavement. She wobbled before catching herself. The smell of ammonia filled the air, and she cursed as she lifted her right boot, hoping urine was the only thing she stepped in.

Dahlia didn't seem to notice. "Thanks for helping me out," she said, about ten feet away but coming closer.

Jaq stepped to the side, worried Dahlia might hug her.

Dahlia stopped in front of Jaq. She was draped in a long army green coat, zipped to her chin. Her cheeks were the color of wild salmon. "I can't believe I lost my pass," she said, staring at Jaq with large brown eyes. "I mean, what an idiot!"

Jaq stared back, not sure how to respond. Their press passes had their names and photos on them. She couldn't just hand hers over, even if she wanted to.

"I don't know what I'm going to do. Do you, Miss Darcy?" Dahlia's mousy brown curls bobbed as she spoke, making her seem closer to sixteen than twenty-something. "My first big assignment, and I blow it!"

Jaq held her gaze, determined to concentrate on her protégé and not the substance soiling her boot. Icy air gusted through the tiny alleyway, and Dahlia shivered.

Just how long had she waited before calling for help?

Movement above Dahlia's head caught Jaq's eye. Window after window across the top floor of The Cornelia filled with a warm glow. Whatever happened had occurred in Cara's penthouse.

"Did you get any information?" Jaq asked. She pointed to the hotel. "I assume this is about Cara..."

"Cara and her boyfriend." Dahlia retrieved a small notebook from inside her coat and fumbled through both pockets, finally producing a penlight.

Jaq willed herself to be patient.

Dahlia flipped open the notebook with one hand and centered the light over the pages with the other. She leaned forward, her eyes resembling the slots at the local arcade as she fumbled to read her handwriting. "A Benjamin... Reynolds?" She gazed up at the lights in Cara's penthouse, thinking. "No, that's not right..."

Jaq gritted her teeth. "Rutherford," she said through pursed lips. "Cara's boyfriend is Benjamin Rutherford."

"Right."

Jaq held her tongue. Ethan had better enjoy his vacation because he was getting an earful when he returned.

"I didn't talk to the manager. Couldn't get past the police tape, remember? I caught one of the deputies—Morales—as he was grabbing a smoke." She pointed to an ashtray near the side of the hotel. "Ever met him? He's kinda cute. Said he works for Andy something-or-other."

Jaq dug her fingernails into her palms, oblivious to the sting of cutting flesh. She could forgive Dahlia for not knowing Ben was her ex. That was personal and had nothing to do with work. But there was absolutely no excuse for her not to know Andy—the Sheriff—was her uncle.

Dahlia re-positioned the light as she flipped more pages. "Chuck Reynolds—so *that's* why I had the name wrong!—is the manager here. He saw Ms. Worthington and, uh, Mr. Rutherford entering the building around nine."

Dahlia swung the light toward the hotel, and Jaq used every ounce of restraint she had to stifle a scream. She didn't need Dahlia to spell out the obvious. She needed her to get to the point!

Dahlia returned to her notebook. "The manager said Miss Worthington was carrying a takeout box. Smelled like steak and lobster when they walked by the front desk. Morales told me—"

"Surf and turf," Jaq said, as much to herself as to Dahlia. She unclenched her hands. Finally, they were getting somewhere.

Dahlia nodded and snapped her notebook shut. "That's all I got."

Jaq's stomach churned at the thought of Ben being wined and dined by Cara, but she ignored it. Objectivity was a journalist's best friend in situations like this, and the only way to extricate herself from whatever mess she had stumbled into, literally *and* figuratively.

Jaq fought the urge to scrape her boot against a dumpster. "Focus on the five W's," she said. If Dahlia asked what those were, she was going to lost it right there in the alleyway.

But Dahlia simply nodded, her curls bouncing in that oh-so-annoying way. "Okay," she said, scrunching her face as she thought it over. "The 'Who' we know. Cara and Benjamin."

Jaq nodded as her stomach roiled in protest. Would it ever stop hurting to hear Ben's name paired with Cara's?

"And the 'When' is now. This evening. At least, that's what Morales told me."

Jaq motioned for Dahlia to keep going.

"That leaves 'What' and 'Why'..." Dahlia chewed on the tip of her pen, thinking.

They wouldn't have an answer for "What" until the police completed their investigation, but the "Why" was no mystery. Cara had been admitted to the hospital more than once for an overdose. It was still undetermined whether those incidents were accidental.

A spark of hope lifted Jaq's spirits. Could this situation be what Ben needed to separate himself from Cara's stranglehold and find his way back to her?

"We won't know those things until later. Right, Miss Darcy?"

Dahlia's voice brought Jaq back to reality. "Yes, but don't forget about the 'Where'..."

Dahlia pointed toward the hotel.

Jaq shook her head. "Assume nothing. It's your job to consider all the possibilities."

A bewildered expression clouded Dahlia's youthful face.

Jaq fought to keep her emotions in check. This was Journalism 101, for crying out loud! "Think outside the box," she finally said through pursed lips.

"Like, what they did this evening?"

"Uh-huh. That's one avenue to consider. So's transportation. Did anyone drop them off at the hotel?"

Dahlia scanned her notes. "I'm not sure..."

Jaq waited as Dahlia flipped several pages, not offering to hold the light. Graciousness was beyond her capacity right now.

Dahlia snapped her fingers. "You're right! Morales said Cara's normal driver was off for the holidays." She eyed Jaq. "Someone else could have driven her, though."

"True."

"Oh, and they were covered in snow." Dahlia stared into the darkened sky. "I didn't get any snow at my place tonight. Did you? Man, that sure would be an awesome way to spend the holidays…"

Jaq glared at her.

"Sorry." Dahlia shifted her weight from one foot to the other. "Um, I managed to talk to a few people outside while I was waiting for you. They said there was a light snow here around eight or eight-thirty. Enough to cover the sidewalk." She flicked her light down the alleyway, where it reflected off small patches of snow and one medium-sized, scummy puddle. "Whatever they got, I guess it melted pretty quick."

"So, steak and lobster for dinner. Within walking distance…"

Dahlia stood by the dumpsters, a confused expression on her face, as Jaq headed for Main Street.

CHAPTER 4

Jaq stepped on the sidewalk and took a right, vigilant of icy patches as she evaluated the row of shops.

White neon signs shimmered against the pre-dusk sky. Treats Galore was every bit what the name suggested, offering the best homemade fudge and pecan-laced donuts for three counties. Maria's Boutique showcased the latest designer fashions, and Derringer's promoted outdoor gear and other must-haves for the adventurers who flocked to Prescott every weekend to enjoy the mountains and waterways.

Other shops had popped up in recent months. Jaq stopped in front of a new sushi place, debating. Would Cara bring her latest conquest there?

Maybe.

She reached the intersection and turned around. A breeze kissed her face as the sign for Maxwell's Steakhouse gleamed at the end of the street. Large Christmas trees lined the entryway, their white lights aglow. Even the valet stand twinkled with festive wreaths and fancy bows.

This had to be where Cara and Ben dined. No other place in town screamed affluence like Maxwell's.

Jaq tucked her head down and made her way back to the alley.

Dahlia was waiting where she left her. As Jaq approached, she pulled a cap from her pocket, a pink and green crochet reminiscent of something Jaq's grandmother knit when she was five. Dahlia tried to position it on her head, but her curls were too thick to be corralled.

Wind gusted through the alleyway, and Jaq shivered.

Dahlia extended the cap, but Jaq declined. She shrugged and shoved it back into her pocket.

"I'm thinking they went to Maxwell's," Jaq said, hugging herself for warmth. "It's the only high-end restaurant on the block."

"So… They walked from the steakhouse to the hotel. Greeted the manager, then headed to the penthouse."

"Sounds plausible."

A loud, forceful voice filled the alleyway. Jaq walked to the edge of the hotel and peered around the decorative bushes flanking the corner. An officer with a bullhorn was directing the mass of reporters away from the entry. Or trying to, anyway.

"Did you know this place before the Worthingtons took over?" Dahlia asked over her shoulder.

Jaq jumped and glared at her before reaching into her camera bag for a pair of gloves. She tugged them on, ignoring the numbness in her fingertips. "I grew up close to here," she said, pointing to the north. "I heard stories about this place—back when it was a no-tell motel—but I've never been inside."

Dahlia's light flickered. She shook it, and the beam solidified, brightening the area where they stood. "I've heard stories, too. *Lots*. Mostly about Cara, though."

Salacious news traveled fast, apparently.

Jaq eyed Dahlia, trying to remember where she was from. Not that it really mattered. She wiggled her fingers in the gloves, willing the circulation to return. "There used to be an X-rated video store there." She pointed down the alleyway to the shop across the street before swinging her hand to the right. "And that way, a liquor store. Kids used to hang out in front, trying to get someone to buy them booze or cigarettes."

"The Worthingtons changed all that?"

Jaq nodded. Despite her personal feelings for Cara, she had the golden touch. News of her involvement in the hotel renovation brought tourists from all over. And it wasn't just Prescott that benefitted. The entire mountain region had seen a revival. Small, struggling towns had adopted the same model, renovating what they could as they sought a connection to the Worthington brand. Revenue was up, even with construction that never seemed to end.

Dahlia flicked the light around the alley. It bounced off the windshield of a parked car, highlighting its web of cracks. "I wonder what made someone like Cara Worthington want to come here, of all places."

Jaq struggled to hide her disdain. Dahlia would never be taken seriously as long as she refused to learn about her surroundings. "Her family was part of the original community that founded Prescott," Jaq said through gritted teeth. "The hotel's named after Cara's great grandmother."

Dahlia thought this over as they watched the lights go off one at a time across the top floor of the hotel until the last window turned dark.

Jaq glanced at her phone. Ten after four. Not much longer and the sun would be up along with the rest of town. The buzz would be unlike anything Prescott had ever seen, and Ethan would expect some type of coverage, even if it were just a blurb and a few photos for the website.

"Everything needs to be ready by eight," Jaq said, although Dahlia had been with the paper long enough to know its deadlines.

Dahlia tucked her notebook and light into her coat. "So, you want me to take a stab at the text first, then send it your way?"

"Excuse me?"

Dahlia looked baffled. "Ethan said you'd help..."

Jaq was speechless.

"Everyone else is out of town." Dahlia shrugged and attempted a laugh. "I guess we're the losers. No place to go, no one to be with for the holidays—"

"Please tell me you're joking."

Dahlia didn't say anything. She didn't have to.

Jaq's glare was icier than the early morning air. "Ethan told you I should help... Knowing full well this story involves Cara Worthington?"

"Uh-huh. I talked to him before I called you."

Ethan might be young, his pimply skin masked by long sideburns and a sculpted goatee, but he had been Editor-in-Chief long enough to know Jaq belonged nowhere near this assignment.

Dahlia leaned forward, her voice muffled. "Between you and me, I think he was a little drunk."

Jaq stood there, hands at her side, too stunned to speak. If Dahlia thought Ethan being drunk was a secret, she really had no clue how life worked.

"So, how do you want to handle this?"

Jaq shifted the camera equipment from her left arm to her right. It was as much a part of her attire as her purse, but right now, it felt like she was carrying a boulder. "We need to let the officers do their jobs. Then, you can request permission to write up what you've got. With some sort of caveat, of course. There are still a lot of questions to answer."

"But—"

"I can't be a part of this, Dahlia. I won't get into the specifics right now, but Ethan knows better. Or at least he will when he sobers up."

"What do you mean? Miss Darcy?"

Jaq did not respond, and Dahlia followed her to the front of the building. An ambulance arrived, quiet against the electricity of determined reporters still huddled near the entrance. Its lights were off. This wasn't Cara's first overdose, but it appeared to be her last.

Good riddance!

Jaq's cheeks instantly turned warm with shame. Cara Worthington was a piece of work, but she was still a human being.

Jaq turned, almost stepping on Dahlia's foot. She cursed under her breath before holding her hands in a makeshift square to highlight different angles. "Take a few photos of the paramedics getting their gear. Then see if anyone from the Sheriff's Office will make a formal statement." She pointed up the street. "Start with Jenkins, then go talk to Morales again. He'll help if it means his name's gonna be in the paper."

"You're leaving?" Dahlia looked like a lost puppy, an innocent against the backdrop of chaos and death.

"You'll be fine." Jaq patted her on the back, as if doing so would somehow make the statement true.

She crossed the street to her car as the flicker of camera flashes and the strobe lights of parked police cars filled the morning air.

She wanted to see Ben, offer him some comfort, but she couldn't do it under these circumstances. Better to give him a few days to process everything. She'd call him after the holidays and suggest they meet for lunch.

Jaq climbed into her car and watched as the paramedics retrieved a gurney from the back of the ambulance. More camera flashes popped as the coroner exited his vehicle and a deputy ushered him inside. With the details of what happened tonight sketchy at best, whatever photos Dahlia took would be all they had to work with on a tight deadline.

Jaq scanned the mob of reporters but didn't see Dahlia's face. Her mind wandered as she waited for the air pouring from her vents to warm. She pictured Ben at her house, making his signature strawberry shortcake waffles or using extra ingredients from work to whip up a five-course dinner. Their laughter as she attempted to help but only made a mess of the cooking area rang in her ears.

If she could just see him again, maybe she could talk some sense into him. Remind him of what life was like then. No Cara. No drama. Just the two of them, facing an uncertain world together.

With one foot on the clutch and the other on the gas, Jaq eased the nose of her car out of the parking space. No matter how much Lawrence Worthington spent trying to protect his daughter, karma had finally caught up with her.

A commotion was brewing near the hotel entrance, and a glint of light in the rearview mirror caught Jaq's eye. Dahlia's face popped out of the fray and was quickly swallowed up by the throng of experienced reporters who granted her no sympathy.

But it wasn't the crowd or even the camera pops that caught Jaq's attention. It was the lights bouncing off brass as an officer in a dark blue uniform crossed the walkway, his hands up as he blocked the reporters' intrusion. He wasn't with the Sheriff's Office. He had to be with the state police or another high-level agency.

A town car idled at the curb, its exhaust forming gray puffs in the early morning air.

Jaq yanked her head around as a second officer trailed behind the first, his hand guiding the arm of a tall, willowy brunette.

Jaq's hand fell from her shifter, and she let off the clutch. Her car stalled in the middle of the road, but she didn't care.

Cara Worthington was alive. And she was alone.

CHAPTER 5

The officer escorted Cara from the hotel entrance. His arm was around her waist, steadying every step.

Cara with her dark, flowing hair and chiseled features, prominent even behind sunglasses designed to mask stoned eyes. She walked like a drugged patient leaving the hospital. Black leggings clung to her lanky figure, and her champagne ski jacket insinuated a trip to the slopes, not an exit from a tiny hotel in an even tinier town.

Jaq's heart raced and her breath fogged the windshield as she willed Ben to appear. Ben with his wavy brown hair, worn longer in the cold months, and broad shoulders. The "next big thing" in restaurateurs, according to her colleague Marcus, who managed the Society section. Cara wouldn't just want Ben by her side. She would insist they be on display for their legion of starry-eyed townsfolk.

A figure emerged, but it wasn't Ben. It was a bald man wearing a thin gray pullover that clung to his sculpted arms. He tapped Cara on the shoulder and handed her a fur-lined backpack.

Jaq gasped as she fought to catch her breath. She flashed to the time Robby Morris pushed her too hard on the swing and she flipped end-over-end, achieving the perfect somersault before crashing to the ground. Her back deep in the soil, the world spun sideways as her lungs refused to do their job. She tried to focus on the beautiful spring sky, the birds chirping in the distance. Anything but the panic as figures raced in her periphery. They were blurred shadows, the blackness of monsters creeping in. Even Robby's garbled voice, hollering for help as he lifted her head from the gritty soil, sounded miles away. "Oof" was the only word she could form then as the breath left her body, and it was the only word she could muster now.

A loud commotion near the hotel snapped Jaq back to the present, but the fogginess of bodies moving in slow motion remained. Her car rumbled as it warmed, sounding more like a cat seeking affection than a poorly tuned engine. Or was it the rapid pounding of her heart she heard mercilessly drumming against her chest?

Jaq struggled for air as fireworks exploded inside her mind. It felt like hours, but the agony only lasted seconds. Her breathing regulated, and the sounds of police and reporters filled her ears, even as the disorientation remained.

What was happening? They weren't supposed to be escorting Cara off the premises. She was dead.

This had to be a mistake! If Cara was alive...

A random photo flitted into her consciousness, something posted online weeks ago. Cara was at the local nightclub, oblivious to the cameras documenting her every move. A group of partygoers surrounded her on the dance floor, dressed in bright purples and blues, sporting jewelry that glimmered beneath the overhead strobe lights. They were in their element, partying with the queen of nightlife.

The body in Cara's penthouse had to be one of those leeches clinging to her side. Someone Cara brought home last night, unaware of the destiny awaiting him or her.

Wouldn't that be the ultimate irony? Seeking fame from Cara Worthington and ending up on the news for an entirely different reason... It would be laughable if it weren't so depressing.

Jaq smacked her hand against the steering wheel, hard enough to leave an imprint. What had happened to the locals once focused on family and community, not the latest society trends?

She massaged the outside of her palm. It would be black and blue tomorrow, but she didn't care. Nothing mattered right now except Ben.

Jaq eyed the entrance with anticipation. Ben would appear any moment now, groggy-eyed and confused by the uproar.

"Get off me!" a man yelled.

Jaq watched as deputies wrestled the overeager reporter to the ground, agitating the others who had braved the cold while they waited for a scoop. They shoved their microphones in Cara's face as her escort fended them off and led her to the idling car. Lights exploded behind her, filling the air like mistimed fireworks.

Jaq scanned the crowd. Dahlia was invisible.

The coroner exited with a body covered by a white sheet, and there was a mad scramble for soundbites and photos. Jaq craned her neck to the right. The breeze flapped at the sheet's edges as a speck of gold glimmered in the police lights. She gripped her seat, usable photos no longer her concern.

Ben's dad had given him a gold chain on his deathbed many years ago. Ben wore it around his wrist as a tribute. Always.

Jaq's lips coiled in horror. "No," she cried, throwing herself against the back of the driver's seat. "No, no, no!"

The coroner climbed into his car and pulled away from the curb.

Dazed, Jaq restarted her car. She slammed the gas pedal to the floorboard, desperate to flee.

The coroner turned right at the edge of downtown. Jaq sat at the stoplight, still stunned, until a car behind her honked.

The sun appeared on the horizon as she pulled into her driveway thirty minutes later, no recollection of how she had gotten there. Streets, stoplights, everything was a blur. A fantastical dream, another world in which she was simply an observer going through the motions.

Jaq put her head in her hands and sobbed. It didn't matter if Mr. Wilson next door saw her sitting there when he walked his dog.

The love of her life was gone, their reunion forever an impossibility.

CHAPTER 6

Jaq sat at her computer, trying to get a grip on the emotions barreling through her.

Ben wasn't her first loss in life, but it sure felt like it.

For some odd reason, she kept thinking of a poster in her high school English classroom. The top half was a sunrise, the bottom a sunset. Scrawling text stating "Time stops for no one" ran between the red and orange splashes of sun. Even back then, she understood the significance, her mom's struggle with cancer a far better teacher that life goes on than pot-loving Mr. Trent would ever be.

Jaq stared at the empty inbox. Dahlia was running out of time.

She opened a blank document and typed a few notes before sitting back in her chair. There was no confirmation the body retrieved from The Cornelia was Ben's. For all Jaq knew, Cara could have given his necklace to one of her acolytes.

The possibility calmed her. Was this spectacle one of Cara's stunts to garner publicity? If so, Ben might be lying low to avoid the fall-out. If those rumors about opening a restaurant were true, this out-of-sight approach made sense. Despite what people said, there actually *was* such a thing as negative press. Especially in small towns, where everyone knew everyone else's business.

Jaq tapped her fingers against the metal arm of her chair. She wanted to believe... But she couldn't. She laid her hands in her lap and hung her head. Years of studying people and documenting their motives had taught her to see the worst in a situation.

Ben was gone. She sensed it, just as she sensed when her mom's final breath was near.

Jaq's email dinged, startling her back to the present. Dahlia had sent a series of photos and a few lines of text for proofing.

Jaq barely glanced at the attachments before uploading them to *The Gazette* website and posting a note for the web developer. He, too, had the misfortune of working while everyone else took time off to be with family for the holidays.

Family... Uncle Andy and Sam were all she had left now.

Jaq swiped at her eyes before the tears could form. This was not the time for softness. It was the time for answers.

As Sheriff, Andy should have been the first person called to The Cornelia. Yet, she never saw him at the scene... Why?

Jaq texted Sam with no luck. She waited a few minutes, finally tossing her phone to the side as she headed for the liquor cabinet.

No good ever came from drinking alone, but she didn't care. Jaq downed the first glass of bourbon in the kitchen. The second, she carried with her to the couch along with a large cookbook. Ben's cookbook. One hundred and thirty-six pages of instructions, photographs, and ideas for culinary exploration.

The glass teetered in her hand as she sank into the worn cushions. She laid the cookbook on the coffee table and took a long swig of her drink before running her fingers over the hard burgundy cover. She traced its embossed gold letters. On a day not unlike this, with bursts of snow and heightened holiday anticipation, Jaq had wrapped this treasure in newspaper, all her money spent on the gift Ben wanted most. What so pleased him last year was left behind in his hurry to start a new life.

In the upper right corner of the first page was her slightly skewed script. A reminder of what used to be, of what she no longer had.

To my dearest Ben,

The greatest chef I know.

Here's to your future and ours.

Yours forever,

Jaq

High-resolution photos of staged foods flooded the pages—main dishes, vegetables, desserts—followed by detailed cooking methods and terminology Jaq didn't understand. Amber liquid sloshed over the edge of her glass, and she stared at the stain as it spread across the recipe for Beef Wellington.

She had trusted Ben. Given him everything. Now, their love was as worthless as the cookbook she clutched with vise-like hands.

Jaq fell asleep on the couch. The cold seeped through cracks she could not see as dreams of dancing with Ben warmed her. Moonlight sparkled on the glass tabletops and crickets chirped from the ground below as they waltzed to music only they could hear atop the terrace of his restaurant.

Jaq welcomed his lips against hers. The kiss was soft and familiar, like her favorite pair of pajamas. She savored the embrace, holding on as long as she could.

When she pulled away, she saw Cara glaring at them from the shadows. Before Jaq could confront her, darkness turned to light, and she was on the balcony alone, listening to cars rush by on the streets below.

Jaq stirred in her sleep. She opened an eye and snapped it shut as the sunlight streaming through her windows blinded her. She sat up and clutched her head, her early-morning indulgence a painful reminder of why it was never smart to drink on an empty stomach. Especially first thing in the morning with no sleep the night before.

The sun danced across the coffee table, highlighting every speck of dirt. Jaq moaned and glanced at the clock hanging on the wall. It was after three. She hadn't slept so long in the middle of the day since preschool.

She reached for her phone, but it wasn't in her pocket. She rolled over and checked the couch cushions before peeking underneath. No luck.

She arched her back as bones creaked from sleeping on her lumpy couch. She wandered through the house, finally finding her phone on the kitchen counter, next to a now-empty bottle of liquor. No wonder she felt like a bronco had kicked her.

Jaq tapped the screen on her phone. Nothing. She grunted and plugged it in before shuffling to the medicine cabinet for something to relieve her headache.

The aspirin didn't help, and she hopped in the shower, her stiff muscles begging for relief. When she returned to the kitchen, there was enough charge to check her messages. Sam had texted while she was in the shower, wanting to know where she was.

"Crap!" The towel draped around Jaq's damp torso fell to the floor. Sam's annual Christmas party was this evening, and Jaq had promised she'd be there.

She grabbed her towel off the floor and returned to the bathroom. She stood half-dry in front of the mirror, droplets of water coating her shoulders. Going to a party—pretending to be okay—was the last thing she wanted to do.

Mr. Trent's prophetic poster filled her mind.

Time stops for no one.

Not even Ben…

Jaq dried off and rushed to the closet. She didn't need an excuse to avoid the festivities. She needed to hurry. If she timed it right, she could make it to the party in that sweet spot between Sam having one too many drinks and being too far gone to help.

This party might be the only way to get some answers.

CHAPTER 7

ನನನ

Sam's party was in full swing, the street a mixture of police and civilian cars. Jaq parked a quarter mile away and tucked her head to her chest to avoid the night breeze. She couldn't decide who she felt more pity for—the poor saps patrolling the streets while senior personnel celebrated the holidays in style, or Sam's neighbors who had to put up with it all.

Sam threw open the door before Jaq could ring the doorbell. Dressed in jeans and cable-knit sweaters, both five foot four with wavy hair and chocolate eyes, they could be twins. The lone distinction—aside from temperament, of course—was Sam's hair, dyed a reddish-purple every few months with the occasional pink or green streaks.

Sam reached for Jaq's hand. "I wasn't sure you'd make it!"

Jaq blocked the doorway and didn't say a word.

"Jaq, get in here. It's freezing!" Sam's cheeks were flushed and she cursed again.

Jaq smelled the alcohol on her breath and smiled as she tried to yank her inside. Sam was right where she wanted her.

"Tell me about Ben," she said and crossed her arms.

Sam grunted and pulled harder, dismantling Jaq from the doorway. She kicked the back of the door with one foot while trying to steady herself with the other. The door gave way, and Sam stumbled backward. Jaq caught her before she tripped on the shoes piled at the entry.

"I got it. I'm fine." Sam shook off Jaq's hands and pointed to the living room. "Dad was just asking about you."

Andy stood behind Sam's movable bar, a dish towel over one shoulder as he prepared drinks. He'd been Prescott's Sheriff for as long as Jaq could remember, but he was also an expert bartender. She smiled, recalling the night Ben tried to stump him with some foreign concoction. Andy whipped it up without hesitation, suggesting Ben try something more challenging next time. They never got the chance to revive the battle of bartending savvy versus culinary expertise... And now they never would.

Jaq willed herself not to cry.

Andy waved and pointed to the bottle of bourbon sitting nearby. Jaq shook her head—her stomach still sour from her earlier binge—and a guest stepped in front of the bar before he could offer again.

Jaq grabbed Sam by the arm and pulled her down the hall to the bedroom.

The door was barely closed before she pounced. "What do you know about Ben?" she said, blocking the exit.

Sam sank to the bed, but before she could plant herself, she slid on the blanket folded over the edge. Jaq helped her up and plopped down beside her.

"I can't tell you anything," Sam said with a hiccup. She wiped at her mouth, her fingers grazing her lips with no purpose. "My dad... He wasn't there."

Jaq patted her leg and tried to mask her sense of urgency. "I know. But please. Anything you can tell me will help."

"Just between us?"

"Always."

Sam responded with a long, loud burp.

Jaq reared back. Bourbon and cigarettes were an awful combination.

Sam snorted and let out a high-pitched, hyena-like laugh, sounding nothing like her normal self.

"Exactly how many drinks have you had?" Jaq asked. It was not unlike Sam to dip into the bottle before the first guest arrived.

Sam ignored the question and closed her eyes. "Morales told me what happened," she said. "But shh! It's supposed to be a secret." She tried to place a finger on her lips but ended up poking herself in the nose.

Jaq frowned. The time for getting information out of Sam had passed. She should have gotten there sooner.

"He was strangled," Sam said, her head bobbing as she turned to face Jaq. "But they don't suspect foul play."

Jaq jumped up, and Sam fell on her side. "What do you mean they don't suspect foul play? How is someone being strangled *not* suspicious?"

It took a moment, but Sam finally righted herself. "It was some sort of sexual incident." She waved her hand in the air. "Auto-erotic something, Morales said."

Jaq's legs gave way. She collapsed onto the bed, feeling light-headed, like she was the one downing the good stuff. Sam's bedroom spun as she struggled with this revelation.

The two of them sat there, the holiday music drifting from the living room the only buffer between them.

"Sam, are you sure?" Jaq's tears were at the precipice, her heart on the verge of splitting in two. Every moment of this day just kept getting worse. She wasn't sure how much more she could take.

Sam sat up straight and looked her in the eye. "I wouldn't lie to you about something like that," she said, sounding more lucid than she had since Jaq's arrival. "But people change, you know?"

Jaq nodded through her tears.

"Having all that money and too much free time?" Sam shrugged. "I mean, we've always known Cara was into some messed up shit."

Jaq fiddled with the edge of Sam's blanket, turning the thread over between her index finger and thumb. Ben had left her for Cara with the barest of goodbyes. Why should she expect any decency in his death when he shunned it in life?

Still, she could not shake the uneasy feeling creeping up her spine. Something didn't add up.

Before she could ask for more details, the bedroom door flew open and Andy walked in, a drink in each hand.

"Muffin!" He took one look at the two of them sitting on the bed, Sam barely able to hold herself up and Jaq in tears, and kicked the door shut. He nodded Sam's way as he handed Jaq a drink. "What'd she tell you?"

"More than I needed to hear." Jaq put the glass to her lips. She hadn't planned to drink anything else, but if ever a situation called for something to take the edge off, it was now.

"I'm sorry, Muffin. Really, I am."

She hated when Andy called her that. He meant it as a term of affection, but it only reminded her of her six-year-old self, awkward and covered in baby fat.

Andy walked over and put his arm around her in a clumsy hug. "I hoped we could enjoy the holidays. Deal with this... Afterwards."

Ice balls jiggled in Jaq's glass as she took a swig. The woodsy liquid burned her throat. "I was at the scene," she said, forcing the words past her lips. "Saw Cara escorted out. Then the body." She looked down. "Ben's body."

"Why on earth were you at the scene?"

"Dahlia needed help. Ethan told her to call me."

Andy smacked his hand against Sam's nightstand. "Your boss must be the dumbest person alive."

Jaq agreed, but Ethan wasn't the issue here. "Sam said it was... Something sexual?" She stood up, unable to remain still any longer.

Andy sighed. "Muffin, I don't think we should discuss this right now."

"I really hate being called that, just so you know."

Andy looked like he had been slapped but regained his composure. "Look, Jaq. I know this is tough. I can't imagine what you're going through..."

"No, you can't." Jaq slid her glass onto the dresser. The room felt wobbly. Andy must have made her a double.

He said nothing but pulled her in for another hug. Jaq tried to resist, but he wouldn't let go. She sobbed loudly, her tears refusing to be stifled any longer. Her head throbbed and her chest heaved as she struggled to catch her breath. She stayed in Andy's embrace for as long as she could stand it, her face wet and scratchy when she pulled away.

"I don't expect you to understand," she said, all trace of emotion gone. "Or even agree with me wanting the details. But I loved Ben. I need to know what happened."

"I get it. But there's not much I can tell you. Not yet, anyway."

Tears pooled in her eyes. "I'm sorry," she said. "About the 'Muffin' thing. I know you mean well."

Laughter emanated from the other end of the house, broken only by the chords of familiar Christmas melodies. Jaq traced the edge of her glass with her finger, avoiding Andy's gaze.

He grazed her chin with his hand, and she looked up. Her eyes were dry, but her stomach still churned like an inferno.

"There's not much I can tell you. But it's not because I don't want to," Andy said. "Lawrence Worthington reached out to the AG. Insisted the state police handle things, not us. So, I sent a few of my guys to help. Figured it was better to have someone there than try to fight it."

This news did not surprise Jaq. Politicians, celebrities, the elitist of the elite. That's who Lawrence vacationed with, formed partnerships with, invested with. When he asked for help, he got it. It wouldn't be that difficult for him to control the situation to protect Cara, although Jaq had been too emotional to consider the possibility until now.

"Dahlia said Cara and Ben went out to eat before..." Jaq's voice trailed off. Before he died, she wanted to say, but couldn't get the words out.

Andy frowned. "You sound like you're gathering facts for an exposé."

"This is Dahlia's story. I just want some answers." She reached for her glass and knocked it over. Brown liquid splashed everywhere.

Andy righted the glass and used a nearby t-shirt to mop up the spill. Jaq offered to help, but he waved her off.

"To Ben."

Jaq and Andy turned to see Sam holding an imaginary glass in the air.

"I think you've had enough," Andy said and shifted his attention back to Jaq. "I think we've *all* had enough. Of work, of this entire ordeal. I don't know what happened. And Morales never should have said anything out of speculation." He paused, waiting for both girls to look his way. "Look, we won't know anything until the coroner finishes his report, right? So, let's not jump to any conclusions."

Morales was more reliable than Andy gave him credit for, but Jaq knew he was right about one thing. No good could come from speculating about events she had no control over.

"How about I let you know when I have something more definitive?" Andy said, picking up Jaq's glass. "This needs to be handled by the book, given our personal connection to Ben."

Jaq nodded. It was all she could manage. Inside, she felt cold. Like she would never be warm again.

Sam teetered as she tried to stand. Jaq put out a hand, but she pushed it away and took a few timid steps toward the door.

Jaq put an arm around her anyway and guided her down the hallway, feeling guilty for cornering her. "How about some coffee?" she asked as they neared the kitchen. Caring for a drunk relative wasn't her idea of a fun time, but at least it gave her something else to focus on. And she needed that right now. Desperately.

Andy set Jaq's glass on the counter, waved in their direction, and made his way back to the bar.

The music was so loud, Jaq could not think. She positioned Sam against the counter and instructed her to stay put.

Sam nodded and pointed to a nearby cabinet.

Jaq found the container of coffee and used the last of it to make a pot. For a moment, she debated about making hers Irish. Anything to take away the nagging questions, to be rid of the desperation simmering beneath the surface. But she did not indulge this desire.

A more pertinent thought consumed her. One she did not need clouded by booze.

How could she get the answers she needed about Ben's death without interfering in a formal investigation?

Music pulsated behind her as more people crowded into Sam's tiny living room. Andy and his colleagues celebrated as Jaq sipped coffee and contemplated her next move.

CHAPTER 8

Birds chirped outside Sam's living room window the next morning as Jaq opened her eyes and groaned. She didn't care what anyone said. Sofa beds were *not* for sleeping.

She kicked off the scratchy blanket and reached for her jeans. She tucked a tee shirt she borrowed from Sam into the waistband and pulled a gray University of Georgia hoodie over her head.

Jaq shoved the mattress into the sofa, covered it with the cushions, and arranged the blanket across the back of the couch. She positioned the throw pillows, stepping over paper plates coated with red and green frosting. Beer cans and soda bottles littered the floor, and a half-smoked cigar lay on the coffee table, ashes strewn around its tip. Wrapping paper and other party favors crunched beneath Jaq's feet as she maneuvered the maze otherwise known as her cousin's living room.

Liquid stained the carpet, and memories of the alleyway behind The Cornelia flooded Jaq's senses. It smelled like beer, but there were no guarantees. Before her gag reflex could kick in, she made a detour around the stain, scooping up a half-filled bottle of rum perched on the edge of the hearth. The glass felt cool against her palm, and she carried the bottle to the kitchen, where the mess continued all the way to the sink. Empty steins and plates were piled atop one another, and Jaq eyed the stack, trying to determine whether she could retrieve the scrub brush without toppling the entire thing.

She peered around the wobbly stack and froze at the sight of a Santa Claus cookie jar by the window. Cheerful, with rosy, red cheeks and a full belly, the oversized container was once a staple in Grandma's kitchen. Nestled inside the entryway, she and Sam used to help themselves to homemade goodies every time they entered.

The dark cloud of sadness returned. It was Christmas Eve, and she had nothing but a cold, empty house to return to. Not at all like years past, when the family gathered at the farm to roast marshmallows, sing off-tune Christmas carols as Andy tinkered at the piano, and make hot cocoa and cookies for Santa from scratch.

Christmas was once her favorite time of year. But the Worthingtons had ruined that, too.

Jaq frowned. This was the first year she hadn't bothered to put up a tree. It was as if a part of her knew there would be nothing to celebrate this holiday season.

Jaq reached around the cookie jar and grabbed Sam's carafe. She filled it with filtered water from the fridge and rummaged around in the cabinets until she found a half-used bag of coffee beans. She glanced at her watch, decided a morning wake-up call would do her cousin some good, and grabbed the grinder, too.

The roar of beans turning to fine particles echoed in the kitchen, and Sam appeared in the doorway before Jaq could finish the grind.

"Seriously?" she said, holding a hand to her head. Her hair was a mess, and she wore a thin robe that did not cover her nightie.

"Got big plans?" Jaq asked with a sideways glance.

Sam shot her a death glare.

"Sorry." Jaq scooped coffee into the basket and flipped the on switch. "This was the only coffee I could find."

Sam scowled and plucked a cigarette from the pack sitting on the countertop. She slid the back door open and leaned out, keeping half her body inside as she lit the tip and took a drag.

The draft was cold enough to penetrate Jaq's hoodie, and she stepped sideways. "Why do you do that?" she asked as Sam leaned outside again.

"Do what?"

"Smoke half-in, half-out. Don't get me wrong." Jaq crinkled her nose. "I appreciate it. But this is your house. Who cares if it smells like smoke?"

Sam shrugged. "I'm trying to quit. I don't want this place smelling like an ashtray when I do."

Jaq couldn't stifle her laugh. Every year, her cousin made quitting cigarettes her New Year's resolution. And every year—often within the first twenty-four hours—she was back to smoking as many cigarettes as before. Sometimes more.

Sam glared at her again but said nothing. She finished her cigarette and bent down to mash the butt against the concrete patio.

"What you got going on today?" Jaq asked.

"Not much." Sam slid the patio door closed and rubbed her hands up and down her arms. "Not until dinner, anyway."

"What time again?"

"Six. Nothing too fancy. Or so he says."

Andy's ability to tend bar paled to his love of entertaining. Every year, it seemed, the festivities grew more elaborate. It had been fifteen years since he and Aunt Mae divorced, but he showed zero sign of settling down. Like Sam, every year was the same as the one before.

Jaq frowned. The inability to change must be a family curse.

Sam disappeared, and Jaq heard a dresser drawer slam shut, followed by the creaking of the closet door. Sam returned wearing leggings, high socks, and an oversized green sweater, looking every bit the poster child for an outdoor living magazine.

She pulled two coffee mugs from the dishwasher. Jaq filled both and handed one to Sam before taking a sip. The dark liquid was bitter, but she forced it down.

Sam surveyed the cabinets beyond Jaq's head. "I think there's some Irish cream somewhere..."

Jaq held up her hand. "I'll survive."

Sam shrugged, and they leaned against the countertop, sipping the black sludge in silence.

"Shit!" Sam jerked sideways and bumped Jaq's arm.

Hot coffee splashed her chin. "What the hell?" she said, wiping the liquid away with her hand.

"I'm supposed to drop off gifts this morning. At the station." Sam reached around Jaq and grabbed the travel mug sitting beside the toaster. "Wanna come?" she asked as she filled the mug and tightened the lid.

Jaq shrugged. "Sure. I'll meet you there." She pushed her empty cup toward the sink and retrieved her purse and keys from the living room. Anything was better than going home.

CHAPTER 9

ಎಂಎಂ

Sam lived ten minutes from the Sheriff's Office. It was both a blessing and a curse, she once said. Today, the drive was quick and easy, almost no traffic clogging the roads as people gathered with their families to celebrate.

Jaq stood in the entryway, preventing the electronic door from closing as Sam lugged a red and green bag stuffed with gifts into the lobby. All she needed was an elf costume and her transformation to Santa's little helper would be complete.

Feeling anything but festive, Jaq waited in Sam's office while she made the rounds. She leaned against the metal desk, listening to the chorus of thanks as recipients ripped open the wrapping paper to reveal their treasures.

Papers shifted beneath her backside, and a large white envelope fell to the floor. Several photos slipped out, and Jaq reached down to retrieve them.

The first print captured an opulent living room, its leather furniture and framed art overshadowed only by a large, glimmering Christmas tree. Jaq pulled it close for a better view. The glimmer was not tinsel, but fine crystal balls distributed throughout the tree's lush branches. A large silver-edged star sat perched atop the tree, with presents three and four deep artfully arranged around the base.

Jaq flipped to the second print. The Christmas tree stood farther away, its lights no longer exuding their inviting glow. A lanky man hung from a dark wooden beam stretching the length of the room. His eyes bulged, and his mouth snarled in a forever grimace. A dark nylon scarf gripped his neck.

"No!"

The photo drifted to the floor. Jaq covered her mouth with her hands, but what she really wanted was to cover her eyes. Forever.

She gripped the desk. She understood the man in the picture was Ben, but her heart refused to believe it. It looked nothing like the man she loved. This man's face was waxy and unnatural, tilted at an awkward angle. His arms, toned as they were, hung limp by his side.

Jaq wanted to look away but couldn't. She stared at the man in the photo, trying to force her brain to accept what her heart knew to be true.

She stared until it was too much. She closed her eyes and felt around on the floor for the picture. She shoved it in the envelope and bolted from Sam's office, unable to get away fast enough.

The automatic door opened and shut behind her. Jaq fished the keys from her pocket and raced to her car, willing herself not to throw up.

She half-expected Sam to come after her and was relieved when she did not. Lukewarm air blew in her face as she forced several long breaths. Finally, her heart rate slowed and the knot in her stomach eased.

She took another deep breath and put the car in reverse. It was time to go home. There, she could shut out the world while she figured out how to forget what she had just seen.

Still, a question gnawed at her. She dialed Dahlia's number as she pulled out of the lot and onto the street.

Dahlia answered on the second ring. "Merry Christmas, Miss Darcy!"

"Did you get any more details from Jenkins or Morales?" Jaq asked, in no mood for holiday chit-chat.

"Not really..."

"Dahlia, this is important." Jaq stopped at a four-way-stop and waited for the car opposite her to go. "Has anyone questioned Cara yet?"

"Not that I heard, but Jenkins and Morales were busy. It took me awhile to find them, and the state police were there, and they were so unhelpful..."

Jaq hung up and made a U-turn at the next light.

The trip home would have to wait.

CHAPTER 10

Jaq pulled up outside The Cornelia with no plan in mind. Just the overwhelming need to find Cara and demand some answers.

Sam called, and Jaq sent it to voicemail. She waited in her car, watching people come and go, the crime scene tape now removed. She turned the press pass over in her lap, running her fingers up and down the lanyard as she debated her next steps. The coarse material snagged a sliver of cracked skin, and she jerked her hand back in surprise.

"Dammit!" She shoved the pass in her coat pocket and stuck the injured finger in her mouth.

The coppery taste of blood only fueled her agitation. She was no coward, yet here she was, avoiding a confrontation with the woman who had stolen the man she loved. What she *needed* to do was march right into that hotel—push through the concierge if she had to—and make a stink with the GM.

Whatever was necessary to get Cara downstairs so she could confront her face-to-face. Somebody needed to ask the tough questions. It might as well be her.

Jaq reached for the door handle as Cara appeared at the hotel entry, surrounded by two burly men in gray polo shirts and black pants. They walked on opposite sides of her, leading her to a dark town car idling just beyond the hotel entryway.

Jaq leaned back in her seat, baffled. Who could possibly want to harm someone so intent upon destroying themselves?

Cara walked to the back of the car, sporting a pair of tight jeans and heeled boots she did not need. In lieu of a jacket, she wore a thick, nubby sweater that clung to her thin frame.

Heroin chic, Jaq thought with a smirk. Cara certainly lived that lifestyle. A staple at every hotspot, she produced a steady stream of images for the tabloids. Dancing with friends. Drinking. Not to mention whatever illicit substances she indulged in at the after-hour venues.

Ben choosing to become a part of that lifestyle, to abandon the life they were building, made Jaq both angry and ill. She started her car, disappointed that today would not be the day she let Cara Worthington have it.

One of the men escorting Cara walked around the front of the vehicle and tapped on the window. The driver cracked it enough to hold a conversation. The other man opened the back door, and Cara climbed inside. A minute later, both men slid into the backseat, hidden behind tinted glass so dark it blocked all outside intrusion.

The town car pulled away from the curb, and Jaq followed it before she could second-guess the decision.

She caught up to the vehicle by the second stoplight. With her right hand, she dug in her purse and pulled out the pen and notepad she carried everywhere. With her left hand gripping the steering wheel, she jotted down the make and model of the vehicle, along with the license plate. The uneasiness in her stomach grew, and she shook her head, determined not to let it take hold as the need for answers overshadowed her usual sense of right and wrong.

The town car continued straight for several lights, eventually making a right turn onto Monroe.

Jaq stayed on the main road, taking a right at the next street. She slowed as she neared a minivan going the 25-mph speed limit.

Cara's driver stopped near a small office building, and a handsome man in professional attire made his way down the steps to the sidewalk.

Jaq eased off the brakes just as the minivan in front of her slowed. She cursed and jerked her car to a stop. The driver continued on, oblivious to the near catastrophe.

Jaq cut to the right and pulled up alongside the curb across the street from where Cara's town car was parked. She killed the engine and scooted her seat away from the steering wheel.

With both hands, she lifted the telescopic lens from her camera bag. It was her one splurge this year, Ethan refusing to let her expense it to the paper. He was clueless about the effort involved in capturing high-resolution photos, but today, the lens was worth the cost.

She tilted her seat back and attached the lens to her camera. She adjusted the aperture, perfecting her view as she took in every detail of the two men, from the bulging veins in their muscular arms to the scar one of them sported on his left cheek.

She watched through her viewfinder as the man greeted Cara with a hug. His hair was curly, falling past his ears, and sun-kissed like his skin. Jaq could only make out his profile, but she pictured his eyes as a bluish green. Maybe hazel.

Jaq rested the camera in her lap and reached for her phone. She typed Cara's name in the search engine, and a few taps later, pulled up a series of thumbnails. With one scroll, she found what she needed.

She opened the image full screen and set the phone on her console while she repositioned her lens. Cara had stepped to the side, giving Jaq an unobstructed view of the mystery man. He looked to be in his late twenties, but next to Cara's chalky skin, anyone with a hint of color seemed young.

She snapped a photo and held the viewfinder and her phone side-by-side. The man at the other end of her camera was Henry Worthington, Cara's older brother.

The heater in Jaq's car circulated warm air as she picked up her lens again to observe the brother-sister duo. Henry was about six feet from Cara, waving his hands about as he spoke. She stood in perfect statue-like formation, her expression that of a child being scolded.

Jaq panned out. One of Cara's escorts stood on the sidewalk, eyeing the occasional vehicle as it passed by. The other kept watch near the town car's back door. In the front seat, an older gentleman wearing mirrored sunglasses rhythmically moved his fingers in the air, enjoying an overture only he could hear.

Jaq returned to the subject of most interest, watching as Henry moved about with a scowl on his face. Or was it disappointment?

Cara folded her arms across her chest. Whatever Henry was going on about, she had no interest in hearing it.

He thrust his hands into the air, and Jaq zoomed in. Reading lips was a trick she learned when her mom was in the hospital and no one would tell her about what was happening. She made out "investigation" and "father" before Henry grabbed Cara by the elbow and pulled her toward the steps. Cara stamped her foot and yanked her arm away, as Jaq zoomed out, following their motions.

The man standing at the back of the car lifted his sunglasses. He turned her way, and the sun bounced off her lens, striking him in the eye.

"Oh, shit!" Jaq put her camera on the passenger seat and slammed her shifter into first gear. She had wedged her car between another vehicle and the curb when she parked, and it took several panicked tries to maneuver a clean exit.

Her windshield darkened, and the man squinted at her through the dingy glass. "You! What do you think you're doing?"

Jaq's instincts kicked in. She yanked her steering wheel to the left and slammed on the gas.

The man ran down the street behind her car, yelling at her to stop.

She was headed the wrong way, but she didn't care. She mashed the gas pedal and sped to the next cross-street, her lungs on fire as she struggled to catch her breath.

A silver SUV approached the intersection but Jaq did not hesitate. She shot forward across two lanes, barely avoiding a collision.

The driver laid on his horn.

Jaq ignored him and pulled into the line of cars headed away from town.

"Nice job, dumbass," she said to her reflection in the rear-view mirror. Some days, she truly did not know what got into her.

CHAPTER 11

Exhaustion and hunger accompanied Jaq through the front door. Bourbon and coffee weren't exactly meal-worthy, yet that was all she had managed to consume in the past twenty-four hours.

Her phone buzzed, and she tossed it on the countertop along with her camera bag. She grabbed the last of the bread and surveyed the contents of her refrigerator. A wilted head of lettuce and a wrinkly tomato wasn't much to get excited about, but with a little mustard, mayo, and a sprinkling of pepper, it would do.

Jaq's thoughts drifted to Ben, as they often did when she was in the kitchen. He could do so much with even the simplest of ingredients. She bit into the stale bread before she could lose what little appetite she had left and reached for her phone.

Sam's voicemail played through the speaker. "Jaq, I don't know what happened earlier, but you need to call me. Like yesterday."

Jaq rolled her eyes. Sam could be so dramatic. She took another bite of her sandwich and tapped the button to return the call.

Sam answered on the first ring. "Jacqueline Marie Darcy, what do you think you're doing?"

Jaq nearly choked on the wad of bread in her mouth. When Sam called anyone by their full name, she wasn't playing around.

"I just got a call from someone with Cara Worthington's security detail. Said a female with light brown hair driving a blue crossover followed them and took pictures of Cara and Henry without their permission." Sam paused. "Please tell me that wasn't you."

Jaq wiped her hands on her faded jeans and retrieved a can of soda from the fridge. She popped the soda top and took a quick swig before pulling the memory card from her camera.

"What the hell were you thinking?" Sam's voice jumped an octave as she spoke. "Those people own this freaking town, Jaq! Why on earth would you pick a fight with the Worthingtons?"

Jaq finished her sandwich and tossed the paper towel in the trashcan beside her desk.

"Jaq..." Sam shifted her tone, realizing a little too late that yelling wouldn't get her anywhere. "This nonsense aside, I'm worried about you."

"Don't be." Jaq walked to the living room. She shoved her desk chair to the side and set her phone and the memory card on top of her desk before turning her computer on. "Really. I'm fine."

"In what universe is stalking Cara Worthington the definition of 'fine'?"

"Sam..."

"I'm serious! You don't know these people, Jaq. You can't do something like that without consequences."

Jaq typed her password into the login screen and popped the memory card into one of the computer's USB ports. "I wasn't stalking anybody."

"But you *did* follow Cara Worthington from The Cornelia to Henry's office on Monroe?"

Jaq clicked on the icon for her camera software. She selected her memory card from the options, and a filmstrip of images filled her screen.

"Look, I gotta go," Sam said with a sigh. Or maybe it was an exhale as she finished a cigarette. Jaq could never tell. "But you're still coming to my dad's tonight, right? We'll talk more then."

Jaq barely noticed the abrupt end to their conversation as the thumbnails filled her screen. She didn't recall taking that many shots, but there they were, lined up in tidy rows.

Jaq scrolled slowly, analyzing each photo. The first few were of Cara sulking, followed by one with Henry waving his hands in the air. In the next photo, he pointed a finger in his sister's direction as she stood to the side, watching, her arms folded like a teenager waiting to find out how long she was grounded.

The last picture featured an up-close image of the large, dark-skinned man about ten feet from the hood of Jaq's car. Cara's security detail, according to Sam.

Jaq clicked the image and zoomed in. The text embroidered across the man's left breast was a dark cursive stitching. With a little finagling of her photo editing software, she could make out the company name. She opened a browser and typed it in the search engine. The first result took her to a web page with an oversized montage of security personnel. "A purveyor of privacy and security, we protect your business and your reputation," the caption read. Below that was information about the company's services and a contact form.

Jaq pulled a notebook out of her desk drawer and jotted down the company's name, address, and telephone number. She clicked the About Us link and scrolled through the contact information, noting the names of the Head Security Officer and the owner of the company. Employee pictures filled the page, but none of them were of the man who chased her down the street.

Jaq closed the browser and returned to the last photo of Henry and Cara. She zoomed in, lingering over Cara's glazed eyes and sad countenance. She looked haggard, especially compared to Henry's youthful appearance.

Jaq clicked on the first photo that captured his face. Sun-kissed hair, a strong jawline, flawless skin. Even his tan seemed more golden up close, like he had just returned from a trip to the Bahamas. And who knows? Maybe he had. It was certainly proportionate to the Worthington jet-setting lifestyle.

Jaq zoomed in again, squinting to make out his eyes. They *were* hazel, with slight crinkles around the edges. From the sun, or life in general? Being related to Cara had to be exhausting.

Jaq flipped to the image of Henry with raised hands, trying to communicate with his sister. Some people turned ugly when they were angry, but not Henry. The outburst of emotion made him seem real. Not artificial, like so many of the people moving to Prescott.

Jaq zoomed out, intrigued. Henry could not have been in town long. She tried to recall if *The Gazette* had run any stories about him. If so, they weren't memorable.

She scanned the building in the background, a two-story red brick structure with jet black shutters encompassing the two large, front-facing windows. The door was painted black, too, with no visible signage to offer any clues to what Henry did for a living. She leaned in for a closer look. There wasn't even a street number on the building.

"What are you doing here, Henry?" she asked the picture on her screen. She traced the side of his face with her finger, trying to imagine what he was like under normal circumstances.

A neighbor rattling around in their yard startled her from her daze. Jaq flipped to an empty page in her notebook and opened another browser. She searched Henry's name with the terms "business" and "Prescott," but what she found centered on Lawrence. Corporate mergers, New York City galas, their investment portfolio. The articles read more like public relation pieces than Intel.

Jaq removed the business term to widen her search. A few items from her paper appeared—charity events sponsored by the Worthington family, notices about their real estate holdings, details on the renovation at The Cornelia. But none of the articles referenced Henry directly or the building where he met his sister. Even a quick search of local tax records told her little more than the building number and its purchase date two months ago.

An hour passed, and Jaq learned little, except Henry modeled as a teen. Aside from his last name, that was his only claim to fame.

Cara, on the other hand… Jaq scrolled through screen after screen of sites filled with news about Cara and her "train wreck of a life," as one blogger put it. Another site detailed her exploits with photos, video clips, and first-hand accounts. Jaq examined the contents of the home screen, discouraged. Sites like this manipulated people into spying on others. All for a sampling of fame.

Jaq held her breath as she scrolled through the feed, worried she might run across a salacious post about Ben. But he was not the topic du jour.

She snapped off the monitor and pushed her notes to the side. Everyone was so wrapped up in Cara. It was easy to see Ben falling victim to the same trap. But was his insatiable desire to open a restaurant worth the price of being with someone so messed up?

Jaq slumped in the chair, her heart heavy. It was a question she might never see answered.

CHAPTER 12

Jaq entered Maxwell's Steakhouse at ten after six, just as Sam called. She put her phone on Do Not Disturb and shoved it in her purse.

A small group of patrons waited near the entry, a mixture of young and old, the blend of rich leather and perfume sickeningly sweet as Jaq passed by. She was out of her element, but she needed to be there, no matter how uncomfortable it was. Cara and Ben had eaten at Maxwell's hours before he died. Surely somebody working there could tell her something—anything—about their visit.

She walked up to the hostess, a young girl with bright red hair swept upward in a taut bun. She looked like a frightened gazelle, on high alert as she surveyed the crowd before her.

"How long's the wait?" Jaq asked.

"We're booked until close." The hostess reached for a stack of menus and waved to a group by the door as another party crammed into the space behind them. "You might try the bar."

Jaq ignored the depressing reality of spending Christmas Eve at a bar and squeezed through tables packed with patrons enjoying the holiday smorgasbord on gold-flaked china.

Her sadness magnified. What ever happened to tradition? If she and Ben were still together...

She stopped herself. There would be no "what if's" tonight. She was there to get information. Nothing more.

The large mahogany bar filled the back section of the restaurant. Only one barstool was empty, and Jaq tapped the woman sitting next to it on the shoulder. "Is this free?"

"Honey, ain't nuthin' in this place free." The woman, middle-aged with hair so dark it had to be dyed, hiccupped and gestured for Jaq to sit.

"Merry Christmas," the bartender said and laid a cocktail napkin on the shiny bar top.

"Cranberry vodka on the rocks. And a menu, please," Jaq said and forced a smile. Tonight was anything but merry.

The bartender slid a piece of printed parchment her way and mixed her drink before turning to the woman beside her. "Need anything else?" he asked.

She shook her head and slipped a fifty into his hand. "Keep the change, love. You know. Happy Holidays, and all that shit."

She hiccupped again, decided the best way to cure it was to down the last of her drink, and teetered away from the bar. She sidestepped a waiter struggling to balance a tray overloaded with food, and he shot her a dirty look. She feigned an apology and continued toward the front door.

"I hope you called her a cab..."

"Miss Jackson? She's a regular." The bartender scooped up the glass and dumped it into a plastic tote with the other dirty dishes. "Her driver waits out front every night."

"Speaking of regulars..." Before Jaq could finish, a man summoned him to the end of the bar and slipped a bill into his palm.

Jaq scanned the menu and almost choked on her drink. Twenty-two dollars for a garden salad? Good grief!

The bartender returned and Jaq ordered miniature crab cakes the cheapest hors d'oeuvres she could find.

A couple crowded in beside her. "Two glasses of your finest scotch," the man said.

Jaq jiggled the ice in her glass and took another drink. Did everyone have money to blow these days?

The floral perfume of the woman next to her was suffocating. Jaq swiveled in the other direction and surveyed the dining room. Every seat was filled. The owners were making a killing off people anxious to spend the holidays anywhere but home.

Guilt stabbed at her heart, and Jaq fished her phone from her purse so she could text Sam. If her food arrived soon, she could still make it to Andy's in time...

"This is complete and utter crap!" A male voice overshadowed the chorus of conversation near the bar, and Jaq looked up.

"Henry, I understand you're upset. But listen to me... There's only so much we can do."

Henry? As in Henry Worthington? Jaq craned her neck for a better look.

Sure enough, he sat just a few tables away, wearing a gray sweater over his blue button-down shirt. Across from him was an older gentleman in a dark suit and gray tie that complemented his full head of silver hair.

"I'm done listening," Henry said. He slammed his fist on the table. "I mean it, Geoffrey. This is the last thing Cara needs right now. It's the last thing any of us needs."

"Understood." The older man stabbed at his filet. Blood oozed from the tender meat and pooled on his plate.

Jaq pushed her bright red drink to the side.

Henry picked up his utensils and cut into a baked potato the size of her fist, loaded with sour cream, chunks of bacon, fresh-shaved cheddar cheese, and chives. Jaq's stomach rumbled in envy.

As if on cue, the bartender arrived with her food. Three tiny crab cakes were artfully arranged on a large lettuce leaf with remoulade sauce drizzled across the top. They were almost too beautiful to eat.

Her stomach rumbled again—angrier this time—and Jaq dug in. She noted lemon, Worcestershire sauce, and a hint of dill. Or was it parsley? The breading was flaky and buttery, the sauce creamy but not too sweet. Each bite tasted better than the last.

Ben would approve.

Jaq dropped her fork, and it clinked loudly against her plate. So much for her appetite.

Henry's waiter appeared with a bottle of wine. He waved him off and tossed his napkin to the table before standing up.

Jaq pretended to pick at her food as he approached the bar.

He mumbled a polite, "Excuse me," and brushed past her, his spicy cologne overriding the pungent crab.

"Can I get you anything else?" the bartender asked.

Jaq motioned for the check. Through the main window, she saw Henry pull on his coat. Snowflakes whirled around his head as he walked to the valet stand.

The bartender handed her the bill, and Jaq groaned inwardly. Thirty dollars for an appetizer and a drink? And that didn't even include the tip.

She grabbed her wallet and plucked out the one card with credit. The bartender ran it and handed her the receipt, along with a smooth black takeout box with Maxwell's stamped across the top. The same box Cara brought home the night Ben died.

Jaq forced this unpleasant reminder from her mind and added a tip and signature to the receipt. She tucked the remaining crab cake into the box and wished the bartender a Merry Christmas. She'd come back after the holidays to ask about Ben and Cara. Right now, she just wanted to get away from champagne toasts and the overwhelming scent of lilac hovering around her barstool.

Jaq pushed through the crowd and slipped on her coat as she exited the front door. A frigid blast slapped her cheeks, startling her. The box of leftovers teetered in her hands, but she gripped it before it could fall.

Henry was still at the valet stand, his coat collar turned up while he waited for his car. He glanced Jaq's way as the valet pulled up in a black sports car.

"Warmed 'er up for you, Mr. Worthington," a stocky man in a burgundy vest said as he climbed out. He handed Henry the keys.

"Call me Henry, Don. Please. Mr. Worthington's my father."

The valet blushed, but before he could walk away, Henry handed him a thick stack of bills. "For your family," he said before making his way around the car to the driver's side. "Merry Christmas!"

The valet waved as Henry climbed in, his smile so big his lips seemed plastered to his face.

Henry's cologne lingered in the air, teasing Jaq's senses. She snugged her coat around her waist, and with her back to the wind, walked to the free parking lot down the street.

Henry passed by and turned on his blinker. He disappeared into the residential section of downtown, a puff of exhaust trailing behind him.

Lawrence Worthington was all about the power, and Cara was all about the fun.

Henry? He was something else entirely.

CHAPTER 13

ನುನುು

Jaq made it to Andy's as he pulled the turkey from the oven. Sam was already two drinks in, so Jaq was able to avoid any questions about her tardiness.

Sam poured her a drink, and Jaq nursed it as she ate, the bourbon a perfect complement to Andy's savory cooking. The three of them spent the evening eating and chatting in front of the fireplace. For the first time since winter began, Jaq felt warm. Alive, even. Was it the fire, the liquor, or the fact a certain gentleman had unexpectedly entered her orbit?

Jaq polished off her drink and handed her glass to Sam for a refill, determined to keep her thoughts of Henry at bay. They hadn't even spoken yet!

Andy went to bed around midnight, leaving Sam and Jaq to tend to the fire and recount stories of Christmas Eves long ago. They giggled at their childish antics—pretending to go to sleep, then checking out their stockings and the gifts under the tree once the adults were in bed. The conversation turned more subdued as they reminisced about the festive meals Grandma used to make. Meals for the entire family that put Andy's skills to shame, although Jaq would never tell him that.

Thoughts of holiday dinners at the farm soured Jaq's mood. "When was the last time you talked to your mom?" she asked Sam as she stood up to stretch her legs. Years later, it was still hard to believe Aunt Mae had run off to the West Coast with her boss.

Curled up in the recliner, Sam answered with a snore.

Jaq poked the logs. The top one fell forward, its edges sizzling as it turned a whitish red. She retrieved a blanket from the ottoman and covered Sam before grabbing another one for herself. She cuddled up on the couch, watching the last bit of wood disintegrate to ash. Around two, she rolled over and fell asleep, determined to put all thoughts of handsome strangers and long-lost family out of her mind.

Jaq awoke the next morning to the smell of coffee brewing. She blushed as Andy stacked several packages at her feet.

"I didn't get you anything," she said, sitting up. It hadn't occurred to her to stop and pick up something on her way over last night. She was too distracted by her not-so-pure thoughts of Henry.

"Don't you worry about that, Muffin." Andy returned to the tree and gathered another stack of gifts. He put one large box and one that looked to be the size of a remote on the table in front of Sam. The others he took with him back to his recliner. "We're just so happy you're here. Feels like old times."

That it did. It didn't matter that the presents were simple—a framed picture of Sam and Jaq in front of their grandparents' Christmas tree as kids, a pair of winter socks, a sweatshirt with a sleeping cat and dog on the front. They were gifts from the people who knew her best. And that made them more special than any fancy trinket or luxuriously wrapped present. She had something people like Cara, for all their wealth and fame, lacked: A family that loved her for who she was.

Jaq ate brunch with Sam and Andy before loading up her treasures. The overcast sky loomed over her car on the drive home, spitting its first flakes onto the warm hood as she pulled into her driveway.

She parked her car in the garage but couldn't resist going back outside to let the snow kiss her cheeks and dampen her hair. This was the first white Christmas Prescott had seen in years. The perfect reminder of childhood, when wonder and anticipation were all she knew.

Her cheeks red from both the snow and her tears, Jaq forced herself indoors. The door creaked shut behind her, and she shivered as she set the gifts down on her way through the kitchen and to the backyard. She uncovered the pathetic remains of a woodpile and lugged a small carrier of logs and kindling to the fireplace.

She made one more trip to retrieve the last bit of wood and shut the patio door with her foot. A bead of sweat rolled down her forehead as she stooped before the fireplace and gathered her materials.

The wad of newspaper sizzled and caught, shooting orange-red flames into the firebox. Jaq added kindling and blew into the fire until the twigs caught, too. She stacked two pieces of wood in the center of the fireplace, tee-pee style like Andy had taught her one summer during a backyard sleepover, and rubbed her hands together above the flames, savoring the warmth.

Outside, the snowflakes grew bigger, turning the ground a chalky white. Jaq cranked up the thermostat. Like the charge at Maxwell's, she would deal with the electric bill when it came due. She couldn't freeze because money was tight. Somehow, she'd find the funds to pay for the unexpected expenses. She always did.

Jaq hung her coat on the hook by the door and kicked her shoes off before retrieving the packages from the kitchen. She pulled the sweatshirt over her head and slipped into the oversized wool socks before stoking the fire once more.

She picked up the picture frame. Her desk was too cluttered, so she settled on the only empty spot on her bookshelf, next to a candle and a picture of her mom. She lingered before the photo, taking in the beautiful ocean background as her mom held up a large fish she had just landed.

Jaq blinked back tears and shifted her focus to the picture Andy had given her. There was no date, but she and Sam were young when it was taken. Her hair hung past her shoulders, partly covering the Santa picture stamped across the front of her green fleece pajamas.

Her younger self smiled at the camera, not yet worn down by life. Tears formed again, and Jaq stared at the picture of Sam, hoping to distract from the emotion building within. Her cousin hadn't changed much since childhood, just a more mature form of rambunctiousness with straighter teeth. But she hadn't experienced the same loss Jaq had, either. Sam had written her mom off while Jaq would give anything to speak to hers again, to feel her embrace as she assured her everything would be okay.

Staring at photos from the past was not a wise way to spend the day. Jaq reached across the desk and turned on her computer. The fan fired up, rattling like her car when it sat in the cold for too long, and Jaq adjusted the logs with a poker while she waited.

It took a minute, but the login screen finally appeared. Jaq input her password and waited for the operating system to finish loading before opening a browser. She typed Cara's name in the search box, followed by the word "scandal."

The browser thought for a moment before spitting out a list of results. Four hundred and seventeen, to be exact. The fire crackled at Jaq's back as she sorted the records, oldest first. The updated list filled her screen, black text against a white background.

Jaq reached for her mouse, but hesitated. That was a lot of entries to sift through, and she was tired.

She headed to the kitchen and returned a few minutes later with an oversized cup of coffee and a splash of bourbon mixed with her creamer. She added another log to the fireplace and pulled a notepad out of the desk drawer. The familiar excitement of starting an investigation overtook her feelings of sadness.

Jaq took another swig of coffee, grabbed a pen, and steeled herself for a tedious journey along the information superhighway.

CHAPTER 14

ನಉನಉ

Hours later, the coffeepot empty and the fireplace nothing but embers as two inches of snow coated the lawn, Jaq still sat in front of her computer.

One after another, she clicked a link, scanned the web page, and noted key phrases and details. She jotted "brought in for questioning" on her notepad when the police questioned Cara about a shoplifting incident at a boutique just across the state line and "questionable circumstances" as she read a blurb about the troublemaker crashing her car into a tree.

None of the incidents appeared in *The Gazette*. They took place in other towns, some in states as far west as Colorado. Aside from the incident with Ben, which Jaq avoided, there was no correlation between Cara's sordid activities and the life she was trying to build in Prescott.

Jaq stretched. There was so much to research, so many scandals to delve into, taking notes by hand was impossible. She tossed her pen to the side and grabbed three pieces of paper from the printer tray. She laid them end-to-end before opening her desk drawer.

Thin notepads—the kind you get from charities, stamped with holiday greetings or cartoon caricatures—sat stacked to one side. Strewn about were index cards and sticky notes with passwords and other tidbits of once-relevant information. Clips, staples, and push pins filled the drawer's built-in organizer.

Jaq eyed the paper on her desk. Clips or staples wouldn't do. She fumbled through the index cards and notes, searching for tape. A steel blade grazed her hand, and she winced. She retrieved the shears and held them to the light. They were stiff with age, belonging to her great grandmother before being handed down to Grandma, her mom, and now, her.

Jaq glanced at the photo of her mom on the bookshelf and crammed the scissors into the pencil cup at the edge of her desk.

The wound on her hand was little more than a scrape, so she resumed her search. A half-used roll of tape was stuck to the back of the drawer, and she yanked it free. She affixed the pages lengthwise before standing back to eye the spread. With a quick glance at the notes on her desk and the search entries displayed in her browser, she attached more sheets to one end.

By the time she was finished, five sheets of paper spanned her desktop. Still, she'd have to write small to fit everything in.

Jaq kicked her chair out of the way and leaned in, her pen in hand. First up was an alcohol-related incident not long after Cara's seventeenth birthday. Next, she added information about a minor fender-bender, followed by the shoplifting accusation and her car accident.

Jaq noted every event she could find related to Cara—from pageants and citations to her involvement with The Cornelia. She drew lines and added dates and keywords to trigger her memory. Any incidents that required further digging, she noted with a star.

By the time she finished, all five pages were covered with markings, dates, and tiny print. A few gaps existed as she moved from the oldest dates to the most current, but she held in her hands a thorough overview of Cara's misdeeds.

Jaq put a star next to a traffic citation from a few months ago. The incident made an online headline or two but was not scandalous enough to generate much in the way of details. But this wasn't the reason she flagged it. A review of the official traffic citation would likely confirm the incident was minor. What stood out was the date. On August third, the day before Jaq's birthday, Cara ran a red light and almost sideswiped a delivery truck. The blurb said she was "agitated" and "irrational" at the scene but offered no additional information. No explanation of where she had been or where she was headed, only that she was in Asheville, North Carolina, when the incident occurred and refused medical assistance.

Another hour passed before Jaq pushed the timeline to the side and stood up to stretch. Her notes ended with October for now, on a drunk and disorderly charge stemming from a bar fight in a neighboring county. That was as far as she could force herself to go.

It was Christmas. The time for peace and gratitude. She had better things to do than dig into the life of a person she despised more with each passing day... Didn't she?

Jaq sat back down. The need to know more about Ben's involvement with this walking disaster—to understand why he left the way he did and how he could ever risk his own life for momentary pleasure—overshadowed everything.

Ben was the type of guy who held the door for others. He went out of his way to be polite to strangers, even giving donations to the homeless men and women who lingered on the street corner near his work.

Bailing on their relationship days after meeting Cara at an event he catered still made no sense.

Had she promised Ben the restaurant of his dreams in return for love and affection? If so, he clearly was not the man Jaq thought she knew.

Jaq picked up her empty coffee cup. Ben's reason for being with Cara didn't matter anymore. Whatever the determining factor was, there was no going back in time to change it.

She set the cup in the kitchen sink and checked the thermostat on her way back to the living room. Surprisingly, the temperature hovered a degree above where she had set it.

Jaq peered out her front window. Darkness hovered over snow splashed in color from her neighbor's Christmas lights.

Under normal circumstances, the scenery would be serene. Not tonight, though. Tonight, it was ominous. A sense of foreboding Jaq could not decipher.

She'd had enough. She returned to the computer and reached for the power button. But before she could shut it off, a string of text from the last article she accessed about Cara caught her eye: "Geoffrey Winters, Esq., named trustee of the Worthington estate."

Jaq thought back to her dinner at Maxwell's. She was fairly certain Geoffrey was the name Henry used to address his companion.

She clicked on the accompanying link, but it took her to an error page. She put the cursor in the search field and typed the words "Worthington trust." Six pages of results appeared. She scanned the first few summaries quickly, learning the trust was formed over twenty years ago.

Jaq added Henry's name to the search string and pressed Enter. Nothing appeared, so she replaced Henry's name with Geoffrey's. The first result was a feature profile in a prominent legal journal.

Geoffrey had served as legal counsel for the Worthington business since its formation. He was named trustee of the family's estate years ago, which meant he played a role in Lawrence's takeover of her family's land.

Jaq felt ill. Everywhere she turned was a reminder of how much destruction this family had brought to her life.

Around eleven, she finally stepped away. Her head throbbed, and she could no longer ignore the chill in her house. She curled up beneath a stack of quilts, their bulk supplying ample warmth as she savored the snow-driven silence.

She pictured Ben lying beneath the same blankets, his breathing slow and steady. She felt peaceful, her world intact.

And then he was gone.

Her thoughts shifted to Henry. Tan and blond, his features a stark contrast to Ben's dark hair and alabaster skin. They sure had the love of money in common, though.

Jaq punched the center of her pillow. How could she lie here and think about either of them? It was inexcusable.

She stared at the ceiling, ignoring the occasional intrusion of headlights against her bedroom walls. Eventually, she rolled over and tucked the pillow between her cheek and her palm. Her breathing slowed as she drifted into twilight, one question lingering at the edge of her dreams.

How far would the Worthington family go to protect its fortune?

CHAPTER 15

Jaq awoke the next morning, the back of her head aching and her senses on fire. The feeling of foreboding had accompanied her through the night, unwilling to part even as a new day began.

It was the same sensation that infiltrated her frightened young mind as she watched the person she loved most be overrun by tubes and treatments and disease. It followed along as she traveled from her grandparent's farm to the hospital. It haunted her dreams. Like her mom's cancer, it was unwilling to relinquish its grip.

This cloud of turmoil was like an imaginary friend, always present. But it was no friend. Friends don't startle you awake in the early morning hours. They don't send your heart into supersonic mode for kicks. And they don't gnaw at you day-in and day-out, determined to retain control.

She was ten, playing near the lake with Sam, when these feelings of anguish first surfaced. The anniversary of her mom's death looming, she hadn't slept well in days. Sam was teasing her about being too scared to jump off the dock into the crisp green-blue water. Jaq had heard it all before, Sam often merciless in her need to agitate. But this time, she wouldn't stop. On and on, Sam agitated her, calling her a baby and a chicken, even making flapping motions with her arms. It was too much. Jaq screamed every obscenity she'd ever heard before fleeing to the woods. Andy found her curled up beneath a large pine tree, shaking and unable to control her sobs.

The episode earned her a trip to the pediatrician's office, where the stench of soiled baby diapers was overrun only by the attempt to mask it with antiseptic. Smooth metal kissed the back of Jaq's dangling legs as she waited for the doctor to confirm she was dying. Only he didn't do that. He looked in her ears and throat and listened to her heart and lungs before proclaiming there was nothing wrong with her.

"It's possible she's suffering from an anxiety disorder," he told her grandmother. "How long since her mom passed?"

Jaq hated when people spoke about her as if she weren't in the room. "I'm not a baby!" she shouted, surprising herself as much as the two adults discussing her care.

Dr. Matthews was a kind man, closer to retirement than medical school. "I know you're not," he said with a pat on her knee. "But sometimes we just need a friend to talk to. It'll make you feel better."

He was wrong. Talking to a stranger about her innermost feelings was a ridiculous waste of time. Week after week, she met with a middle-aged heavyset woman in a dingy office across town. At every visit, she asked how Jaq was doing, and the response was the same: "I miss my mom." Only when Grandma fell ill and Jaq convinced Andy she needed love, not a rehashing of everything wrong in her world, did the feelings of panic finally diminish.

Jaq pulled the covers tight. Being with Ben offered the same sense of hope. After he left her, she wandered through the days, weeping and lashing out at the simplest of things. Symptoms of her inability to accept that life had robbed her yet again of what she held most precious.

She rolled over on her side. So much time had passed since she lost her mom, but she could still picture her laughing at Andy's jokes. Could still see her smiling as she sat in Grampa's small boat, teaching her how to fish. Her mom was fierce, never once giving in to the misery of her disease. This example of how to deal with adversity carried Jaq through the initial breakup and served as her source of strength when the Ben and Cara sightings filled the papers and social media.

Sunlight filled Jaq's bedroom, and she glanced at the clock. It was after eight, and she'd lingered in bed for two hours. No wonder her headache wasn't getting any better. She was normally on her second cup of coffee by now.

Jaq threw off the covers and snatched her robe off the end of the bed before padding down the hallway, still wearing the thick socks Andy had given her. They did little to protect against the air chilling her house as she slept, but they were warmer than her ratty slippers.

Jaq bypassed the thermostat and made her way to the kitchen. She turned the coffeemaker on and listened to the burner sizzle as the familiar aroma tickled her nostrils and set her at ease.

Her phone buzzed as she poured her first cup. Jaq glanced at the caller ID and groaned as she tapped the phone screen. So much for tranquility.

"Did you know anything about this?" Ethan asked.

Jaq grabbed a spoon from the silverware drawer. "Anything about what?" she asked, determined not to let him snatch her last vestige of peace.

"The write-up. In today's paper."

Jaq could picture Ethan on the other end, his face frozen from years of Botox injections. Why someone his age fretted about frown lines was a mystery, but no one at the paper dared ask. Instead, they tiptoed around him whenever he was in a mood. Like now. Jaq held her tongue as she waited for him to explain whatever nonsense he was going on about.

"This is so unlike you, Jaq," he said. "I mean, you've been with the paper how long? What were you thinking?"

"Ethan, I have no clue what you're talking about."

"The O-bit-u-ar-y." Ethan always enunciated his words when he was irritated... Or drunk. Lately, it was hard to tell which state he operated from more.

Jaq set her spoon and coffee cup on the counter and walked to the front door, cracking it open just wide enough to grab the newspaper off the stoop. The frost-covered bag burned her fingertips, and she carried it into her house by the edges.

Ethan rambled on as she fought with the wrapper. Something about how this time of year was too busy with suicides and deaths of the elderly to waste space on such an elaborate spread.

Jaq finally got the paper out and flipped to the Obituary section. She gasped. Ben's full name appeared in block letters across the top of the page, followed by a list of his accomplishments and next of kin. Below that was a collage, the first photo a young schoolboy with prominent dimples and teeth too large for his face sporting a lopsided grin. Another photo of Ben and Cara in a designer suit and lavish gown must have come from a recent society event. Information about the funeral arrangements appeared in fancy script across the bottom.

Jaq grabbed the edge of the counter. Funerals. Obituaries. This had to be a dream. A horrible, heartbreaking dream.

"Jaq, you there?"

Her saliva tasted metallic, and her voice cracked as she spoke. The walls contorted, and she fought to stay on her feet. Every movement felt deliberate, like she was trying to steady herself in a fun house as the floor rippled beneath her. "This looks like something Marcus would put together," she finally said.

"Not him. I already checked. And his staff is out until next week."

Dahlia was the only other person working. Surely, she wouldn't approve something so outlandish... Would she?

"I guess I'll call Dahlia," Ethan said, reading her mind.

Jaq closed the paper and massaged her neck, the pain in the back of her head escalating. Ethan had a lot of nerve accusing her of something so ridiculous, especially after the position he put her in the other night.

"Hey," he said, all traces of agitation gone as his voice oozed with fake sincerity. "You'll go to the service, won't you? I was thinking... Since you'll be there and all, why don't you gather some info for the website? I know you won't be able to take photos or anything, but an article like this could get us a lot of positive attention."

It was bad enough he called to accuse her of something she would never do. Now he wanted her to attend the funeral of her ex-boyfriend to boost paper sales?

It was unprofessional to hang up on one's boss, but Jaq didn't care. It was that or call him a few names she couldn't take back.

She ended the call and stared at her phone in disgust. Before he was Editor-in-Chief, Ethan's career consisted of writing copy for those classified books people picked up when they needed a used lawn mower or car part. The only reason he had this job was because of his mom's marriage to the publisher. And everyone knew it.

But this? It was over the line, even for him.

Jaq reached for her coffee, now lukewarm. She popped it in the microwave and dialed Dahlia. If she broached the subject carefully, she might find out who requested such an elaborate spread. There had to be an invoice in the computer system somewhere.

The call went to voicemail.

Jaq tried Sam with the same result.

"Dammit!" She banged her hands against the countertop and sent the newspaper cascading to the floor. She yanked on the cabinet doors, opening and slamming them shut. She jerked on the junk drawer and lost her balance as her feet slid on the paper and almost sent her crashing into the edge of the countertop.

She cursed again and snatched the paper from the floor. It had ripped in two, but the text below the crease was still legible. Ben's funeral service was at two o'clock, in the same church where she said goodbye to her mom.

Jaq sank into a kitchen chair. She hadn't been to church in years. Certainly not this one. Her grandparents were laid to rest on the farm, negating the need to return to the scene of her mom's farewell.

She grabbed her cup from the microwave and added a dash of liquid fire, consuming it quickly despite the burning in her throat. She plunked the cup in the sink and shoved the newspaper in the recycle bin before stomping to the shower.

Days like this really tested her limits.

Hot water splashed Jaq's face and chest, but she could not process even the simplest sensations of wetness and warmth.

Her mom's death was like a wound scabbed over, but Ben's was still fresh. Despite his sudden vanishing act, she had been certain

Cara would alienate him, and he would eventually find his way back to her. But now...

Her tears blended with the spray as she slumped to the shower floor, unable to hold off the flood of pain any longer.

Ben was gone, their time together officially a part of her past. No second chances lurked around the next corner.

It was over.

Jaq hugged her knees and cried, hot water rolling off her shoulders and down her back. She cried for her mom, for Ben, for what they once had, now forever lost. Jaq cried until the hot water turned cool, leaving her a sniveling, chilled mess, curled in a ball on the slick shower floor.

She pulled herself together and washed up. Moments later, staring at her puffy red eyes in the mirror as steam dissipated around her, Jaq decided she would go to the funeral.

Not because she wanted to. But because it was her last chance to give her relationship with Ben a proper goodbye.

CHAPTER 16

ನಟನಟ

The church overflowed with mourners from Cara's circle of influence. They filed in, the smell of high-end perfume and rich leather clinging to the air as Jaq stood outside the church waiting for Sam.

Andy dropped her off near the front door, and Jaq held her arm as they walked in. Several young men stood before the sanctuary, solemn as they offered condolences and handed programs to all who entered.

Jaq's heart raced as she passed through the ornate wooden doors for the first time in over twenty years. The space was small, with ten rows of formal seating. The back rows were sparse, but the front half overflowed with people wanting to pay their respects. Dim fixtures lit the perimeter, keeping the pews dark out of respect for the grieving.

Jaq stared at the first row. She wanted to feel something but couldn't. Was this where she sat with her grandparents and Andy? Or were she and Sam allowed to roam, a way of protecting them from the sadness permeating the holy space? She couldn't remember.

To the right, several women clutched tissues in their hands, surrounded by stoic men in dark suits. A teen who once worked with Ben nodded in her direction, but even this act of recognition could not distract from Cara, seated near the pulpit in a black dress so simple, Jaq thought she was mistaken. But then she turned, and even the intricate lacy veil could not mask her sharp profile.

"I'll bet you ten bucks she's high beneath that thing," Sam said, her voice not as quiet as she intended.

An older woman turned from the third row and glanced their way. Her chest heaved as she lifted a handkerchief to her face.

Jaq waved in apology and tugged at Sam's arm. They made their way around the pews and to the left, where several metal chairs sat empty, waiting to hold any overflow.

Sunlight pierced the stained-glass window that encased the sanctuary, casting blue and orange light over the closed casket, as if to say farewell to the man inside.

Jaq fought off her memories of the photo from Sam's desk— Ben's unnatural color, his contorted face. She ached to see him once more. To hold him, to replace the memory of that horrendous crime scene photo with the face she once knew by heart.

The metal chair was cold against Jaq's legs, but she didn't care. Sitting away from the crowd allowed her to mourn in private.

The reverend's speech was brief, a recitation of scripture and the need to seek comfort in God's grace after death. Jaq wanted to believe the words but struggled to do so. Tears stung her eyes, and she forced her attention elsewhere. On the cigarette smell of Sam's winter coat, how the dress on a woman seated nearby bunched in all the wrong places. Anything but the onslaught of memories flooding her soul... Of Ben *and* her mom.

Jaq took a deep breath and willed the flood of emotion to pass.

Cara approached the pulpit, and two men in dark suits escorted her up the steps.

Sam raised an eyebrow, and Jaq shared her sentiment. Cara was too high to walk without help.

Cara reached the pulpit and lifted her face covering with the dramatic flair of a bride preparing for the consummate kiss. If ever there was a woman who didn't let a tragedy go to waste, it was Cara Worthington. She swayed slightly, her expression glazed from whatever substance she indulged in beforehand, before steadying herself against the tall wooden structure. The ushers retreated.

"Benjamin..." Cara said, dabbing at her eyes with a crumpled tissue. "Was the most decent man I've ever known."

Jaq stared at the paper in her hand, willing herself not to lose it. What did Cara know about decency? She had stripped Ben of any he had left.

The print on the program blurred, and a drop of moisture stained the edge. Sam grazed Jaq's knee, and she nodded she was okay. She wiped the wetness from her cheeks, determined to save the sorrow-fest for the privacy of her home.

Cara stumbled over her words, and Henry appeared from the shadows to help her.

Jaq's heart skipped at the sight of his handsome face.

"Who is *that*?" Sam nudged Jaq in the ribs as she nodded her head in approval. Leave it to her cousin to think about men during an otherwise somber event.

Jaq kept her eyes forward, opting not to engage.

Henry took Cara by the arm and guided her to her seat, his movements gentle, a brother protecting his sister. She flopped into the chair like the ordeal was too much for her to handle.

"Puh-lease." Once again, Sam misjudged the volume of her voice.

The same woman as before looked their way and held a finger to her lips. Sam's face turned red, and she found something interesting to stare at in her lap.

"Mrs. Rutherford?"

The reverend motioned to the older woman, and Jaq's breath caught in her throat. They had met only once, over a quick meal where Ben last worked.

Sam touched her knee again, and Jaq ignored her as an usher guided Ben's mom to the front. Heavyset, with graying hair and sharp glasses, she looked twenty years older than their first encounter. She took a deep breath and tried to speak, but sobs overtook her before she utter a word.

Henry was by her side in an instant, helping her return to her seat like he had Cara. He whispered something in her ear and placed his hand over hers before disappearing once again into the shadows.

Cara sat with her veil raised and her eyes forward, oblivious to any pain but her own.

A few people Jaq did not know paid tribute to Ben, and the reverend offered a closing prayer as the service ended.

"I'll be back," Jaq said before Sam could object. She slipped through the procession of mourners and made her way to the front of the sanctuary. Ben's mom was struggling to get up, and Jaq extended a hand. "Here," she said. "Let me help."

"Jaq, dear. I thought that was you, but these old eyes aren't exactly reliable anymore." Her voice was pleasant, but the smile did not extend past her lips.

"Is there anything I can do for you?"

Ben's mom motioned for her coat and purse. Jaq picked them up and steadied her as they made their way to the aisle.

"I was really hoping you and Ben would work things out, dear," she said as she stumbled along. "I can't help but wonder..." Her voice drifted off as she stopped and turned toward the casket.

"Me, too." Jaq put her hand on her lower back and nudged her forward.

"Coming through!" Cara pushed past them and through the small crowd gathered at the end of the aisleway.

Ben's mom clenched her hands. "That woman! I swear. If she weren't helping my Benjamin open his restaurant..."

Jaq felt no pleasure at having her hunch confirmed. Ben was willing to pimp himself out to someone with money and power to fulfill his professional dreams. So much for decency.

"He loved you, you know."

Jaq stared at Ben's mom. Black bags adorned her puffy red eyes, and her brow furrowed with wrinkles from too much sun over a lifetime. No wonder she hadn't recognized her. It was like placing a ghost.

"You were the love of his life," she said and continued on without Jaq's help. "He told me that the last time we spoke."

Jaq caught up to her in two strides. "When was that?" she asked. Her heart felt like it would jump out of her chest.

An usher scurried between Jaq and the empty pew. "Lean on me" he said, leading Mrs. Rutherford away before she could respond.

Jaq drove to the cemetery in silence.

Ben loved her. Or so his mom had said. Assuming their conversation was recent—a real possibility since they used to talk at least once a week—had this confession somehow contributed to his death?

The sky seemed grayer as Jaq climbed out of her car. "Is it supposed to snow?"

Sam shivered and dug in her coat for her gloves. "I don't think so. But it's certainly cold enough to."

They crossed the street in silence. When they reached the grassy area, Sam touched her arm. "Are you sure you want to be here?" she asked. "I know I wouldn't want to be."

"I'm fine. Promise."

Jaq wasn't fine, but it didn't matter. This was something she had to do. They trudged up the small hill to the plot Ben's mom selected, surrounded by tombstones for his father, older brother, and both grandparents. Ben had no other siblings, so it was just his mom left now.

More people arrived and Jaq and Sam stayed at the periphery, allowing them room. The same usher that escorted Ben's mom out of the church led her to a spot in front of the casket. The reverend spoke, and she sobbed as the funeral director lowered Ben's casket into his grave.

Cara stood opposite his mom, huffing and tapping her foot as she waited to toss dirt on the gravesite. Henry was a few feet behind her. An older man stood to the right, refined in a tailored three-piece suit, his gray hair parted to the right and smoothed to perfection.

Lawrence Worthington.

He leaned over and said something to Henry, who nodded and ran his fingers through his hair as he listened. He looked every bit the model in his own dark suit and steel gray tie.

Cara wobbled, her pointy heels no match for the frozen ground. Henry put out a hand to steady her, and Jaq's heart fluttered at this simple but considerate action. For a fleeting moment, thoughts of Ben fell away as she pictured herself in Henry's arms, his calm strength steadying her, not Cara.

"Jaq?" Sam touched her arm. "You all right?"

Jaq nodded, her cheeks red from more than the cold.

Ben's mom was the first to toss dirt on the casket. She lingered near the edge, her shoulders heavy with grief, until the usher convinced her to leave.

Cara wrapped her long fingers around the handle and flung dirt over the cream box, her face expressionless. She handed the shovel to the funeral home director and wiped her hands on her coat. "Am I glad *that's* over," she said to no one in particular.

Sam made a face behind Cara's back, and it took every ounce of Jaq's restraint not to trip Cara as she passed by.

The wind picked up and Jaq repositioned her scarf before shoving her hands into her coat pockets. If there were any justice in this world, Cara would stumble head-first on her way down the hill. But Jaq knew all too well karma was a finicky master.

Cara, Henry, and Lawrence made their way down the embankment to the limousine parked across the street. The driver stood near the back door and opened it as they neared. Cara climbed in first, followed by Henry. Lawrence said something to the driver before getting in himself.

"I swear," Jaq said as they, too, headed down the hill. "I'm going to take that woman down if it's the last thing I do."

"I doubt you're the first person to feel that way."

Jaq stopped short of the car. "I mean it, Sam. Cara's a disease."

"No argument there." Sam waited for Jaq to unlock the doors and slid into the passenger seat. "But what makes you think you can do anything about it? The Worthingtons are like Fort Knox around here, you know. Impenetrable."

They waited for a break in the line of cars leaving the cemetery. A green minivan paused long enough to let them out, and Jaq waved her thanks to the driver.

"You'd be surprised," she said, picturing the timeline sitting on her desk. "Nobody escapes their past forever."

CHAPTER 17

Jaq dropped Sam off with the assurance she was okay and drove north before she could change her mind.

Twenty-six miles later, she turned onto the narrow road that once connected her grandparent's farm to the rest of the world. A quick turn at the thicket of pine trees, a long, winding stretch, a split to the right for one point two miles... The route was imprinted on Jaq's brain. Not only had she and Sam walked the long, gravel stretch often as kids, but Andy also measured it one spring when, for reasons unfathomable now, they decided to join the track team.

Those aspirations faded, of course, when they learned how much conditioning was involved. But the bright orange markers Andy used to line the road persisted. Remnants peeked through tall, tangled weeds just beyond the shoulder. The Worthington family had tried to erase the past but fencing and a layer of asphalt were nothing more than ornaments desecrating the memory of this once thriving farmland.

A lawsuit filed by the local wildlife organization halted construction until Lawrence's company conceded to build its multimillion-dollar community on but a portion of the acreage. Within six months of signing that agreement, a community of wealth was born... And the land Jaq and Sam once played on was no more.

Jaq parked her car on the shoulder and hiked the brief stretch to the entrance. A large, wrought-iron gate with the Worthington family insignia loomed over the drive, protecting the community occupants from the meddling of outsiders. A security guard sat in a tiny building just before the entry, his chest moving up and down as a space heater droned at his feet.

Jaq tiptoed past the guard and eyed the vertical slats. It was a tight fit, but she managed to squeeze through the gate.

In the distance, she could see the lake where she learned to swim. Where she fished with her mom until the very end. And where she sat with Andy on the dock as they discussed the possibility of coming to live with him and Sam when Grandma got sick.

This place was so much more than a plot of land. It symbolized every important event in her childhood, yet she had no means to fight for it when the time came. Neither did Andy, responsible for her and Sam and a mortgage of his own. But he scraped together the funds needed to pay the estate tax. Had the bank manager processed his paperwork instead of holding it while Lawrence made an offer the bank would never refuse, she would be celebrating the new year here with Sam and Andy, not by herself in her small, frigid house.

Lawrence Worthington displaced her family... And for what? Yet another private community for his friends and business partners. A place the rich could frequent for vacation or send their pampered children when they needed some "space."

Jaq's blood boiled. Just like that, generations lost their heritage while the bank manager packed his belongings and bolted to some place far away before the news of the transaction went public.

Her pace quickened as she walked down the center of the street, daring a resident to confront her. It didn't matter to her how rich or powerful these people were. They would get an earful… Of how unwelcome they were and how much their greed had cost her family. It was time they understood the truth. With every entrance or exit of their lavish homes, they were tromping on her legacy.

No one noticed her, or if they did, wisely stayed indoors. Jaq's fury only deepened as she walked, each residence larger than the last. At the end of the half-mile stretch, just beyond a dip in the road, was the largest of all—Lawrence's mansion, built on the exact spot where her grandparent's modest cabin once stood. To the right, where the fort Grampa built for her and Sam used to be, stood a steel five-car garage.

Jaq stood at the top of the hill. Spotlights reflected against the front of Lawrence's house, lighting up the landscape. The surrounding shrubs and flowers were trimmed back and covered with wire to protect them from frost. Christmas lights lined the expansive roof, twinkling as the sun started its descent. No one was home, and maybe that was for the best. Even the sight of Henry would not deter her from telling his vulture of a father what she thought of his business practices.

She glanced at her watch. It was getting late, and she had to make it past the security guard before he awoke from his nap. She scurried toward the entrance and exited the community as discreetly as she entered. Her car still sat parked on the shoulder, undisturbed. She crawled in and made a U-turn as the lights of a large SUV appeared in the distance.

Jaq kept her head down as the vehicle passed by. She cranked up the heat and drove the long trek home, injustice and revenge riding shotgun.

CHAPTER 18

The Sheriff's Office was quiet, the anticipation of Christmas overtaken by exhaustion as deputies prepared for the arduous task of welcoming in the new year.

Sam greeted Jaq at the entry and escorted her inside.

Normally, the lobby overflowed with family members trying to post bail as officers struggled to manage the onslaught of questions, demands, and radio call-outs. Not today. Only a single unlucky officer sat at a small metal desk in the middle of the room, surrounded by a stack of papers waiting to be processed.

Jaq waved as they passed by, and he nodded as he reached for another form.

"This way," Sam said, weaving through the empty desks.

Jaq followed her to a small room down the hall.

"I got to thinking about what you said yesterday... About a person's past catching up to them?" Sam stopped outside a navy door with the words "Meeting Room" etched on its placard. "I pulled a bunch of stuff that might interest you."

"You didn't have to do that." Jaq touched Sam's arm. "Seriously."

Sam shrugged and raised a card to the gray box attached to the door. A green light glowed, and she waved Jaq inside. "I always liked Ben," she said. "It was the least I could do."

Jaq surveyed the room. It was as small as her kitchen, with an oversized wooden table shoved against the far wall and three metal chairs opened for seating. More folding chairs were stacked nearby.

Papers and folders littered the tabletop. On the wall to the right was a large whiteboard filled with Sam's handwriting.

Jaq spun on her heel and banged her hip against the table corner. "Ow!" she said, rubbing the spot. "When did you say you came in?"

Sam scooted a chair from beneath the table. She plopped down and motioned for Jaq to do the same. "Last night. Wasn't planning to be here that long, but once I started pulling stuff, it was hard to stop." She gestured toward the table. "Never imagined I'd find so much dirt on one group of people."

She was wearing jeans and a long-sleeved tee, with no makeup and shadows beneath her eyes. A rarity for someone who insisted on always looking her best.

"Did you get any sleep?"

Sam avoided the question and stood up. "Coffee?"

Jaq nodded and pulled a notepad and pen from her purse. She tossed her bag and coat onto the extra chair and opened the notebook to a clean page. None of what she viewed would ever see print. She could use it, however, to dig into other leads.

Sam plucked a folder from the mess on the table and handed it to her. "Be back in a sec," she said. "Start here."

Jaq opened the file as the door shut behind her cousin. It was the report from Cara's traffic accident in August, but this time, she was privy to all the details. Not the watered-down version approved by the Worthington public relations machine.

Jaq scrolled the contents. As suspected, the incident was minor, only the timing suspicious. She noted the location and the citing officer's name and badge number.

Sam banged against the door, and Jaq let her in.

Tendrils of steam floated above two cups. Sam handed Jaq the coffee with cream and scooted by her. "Cara's legal troubles go back years," she said, wagging a finger at the whiteboard before sipping her coffee. "Pretty much since she was old enough to leave the house on her own."

Jaq reached for her phone and scrolled through the photos, hoping she had captured a shot of the timeline at home and just forgotten. No such luck. "Crap," she said under her breath, but Sam turned around in surprise.

"You say something?"

Jaq shook her head. "Okay if I take a picture?" she asked.

"You know the drill."

Jaq winked. "I'd never give you up," she said and snapped a full view of the whiteboard before capturing close-ups of both sides. She always took multiple views from every angle, no matter the subject. Sometimes, it was overkill. But, other times, it captured elements she didn't notice at first... Like the eraser marks still visible in Sam's notes. Jaq shifted her attention from her phone to her cousin and nodded toward the whiteboard. "Why the change?"

Sam stepped back. "You mean here?" She pointed to the spot where she had written something over the eraser smear, and Jaq nodded. "I thought the first incident last year was April, but turns out, it was March."

"Not long after Cornelia Worthington died." That much Jaq recalled from the news. It was all the local reporters could talk about for a week leading up to the funeral.

Back then, Cara was nothing but a blip on her radar. Another attention-seeker she could ignore. How things had changed.

"Cara ran into some trouble not long after," Sam said. She turned and faced Jaq again. "You'd have to be living under a rock not to remember the stink her dad made when they picked her up for questioning."

Jaq nodded, keeping it to herself that she only learned about Cara's criminal transgressions the other day. "Did you find anything around the time she and Ben got together?" Jaq's lips felt dry, the words stinging as they escaped. She reached for her coffee.

"Surprisingly, no. Not until..."

Jaq wiped a drop of liquid from her top lip. "So, she meets Ben a year or so after she gets into all sorts of trouble and magically turns her life around? You're not buying that, are you?"

Sam downed the rest of her coffee and shrugged. "People change."

Jaq winced, the memory of how Ben died still as breathtaking as a splash of icy water.

"Oh, geez, Jaq. I'm sorry. I didn't mean—"

Jaq held up a hand. "It's okay," she said, leaning back in her chair and thinking of the pictures of Ben she found on Sam's desk. "Yeah, people change. Sometimes for the better. Sometimes... You just don't know what the hell's going on with them."

With Sam's permission and a sworn promise to secrecy, Jaq took photos of several incident reports for further investigation. Most were minor infractions. Parking in a handicapped space then arguing with the shop owner about it, missing a scheduled court date. Things like that.

Aside from the DUI and Ben's death, the picture painted by Cara's run-ins with the law was that of a child seeking attention, not a hardened criminal. Had Cara not stolen Ben away, Jaq might even feel sorry for her.

But Cara *had* stolen him away, and she would find no forgiveness with Jaq. No pity or compassion. She deserved none of those things.

What she did deserve was a dose of reality. To come face-to-face with a member of the press who had nothing to lose in her pursuit of the truth.

"Don't do anything stupid," Sam said that afternoon as she walked Jaq out. "Please."

Jaq gave her cousin a quick hug and bounded for the steps, keys jangling in her hand. "Not making any promises," she said with a wave goodbye. "But whatever happens, I'll be sure to keep your name out of it."

CHAPTER 19

Twenty minutes later, Jaq idled on the street in front of The Cornelia, Sam's reputation the furthest thing from her mind.

She settled into her seat as cars of various makes and models drove by and reached for the bottle of water she pilfered from Andy's office. Unless Cara decided to eat in—a concept so ridiculous, Jaq nearly choked at the thought—she would appear any moment now.

The sun continued its slow descent. Jaq got her coughing fit under control and shifted in her seat. The heater blasted warm air around her legs and her head drooped toward her chest.

A car honked nearby, startling her awake.

"Watch it, you jack-off!" Cara gave the driver the middle finger and stumbled through the crosswalk, no bodyguards in tow. Her boot caught the edge of the curb, and she flailed about, fighting to keep her balance.

"Hey, lady. You okay?"

"Mind your own damn business!" Cara flipped him the bird again and disappeared between two parked cars. The driver rolled up his window and drove away as she lurched down the sidewalk.

Jaq groaned. Of course Maxwell's was where Cara would go to eat. She should have expected nothing less.

Jaq shut off the engine and grabbed her coat and purse from the passenger seat. She paused at the crosswalk, barely averting a speeding driver on his phone. The sidewalk teemed with passersby undeterred by the wintry weather, and Jaq maneuvered her way through a group of people as Cara entered the restaurant.

Another group gathered at the entry, and Jaq forced her way through as she tried to keep her cool. Maxwell's was the last place she wanted to be—again—but she had to confront Cara if she ever stood a chance at finding out what happened to Ben.

When the hostess greeted her this time, Jaq knew what to say. Moments later, she was asking the bartender for a club soda and a loaded baked potato.

He nodded and fixed her drink before turning to a woman sitting at the other end of the bar. He leaned in as he answered her questions and shared a few recommendations from the menu.

Jaq smirked. Either he recognized the tip potential with the other patron, or he liked his women older and lonelier. She didn't care as long as she didn't waste another thirty bucks in this place for what barely qualified as a meal.

Jaq plunked a slice of lime in her glass and eyed Cara, sitting alone at a table for four.

Two waiters hovered nearby, in a heated discussion. The younger one walked to the server station, grabbed a menu, and gave the other waiter the finger behind his back.

Jaq stifled a snort, happy to learn someone else in town shared her sentiment toward the youngest Worthington. Her baked potato arrived, and she gobbled several bites of the soft, cheesy filling, monitoring Cara out of the corner of her eye.

"I said, 'Bring me another,' you moron!"

Jaq looked over as Cara raised her glass above her head. Liquid sloshed over the side and splashed to the floor.

The waiter removed the glass from her hand with care, as if he feared she might throw it at him.

"Yo," the bartender said as the waiter approached and Jaq tried to appear preoccupied with her food. "I think she's had enough."

"Maybe you can tell her that," the waiter said with a scowl as he set Cara's glass on the bar. "She sure as hell won't listen to me."

Jaq could smell the bourbon. Warm and elegant, it had to be high end. Cara was not one to resist the finer things.

The bartender made a face and pulled the towel from his shoulder. He was halfway around the bar when the waiter held up his hand.

"Never mind." He pointed toward the front of the dining room. "Looks like it's our lucky day…"

Jaq almost dropped her fork as Henry walked in.

He looked around, his eyes landing on Cara. He waved to the waiter and headed for her table.

The bartender retrieved Cara's glass and asked if Jaq needed anything else before closing out her tab.

She shook her head and reached for her purse. Any hope of fulfilling her mission was gone now that Henry had arrived.

Jaq took one last bite of her potato and a final swig of her drink before leaving a twenty on the bar. She had one arm through her coat when someone bumped her from behind. Her purse went flying, and she smacked her knee hard against the thick wooden leg of the barstool.

"Miss, I am so sorry." A flustered Henry held Cara by the elbow. He was so close Jaq could smell the peppermint on his breath.

"What the hell you looking at her for?" Spit flew from Cara's mouth, and Jaq reared back. They were close in age, but Cara could pass for ten years her senior, gray hairs protruding from the part in her otherwise dark hair, the wrinkles around her eyes and mouth undeniable, even in the dim bar light. Either an expert make-up artist was paid to perfect her youthful look for public consumption, or the events of the past week had aged her.

Jaq felt the weight of Ben's death, too, but sadness and guilt were different animals.

"Are you okay?" Henry asked.

Jaq realized she was standing with her weight on one leg, and her hand on her injured knee. She dropped her foot and nodded, even though her knee throbbed.

Cara tottered, and Henry struggled to keep her from falling face-first into the bar.

"Let me help." Jaq finished putting her coat on and yanked her purse over her neck and arm. She gripped Cara's waist and tried not to recoil at the stench of alcohol on her breath and clothes.

"Thank you," Henry said. "But you don't—"

"Henry. The girl wants to help." A line of drool formed at the edge of Cara's lips and threatened to mar her designer blouse. She snorted as she eyed Jaq in her sweater, boots, and faded jeans. "Maybe you could thank her for me later."

Jaq blushed and tried to ignore Cara's intrusive stare.

"I'm really sorry," Henry said.

Cara sneered at him. "Stop apologizing. You always do that."

Jaq tightened her grip, finding some pleasure in Cara's cries of discomfort. Slowly, she and Henry led her through the dining room and out the front door, ignoring the stares as people moved out of their way.

"I can take it from here," Henry said as Cara unexpectedly threw her weight forward. He caught her before she knocked Jaq over, and the two of them grappled to keep her upright.

Cara tugged until she broke free. She collapsed to her knees by the curb and threw up in the street.

The valet on duty stayed at his podium, suddenly occupied with organizing the keys in the rack. Henry looked ready to leave his sister crumpled at the edge of the road.

Jaq ignored every part of her that screamed Cara was getting what she deserved and helped her up.

Henry gripped Cara's waist. Jaq did the same from the other side, aware of the warmth of his skin near hers.

Henry nodded toward The Cornelia. "Just a little further," he said, and the three of them made their way down the sidewalk, across the street, and up the steps to the lobby entrance.

"Everything okay, Mr. Worthington?" the concierge asked as they stumbled through the front door.

Henry nodded, and they led Cara to the elevator.

She did not put up much resistance while they waited. "You should ask her out, Henry," she said with a nod in Jaq's direction. "She looks like your type."

Jaq did her best to keep a solemn face. What was Henry's type? Normal and sober? She stared ahead, willing the elevator to hurry before she gave into the urge to knock Cara onto her obnoxious behind.

How had Ben ever chosen this vile woman over her? Jaq bit her lip as her baked potato threatened to surface.

The elevator doors opened, and they helped Cara inside.

"I got it!" Cara said, yanking her arms from their grasp and snarling in Jaq's direction. "This ain't a prison!"

Jaq let go, her hands on fire, like Cara's rage had seeped into her pores.

Cara whipped around and lunged at the closing elevator doors, but Henry blocked her exit. If Cara was five-eleven, as several outlets proclaimed, Henry was six-one or six-two.

"Sis," he said, gripping both shoulders. "We've talked about this. I'm only here to help. Not judge."

The elevator rattled and began its journey to the top floor.

Cara stopped struggling. "You know what you need?" she said, waving a hand in Jaq's direction. "A good lay. You're too uptight."

Henry turned every shade of red, and Jaq wished she knew him well enough to offer some words of comfort. Instead, she held his train wreck of a sister steady as the elevator lurched toward its destination. The rumors about her childish behavior were no exaggeration. It was easy to picture Cara doing all the things she had uncovered in her research.

The elevator came to a stop and the doors opened. Jaq and Henry escorted Cara through the foyer to the living room, where they seated her on the oversized sofa. She flopped backward onto the plush cushions, oblivious to the slush coating her boots and staining the cream fabric.

Jaq clenched her fists. Cara was every bit as awful as she imagined, yet she would face no consequences for her behavior. Not with her dad funding her every move and Henry insistent upon protecting her.

Jaq scanned the surroundings. To her left, stainless appliances sparkled against the white marble kitchen countertops. A crystal chandelier, at least six feet above the cherry dining room table, shimmered as streetlights refracted off large casement windows. A stocked bar stood to the right, with several glasses overturned and liquid pooling on the marble top. Nearby, the gas fireplace flickered as Henry adjusted its settings.

Jaq panned from the fireplace to the sofa. Cara was sprawled on her back, eyes closed. The fingers on her left hand twitched as she let out a little moan.

Jaq leaned forward.

Cara's dark, piercing eyes shot open, and she stared at Jaq like she could see her soul.

Jaq stumbled backward, nearly tripping over the jagged coffee table. Its glass edge pierced her flesh, and she flailed backwards as a warm wetness trickled down her leg.

She gripped the edge of the sofa, noticing for the first time the large walnut beam spanning the length of the room. She craned her neck to see around the fireplace.

A silvery Christmas tree stood just out of sight, rows of decorative packages artfully arranged beneath its artificial limbs.

Jaq willed herself not to scream.

She was standing less than twenty feet from where they found Ben.

CHAPTER 20

"Are you all right?"

Jaq stared at Henry, too stunned to speak.

"I'm sorry, I didn't catch your name," he said, his hazel eyes appearing blue against his dark polo shirt.

Jaq blinked away the tears stinging her eyelids and forced herself to focus on Henry, not the beam above her head.

Anything but that.

"Jaq," she said, trying to throttle the emotion raging within.

"Jaq?"

She nodded and brushed the tinge of wetness from her cheek. "And, yes, I'm okay."

Cara mumbled something, her eyes closed once more as she flailed her hand about, trying to find Henry's leg.

He sidestepped her touch and reached for a nearby throw. He slipped her boots off and put them to the side before tucking her feet beneath the blanket and whispering something in her ear.

Jaq stared. Cara was wearing the same leather boots with chunky heels she told Ben she wanted for Christmas last year.

"One day, babe," he had said, kissing the top of her head and dishing stuffed pesto shells with sauteed vegetables onto her plate. "I see nothing but good things in our future. Everything we've dreamed of."

Jaq gripped Cara's sofa, afraid she might pass out if she didn't get out of there soon.

Henry touched her arm, and she jumped.

"I'll walk you out," he said.

Jaq didn't trust herself to speak. She stared at the man before her, dapper despite the purplish-blue circles beneath his eyes. He motioned toward the entryway, and she followed in silence, afraid if she opened her mouth, she might reveal her connection to Cara.

"Thank you again," Henry said when they reached the elevator. He pressed the down button, but before the doors could open, stepped in front of Jaq. "How about a cup of coffee?" he asked.

Jaq was speechless. Here was this incredibly handsome man, asking to spend more time with her... Yet she could not ignore her feelings about his family.

"Please," Henry said and flashed her a charming smile. "It's the least I can do."

Jaq nodded, and he ushered her inside and pressed the button for the first floor. She stared at the metal doors as the elevator shuttled them downstairs.

She was in unfamiliar territory, but there was no turning back.

Only a few people milled about in the lobby. Henry led Jaq to a leather couch beneath a large picture window.

She paused, taking in the sight of snowflakes flitting across the building's exterior lights.

Henry stood with her until someone approached from behind.

They both turned, and Henry stuck out his hand. "Good evening, Frank," he said with a quick shake. "I'll have an Irish coffee, please. And you, Jaq?"

The way he said her name sent a jolt of electricity through Jaq's body, but she kept her composure. "That sounds great."

"Homemade whipped cream?" Frank asked.

Henry looked at Jaq, and she nodded.

Frank disappeared into the kitchen, and Jaq raised an eyebrow.

Henry chuckled. "When you practically own the place, they'll make whatever you want." Unlike Cara, he did not reek of entitlement. He was merely stating a fact.

Jaq tried to pull off her coat, but the right arm caught on her watch. Henry leaned over to help, giving her another whiff of his cologne as his hand grazed her arm. Cinnamon mixed with a tinge of orange. Maybe vanilla. It smelled fantastic, whatever it was.

"Thank you," Jaq said and looked away before he could detect the color in her cheeks. Cozying up to Henry was a line she could not cross.

Frank returned with two cups of steaming, caramel-colored liquid, topped with silky cream and a dusting of sprinkles. Jaq took a sip and smiled at him. It was just the right blend of bitter and sweet.

Henry shook Frank's hand again, this time with a bill in his palm.

Clearly, he was raised proper. So, what had happened with Cara? Jaq pondered this question as she cupped her beverage.

Henry took a drink and sat back on the couch, more visibly relaxed.

Jaq studied his profile. Who was she kidding? This wasn't about Ben. Or Cara. Henry was handsome and single, and here they were, sharing Irish coffees like two old friends catching up. What difference did it make if his world revolved on a different axis?

Henry took another sip. His shirt bunched above his belt where Cara had gripped him, but even that did not hide his toned physique.

Jaq forced herself to look away. "It must be weird living in a hotel," she said. She scanned the lobby, noting the fancy columns, the fresh flowers, the intricate oriental-style furnishings. "I mean, I'm sure it's nice and all. It just seems so... I don't know. *Cold.*"

"It's not that bad, having someone on hand to make meals and take care of your laundry." Henry smiled as his eyes took on a faraway look, like he was reliving a part of his past. "Makes things simple. Especially when you're a kid."

Jaq didn't respond, her childhood spent playing with worn stuffed animals and wearing hand-me-downs fitted by her grandmother. Money was as tight back then as it was now.

Her next sip of coffee tasted bitter, and she set her cup down with more force than intended.

"Did I say something wrong?"

"No, you're fine." She waved toward the cup. "I'm gonna have to drive home, though. Better to quit while I'm ahead."

"Our driver can take you." Henry set his cup on the table beside hers. "Or I can give you a ride myself?" He ran his fingers through his hair, and his loose curls bounced back into position with ease.

Was there anything about this man that wasn't perfect? The thought should not have irritated her, but it did.

Henry stood up. "Really. I don't mind."

"Thank you. But I'm okay." Jaq tucked a strand of hair behind her ear and reached for her coat. It was the same one she had worn for three winters now, the trim around the collar frayed and several buttons in need of repair. She could not let him drive her home.

Henry touched her arm. "I'm sorry if I said something to offend you." He sat back down. "Please. Won't you stay? I haven't spoken with anyone but lawyers and family in days."

The tortured look on his face pricked at her heart, and Jaq relented. She draped her coat over the arm of the couch and faced him as she sat down. "I would love nothing more than to continue talking with you."

Henry smiled, but it faded as Jaq held up her hand.

"I would love to stay, but you need to know something first." She picked at the orange stitching in the leather. "I go by Jaq, but my full name is Jacqueline Darcy. I work for *The Gazette*."

The look of horror on Henry's face was unmistakable.

"I'm not writing a story about you or your family, if that's what you're worried about."

He stayed seated but looked like he wanted nothing more than to bolt from the hotel lobby.

"I was at the restaurant tonight, hoping to learn more about your sister because, well..."

Henry slapped his palm against his forehead. "You're Benjamin's ex." His voice was barely a whisper. "I can't believe I didn't recognize the name." He ran his fingers through his hair again and polished off his drink in one gulp. If the hot liquid burned his tongue, he gave no indication.

"Henry—"

This time, he was the one to put up a hand. "I agree, it's time for you to go." He laid a twenty on the table next to their cups and stood up. "Thank you again for the help with my sister."

"Please don't leave, Henry..."

Henry stared at her. "Just once," he said, "it would be nice to meet someone with no ulterior motive."

He strode to the elevator, leaving Jaq alone on the couch.

Frank walked over and cleaned off the coffee table. "Anything else, Miss?" he asked.

Jaq shook her head and gathered her things. She exited the lobby and walked to the parking lot, her eyes cast downward. On the way home, the tears she held at bay in Cara's penthouse finally fell without restraint.

CHAPTER 21

ﭏﭏﭏﭏ

Jaq rarely dreamed, but that night, her imagination swirled about like a tempest. She snuggled with Ben on the couch as a movie played on the TV, comforted by his deep rhythmic breathing. Only it wasn't Ben, it was Henry beside her. Henry with his sandy hair and smile so warm, her stomach fluttered.

Jaq reached for him, and just as she felt the softness of his skin, Cara's sneering face jolted her awake.

The room spun as sweat glistened her brow.

Jaq rolled over and curled her legs toward her chest, willing herself to stay calm.

Gray sky filled the bedroom windows, a perfect complement to her mood. She buried her face in the pillows as the outside world came to life. A neighbor down the street revved his oversized pickup, the loud intro to a heavy metal song barely overtaking the rumble of his V8. Mrs. Jenkins, her neighbor to the right, yelled at her grandson to get moving or he'd be late for work.

Jaq's phone vibrated on the nightstand, but she ignored it. Instead, she closed her eyes and pictured the hurt look on Henry's face. Ben had hurt her enough while he was alive. Did she really have to let him dictate her future, too?

Jaq punched her pillow. She didn't even know who Ben was anymore. Certainly not the person she had planned to spend her life with. *That* person never would have taken up with someone like Cara. At least not the drunk version she'd had the misfortune of meeting last night.

Henry's kind face replaced the memory of Cara leering at her in the elevator, and Jaq bit her lip in frustration. Or was it desire?

She closed her eyes. Henry seemed far kinder than she imagined someone with wealth could be... Her attraction to him was like an intoxicating fog she could not escape.

Her phone buzzed again, and Jaq snatched it off the nightstand. It better not be Dahlia. It was way too early to field calls from work.

Jaq didn't recognize the number. She dropped it to the bed and reached for her quilt.

Her phone buzzed again, indicating she had a voicemail.

Jaq dug her phone from beneath the covers and played the message. A loud female voice screeched in her ear, and she scrambled to adjust the volume.

"You leave my brother alone, you hear? Ben left you for me. Get over it, you stupid—"

Jaq's stomach did somersaults, and her hand shook as she deleted the message. How had Cara gotten her number? She rarely gave it out. Not even for professional reasons.

The blaze in her stomach intensified.

Someone with that information might share it for a price.

What a depressing thought.

Her phone buzzed again, and Jaq ignored it. She crawled out of bed and made her way to the bathroom.

She would figure out a way to block Cara later. Right now, she just wanted to wash away the past twenty-four hours and get on with her life.

Even if that meant never seeing, talking to, or thinking about Henry Worthington again.

An hour later, Jaq returned to the bedroom, clean and two cups into her morning brew. She found her phone beneath the covers and turned it over, one eye closed as if this would somehow protect her from Cara's wrath.

But messages from Cara weren't all she missed. Ethan had called twice and sent her a text to contact him ASAP.

The calmness she had worked so hard to achieve evaporated. Jaq accessed her voicemail. Her mailbox was full, the last of Cara's messages saved around the time Ethan texted her.

She tapped Ethan's number. The creamy coffee that soothed her now soured her stomach.

"You've been a busy little bee," he said before she could speak. "My phone's been on fire all morning."

"Mine, too." Jaq's shoulders felt like blocks of cement. If Ethan were part of this, things had officially escalated from bad to worse.

"So... Tell me about Henry Worthington."

"Not much to tell." Jaq tried to sound nonchalant, but it was difficult when her heart threatened to explode in her chest. The headache that subsided in the shower was back and more intense than before. Her hands felt clammy as she stood in her bedroom, holding the phone as she listened to Ethan over the speaker.

He started with a lecture about the Worthingtons and how important they were to Prescott's future.

Jaq didn't bite. This was his usual song and dance—digging for information while tiptoeing around the real reason for his call.

"Jaq, don't play dumb. I know you met with Henry last night."

"I didn't 'meet' with him, Ethan. I was at Maxwell's, when—"

"Why the hell were you at Maxwell's? You're not responsible for the Worthington story, remember?" Ethan slammed his hand against something hard. "Dammit, Jaq. The conflict of interest alone could sink us. The negative publicity... What were you thinking?"

Her eyes sparked with anger. He had some nerve!

"Jaq—"

"You're the one who sent me to the crime scene in the first place, Ethan! Or don't you recall that brilliant decision?" Normally, his drinking habits were off-limits, but propriety was the least of her concerns at the moment.

Ethan spoke with deliberation, like he was talking to Dahlia. "I sent you there to take pictures, Jaq. Nothing more. You, of all people, should get that."

His condescension was infuriating. He put her in this mess to begin with, and yet...

Jaq's head throbbed. He was going to blame her for everything, wasn't he?

"You knew better than to put yourself in the middle of this."

She couldn't argue with him on that point. She *had* known better. But it didn't change anything now.

She needed to move. She paced the hallway between her bedroom and the kitchen as Ethan went on about journalistic integrity and why it was not wise to upset powerful people.

Ethan preaching integrity was laughable, but Jaq bit her tongue. Sometimes it was best to just let him rant and get whatever he had to say off his chest.

She stopped at her desk, the notes on Cara's exploits stacked in a neat pile. Folded up beside the papers was the timeline she compiled but had not yet compared with the information from Sam. If Ethan could see these files or the search history on her computer...

"Jaq, did you hear me?"

She fiddled with the shears, still sitting in the decorative cup on her desk. "The Worthington story is off limits to me. Yes, Ethan. I heard you loud and—"

"It's more than that, Jaq. I can't have you anywhere near the paper right now."

Jaq collapsed in the desk chair. She cracked her elbow against the metal arm, but the pain barely registered. "You're... Firing me?" She choked as she spit out the words. What had she done?

"Not firing you. Telling you to take some time off." Ethan paused. "*Mandatory* time off."

"You're suspending me."

"You haven't given me much choice, have you? Battling the Worthington empire is a losing proposition, Jaq."

Maybe for you, she wanted to say, but kept her mouth shut.

"Your suspension is immediate," Ethan continued. "Without pay. And, as of right now, indefinite. I don't know how far the Worthington lawyers are going to take this." He concluded with a directive to use the time off to reevaluate her personal and professional priorities.

Jaq stared at her phone. Ten minutes ago, the prospect of anything worse than Cara's voicemail seemed impossible. But now she was on the brink of losing everything she had worked so hard for. All because she made the mistake of telling Henry who she was.

Jaq didn't know what upset her most—her suspension, or the realization Henry was as awful as the rest of that hideous bunch.

CHAPTER 22

"Tell me everything," Sam said when Jaq opened the front door.

Ice pellets lined her coat, and Jaq shivered as the frigid air swirled around her legs. "Not much to tell. Ethan's a jerk, but what's new?"

She kicked the door shut and shoved a small, braided rug against the opening between the seal and the floor to block the draft.

Sam followed her into the living room. She snugged her coat around her waist and walked over to the cold fireplace. "Geez, Jaq. No wonder it's so cold in here!"

Jaq shrugged. She had called all the usual places, but the holidays, coupled with the early winter blast, had depleted everyone's stockpile. She did find one seller with firewood just across the state line, but he demanded three times the normal rate. Jaq didn't care if she froze. She refused to give money to anyone who thought it was a good idea to price gouge at Christmas. She'd already been robbed enough this season.

"They're talking teens tonight, you know." Sam stared at Jaq. "The coldest in twenty years."

Jaq's face darkened, and she collapsed on the couch.

What difference did it make? Ben was gone. Whatever connection she might have had with Henry faded before it even began. And now her job was in jeopardy.

Sam fished her phone out of her pocket. "I'm calling my dad. He'll know what to do."

Jaq leaned against the cushions and closed her eyes as Sam's indignant voice filled the hallway. She had just over a thousand dollars in the bank. Barely enough to pay the next month of bills. Like so many other cold fronts she had faced since buying this poorly insulated house, she would just have to weather the next few days by bundling up. Of course, the last time it got this cold, she had Ben there to keep the fire going...

Jaq sank deeper into the cushions. It was a depressing thought to end a depressing day.

"My dad's sending one of his deputies with some firewood," Sam said when she walked back into the living room. She shoved her phone in her pocket and walked over to the windows. She pulled one of the beige curtains to the side and peered at the glass before yanking the material closed. She turned to face Jaq, her arms crossed. "You didn't put up the plastic this year, did you?"

"I ran out." Jaq crossed her arms, too, tucking her hands in her armpits for warmth. "Besides, Ben always took care of that for me."

"Well, Ben's not here."

Jaq's lip quivered. Everything was falling apart.

Sam sat down and put an arm around her.

Jaq wanted to pull away but could not. She stayed in her cousin's embrace, shaking with sobs and hating herself for it.

Even more than she hated Cara.

Jenkins arrived an hour later, his trunk stuffed so full he had to use bungee cords to secure it. The tears dried up, Jaq offered to help, but he insisted he had it. She and Sam stood against the garage wall, out of his way.

"This should keep it dry," Jenkins said after making several trips. He stacked the last of the wood against the wall. "And you're gonna need it, too. Another blast is heading our way, I hear."

Jaq nodded, amazed he found a stick of wood, let alone enough to fill the side of her garage.

Sam thanked Jenkins for the help and shut the garage door behind him. "Get a fire started," she said, pointing to the stack of wood. "I'm ordering pizza."

Jaq didn't have the heart to tell Sam she felt too sick to eat. She grabbed a handful of scraps for kindling and stacked them in the firebox before returning to the garage. Within minutes, a fire blazed, and Jaq sat on the edge of the hearth, staring into the orange and yellow flames.

"Food will be here soon," Sam said upon her return.

Jaq added another piece of wood. The area where she sat heated quickly, and she held her hands up to the fire. Her fingers tingled as they warmed. "You didn't have to do this," she said.

"I did if I wanted to eat." Sam rifled through the papers on Jaq's desk. "You still thinking about pursuing the research on Cara?"

"I don't know. Maybe." Jaq used the poker to reposition a piece of wood. "I mean, there's not much else I can do right now, is there?" The words made her stomach hurt more.

The firelight cast a weird shadow across Sam's profile.

"You look like a ghost," Jaq said with a faint smile.

Sam made her spookiest face, and Jaq laughed as she watched her unfold the timeline.

"Impressive," she said, scanning Jaq's notes. "You've got everything stored somewhere, I assume?"

Jaq nodded. Her standard practice was to save everything to her computer, with a permanent backup on an external drive. She'd never been sued—knock on wood—but her files were her protection if anyone ever questioned her sources.

Sam laid the timeline across Jaq's desk and pulled out her phone. "I have an idea," she said and reached for a scrap of paper and a nearby pen. She wrote something on the paper and slid it Jaq's way.

Jaq glanced at the name and phone number. "What's this?"

"Mack runs a local website. I'm sure you've heard of it… The Prescott Diaries?"

It sounded familiar, but what did this have to do with her current situation? Jaq shot Sam a quizzical look.

"Where's the friggin' pizza? I'm starving!" Sam checked her watch and walked to the front door. She stared into the peephole. "They gather information about people in the public eye. Celebrities, socialites. Pretty much anyone rich and powerful."

People like Cara Worthington. Now it made sense.

"He's run the site for a few years now," Sam said, an exasperated look on her face as she checked her watch again and returned to the living room. "It's a gossip site, but his work is solid." She snapped her fingers. "Hey, he helped us crack that drug case last year. Remember? The one with the lead drummer for—"

There was a loud knock.

"About time!" Sam rushed to the door and returned with two pizza boxes.

Jaq grabbed plates and napkins from the kitchen. The smell of pepperoni and sausage filled the living room upon her return, making her stomach growl. Maybe she could eat after all.

Sam went home around eight, and Jaq stayed on the couch to tend to the fire. For once, the local weatherman was right. The temperatures plummeted into the teens. Ice formed on the windows and power lines, knocking the power out around two. Jaq nodded off, the crackle of the fire lulling her into a dreamless sleep.

The electricity kicked on the next morning, and Jaq awoke to a trickle of warm air kissing her face. She stared at the vent above the couch. Her neck and back ached, but she was warm.

She glanced at her watch and shot up when she saw the time. If she didn't hurry, she'd be late for work...

Her disposition shifted from warm and hopeful to gloom and doom in record time. "Screw you, Ethan," she said, stabbing at the embers in the fireplace. "You *and* your stupid paper."

Jaq added kindling, followed by two medium-sized pieces of wood. Her mind sparked alongside the flames. She could reach out to another newspaper or one of the regional magazines. Perhaps offer her services as a contractor.

Her head throbbed as the reality of crossing the Worthingtons settled in. Ethan wasn't right about much, but he had nailed his assessment of their hold over Prescott. Any professional opportunities in town were off-limits now. If her reputation wasn't ruined yet, it was only a matter of time.

She thought of Dahlia filling in for her and suppressed a laugh. That girl could barely make her way around a crime scene, let alone manage a software program or high-end camera equipment.

Jaq got up to make a pot of coffee. Her socked feet offered little warmth against the cold kitchen tile, and she hurried to make the brew and return to the warm, carpeted living room.

The smell and glow of the fireplace put her at ease even as she sat at a desk overrun with evidence of Cara's shenanigans.

"Not today," she said, shoving everything to the side. She booted up her computer and sipped the creamy liquid while she waited for it to complete the start-up cycle.

First, she checked the job boards in neighboring towns. Surely, not every town was corrupted by the Worthington influence. She scrolled through a few postings, lingering on one for a part-time photojournalist. But the description stated it was entry level. An extreme cut in pay wouldn't help her any.

She took another swig of coffee as she eyed the posting on the screen. There was no telling how this whole Worthington thing would play out. Better to save the listing in case she needed it. Less pay was better than no pay at all.

Depressed, Jaq refilled her mug and returned to the computer. She scrolled through a few more postings for copywriters and web content specialists before landing on a freelance journalist position.

She perked up. The requirements noted three years of experience, preferably in the field, with a background in photography. And the pay was remarkably decent.

Intrigued, Jaq scanned the About Us section. In small print was the contact information for the job: Mack Lundgren with The Prescott Diaries.

CHAPTER 23

৩৩৩৩

"Jaq, I'm so glad we could meet."

Mack's smile stretched from the corners of his mouth to his ears. His chestnut hair was cut close, tinges of gray complementing eyes as blue as the lake on a perfect summer day.

"Me, too." Jaq returned the smile as she shook his hand. Sam had really come through, arranging a meeting today instead of after the first of the year.

Mack had chosen a mom-and-pop restaurant thirty minutes east of town. Jaq did not complain. Given the current atmosphere in Prescott, the locale was ideal, even if it cost her a tank of gas.

She hung her coat on the back of a chair and sat across from him at the small bistro table. She stared at his electric green sweater, and he laughed as he slid a menu her way.

"I'm headed to an after-Christmas party later. A bunch of us get together every year around this time of year. We wear these"—he tapped the coffee-colored reindeer in the center of his sweater and its nose lit up—"for good luck. Kinda like eating black-eyed peas on New Year's."

Jaq nodded. Andy ascribed to the same tradition. She suffered through a few bites every year, mostly out of superstition and only with a healthy dose of hot sauce and a side of applewood bacon.

The waiter arrived and took their drink orders.

"So, this was a good year for you, then?" Jaq blushed at her awkwardness. She'd never been good at small talk, unlike Ethan, who could schmooze potential advertisers with empty promises and somehow get away with never meeting their expectations.

Meeting new people wasn't easy, especially with so much on the line. Jaq squirmed but kept eye contact. That much she could manage.

Mack didn't seem to notice her discomfort. "It was! Best year to date, in fact. It's even got me thinking about opening another office."

"You have an office?" Jaq stared at the menu and willed herself to stop saying idiotic things. "I just assumed everything was online."

Mack laid his menu on the table. "We were at first. But we've tripled in size. You'd be amazed at how much people will pay to stay on top of the latest gossip. Even someplace like Prescott."

Jaq nodded as the waiter returned with their drinks. Mack ordered a Reuben with fries, and Jaq settled on a chicken salad sandwich. She unwrapped her straw and sipped her water as Mack continued.

"We started out small. Me and another reporter from undergrad. I had a few connections in the industry. She did, too, but her expertise is web content." He took a quick sip of his Arnold Palmer before setting it back on the table. "Before I knew it, we were one of the most visited sites in the southeast. And not just for the latest gossip. We cover criminal investigations, too."

"Yeah. Sam said you've been a big help."

Mack shrugged. "It's my way of giving back."

Jaq studied his body language. His motivation seemed personal.

"How long have you been at *The Gazette*?" Mack asked.

"A few years now." Jaq wadded the straw wrapper into a ball and rolled it between her index finger and thumb. "I started out as a junior reporter. Then my boss learned about my photography background and sent me to a few scenes. I've been the lead ever since."

"You still write?"

Jaq nodded. "I'm also tasked with training new employees on the ins and outs of the paper." What she believed were the ins and outs, anyway. Apparently, she had overlooked a lot during her tenure.

Jaq tossed the wrapper onto the table and leaned forward. "Between you and me, not everyone's cut out to be in the field. One of our new reporters beat me to the scene a few months ago, and would you believe I found her sitting in the exact spot where a drug deal had just gone down?" Jaq chuckled as she recalled the look of horror on Dahlia's face as she realized the bench she was sitting on was inside the yellow police tape. "I tell you, she had those drug dogs so confused! I finally had to send her home just so they could do their job."

Mack laughed, and the tension in Jaq's shoulders eased.

"So, why are you thinking about leaving?"

And there it was. No amount of prepping could help her tiptoe around that question.

Jaq retrieved the wad of paper. Whatever came from telling the truth, she'd just have to deal with it.

Like her conversation with Henry?

Jaq clenched her jaw. She couldn't afford to think about Henry or anyone else from the Worthington family. Not right now.

She forced herself to look Mack in the eye. "I'm sure you've heard about the latest drama involving Cara Worthington?"

His face lit up, and he nodded.

Jaq continued rolling the paper between her fingers, the simple back-and-forth motion soothing. "The man who died?" The paper ripped between her fingers. "He was my ex."

Mack took another sip of his drink, his eyes fixed on hers.

"I ran into Cara and her brother the other night. Ended up helping him get her home, actually. I don't know what happened, but she flipped out the next day. Said I was stalking her and whatnot."

Mack raised an eyebrow but once again refrained from commenting.

"Cara called her dad, and he raised all kinds of hell." Nothing would please Jaq more than to share with Mack what a scumbag Ethan was, but it was bad form to bash one's boss during an interview. She sipped her drink to avoid the temptation of divulging any further details.

She needn't have worried. The waiter arrived with their food, halting the conversation.

Jaq bit into a thick steak fry, and her stomach rumbled with gratitude. Was it really two nights ago with Sam when she had her last meal? She swallowed the rest of the fry, the hot oil burning her tongue.

"So, you're suspended, I take it?"

"Sam said you were a straight-shooter." Jaq reached for another fry. She nibbled at it, trying not to burn herself this time.

"In this line of work, there's no other way."

Jaq unwrapped her silverware. "Not saying it's a bad thing. You don't run across many people so forthcoming." She pictured

Ethan partying with the upper echelon, selling his smooth lies, and jammed the knife into her sandwich, splattering chicken salad across her plate. "And yes. I was suspended." She kept her eyes down, unable to bear the look of disapproval in someone else's eyes. Disappointing herself was bad enough.

"The job I posted is more of an entry-level position," Mack said.

Jaq's heart sank. She gathered what she could of her chicken salad and slid it back onto the ciabatta bread. The blend of herbs and seasonings was pleasant, but it could not erase her disappointment.

"I do have a contractor position available, though."

Jaq looked up in surprise.

"I think it would be perfect for someone with your experience."

"What's it entail?"

"Research and field work, mostly. I already have several people on staff that excel at web copy. Keywords and search engine stuff." Mack stretched, grazing Jaq's boot under the table. He didn't seem to notice, his eyes cast upward as he spoke, like he already envisioned her in the position. "What I need is someone on the ground. Someone who can gather Intel, take photos. Assess the scene. You know, give our people the info they need to put together content for the site and convince our subscribers to share their own stories and information."

Jaq nibbled on another fry as she contemplate the opportunity.

"There's one thing, though." Mack wiped a strand of sauerkraut from his hand before setting his napkin on his plate. "We pay per story, not the hour. So, there's no guarantees. But depending on the topic—and whether the story is an exclusive—you can definitely make some cash. I'm toying with a per-click option, too, that would benefit everyone. Like what bartenders or waiters do when they pool tips."

Jaq nodded. Pooled tips helped get her through some tough times during college. If this meeting didn't go well, going back to that type of work might be her only salvation.

"Based on what you've told me and your connections, I think you'll do quite well. Especially since you're just looking for something extra."

Mack called the waiter over and asked for a to-go box as he handed him a credit card.

Jaq blushed. She'd only eaten half her sandwich.

"Sound like something you'd be interested in?" Mack asked.

"Absolutely," she said, swirling a fry in the pool of ketchup on her plate before popping it in her mouth. The opportunity wasn't ideal, but what other choice did she have?

Mack emailed her a link that evening, along with several documents. Jaq sat on her couch, the last of the firewood keeping her warm as she flipped through the printouts. She studied the legalese built into each document and set aside the pages requiring her signature.

There was so much to absorb, so much anticipation at taking on something new. It was a feeling she hadn't experienced in a long while. Not since she first met Ben.

Well, that wasn't entirely true. Henry brought forth the same sense of wonder and excitement...

Until he'd gone and ratted her out, anyway.

Jaq shoved that thought from her mind and flipped to the payment table. She ran her finger down the list of rates. Mack was right. The pay was nothing spectacular, but bonuses kicked in the more you produced. She skimmed the disclaimer about a proposed pay-per-click structure and smiled at the note about incentives for high-resolution photos.

She moved from the couch to her desk, the fire now warming her back as she filled out the tax forms and signed the legal agreements and disclosures. She read over the non-compete agreement again but still felt uneasy signing it.

She opened the cabinet that served as one of her desk legs and flipped through her files until she found her paperwork for *The Gazette*. She scanned the documents, relieved to find nothing that prohibited moonlighting with other organizations. As long as she didn't share any proprietary information or intermingle content, she'd be okay.

Jaq shoved the documents back into the file. Although only Mack and his accountant would have access to her identity, knowing she was on solid legal ground eased her anxiety a bit. Things had a way of getting out, and the last thing she could afford was a lawsuit.

Jaq flipped to the final document and chewed on her pen as she considered various pseudonyms. Whatever name she chose would be the basis for her email address. She would have access to the website and email via VPN so no one could trace her IP. Mack had invested a lot of time and resources into creating an anonymous structure for his business.

Most of the journalists were remote—some from other parts of the country—so Jaq would never meet her colleagues. She could be whomever she wanted. She stared into the air, thinking as the logs in the fire shifted one last time.

Becca Allen, she finally wrote in the Alias field. It sounded like a fitting name for an undercover gossip reporter.

Ugh. Jaq tossed her pen onto the desk. Was her life's purpose truly relegated to this?

The phone rang, and Jaq took that as a sign to step away from her desk and clear her head.

"How'd it go?" Sam asked.

People talked in the background amid the clinking of glasses. "Sounds like you're at the bar."

"I am. Wanna join me?"

Jaq glanced at her watch. It was ten after seven, and half a sandwich was all she had to look forward to in the fridge. "Sure. See you in a few."

She adjusted the thermostat and put the grate in front of the fireplace. The coals glowed as she grabbed her phone and purse. A warm front was supposed to move in tomorrow. She could think of no better way to ring in the year... And her new identity.

"Becca Allen," she said, testing it out as she climbed into her car.

Undercover gossip reporter or not, she had nothing to lose.

CHAPTER 24

ꂌꋊꂌꋊ

"I'm something of a computer geek," Mack said the next morning when Jaq answered the phone. "I set up your access. Figured you were raring to go, given the situation and all."

Yes. The situation.

Wind whipped against Jaq's house as if pursuing a personal vendetta.

She glanced at the empty fireplace and shivered. So much for the weatherman's promise of a warm front.

"Check your email," Mack said. "I just sent you two files."

Jaq pressed the phone between her ear and shoulder as she logged into her personal email account. Mack's message appeared at the top of her inbox. Her anti-virus software assured her the attached files were safe, and she clicked on the first document. It was a detailed checklist to set up access to the website. The other document detailed the instructions for accessing the company's private network.

"Got it," she said. "It's been a while since I set up a VPN, but I should be able to figure it out."

"It's not complicated but let me know if you have questions. You've used FTP, too, I take it?"

"Uh-huh. I use it sometimes when we're close to a deadline, or our web developer is on vacation."

The sound of running water and rattling dishes filled the background. Jaq smiled. Ethan was probably hungover somewhere or sleeping off a bender in his office while Mack setup her credentials and talked shop despite his personal commitments. He might be a workaholic—most successful people were—but he was the antithesis to her do-nothing boss. Thank goodness.

"Excellent." Mack sounded pleased. "Now, don't forget. You need to use the VPN for everything. To access the site. Save your work. Ask questions."

"Questions?"

"Yeah. That's how you get the public involved. Post a question to set up a forum. Those instructions are in the files I sent you, too. Our readers love it when we ask for their help. Sightings, photos, videos, you name it. Everyone wants a piece of the rich and famous."

They chatted a few minutes about documentation requirements and when Jaq could expect her first pay-out. The sound of dishes clinking in the background ceased, and Mack wished her luck before hanging up.

Jaq stared at the documents opened on her screen. No matter how much she tried, her misgivings about the position weren't going away. Sure, working for Mack meant a paycheck—something she needed desperately—but at what cost?

Thoughts of Ben filled her mind. He paired with the disaster queen for similar reasons. She was no better than him, pimping out her soul to pay her bills.

She felt sick.

Before she could dive too deep into her thoughts, Jaq printed the instructions for accessing the VPN. She downloaded the files and mapped the shared drives to her computer. Ten minutes later, she connected to the network, her Becca Allen persona official.

She scrolled through the secure portions of the website before landing on the forums page. Prompts filled the screen. The first was an inquiry into a celebrity's recent stint in rehab, followed by a request for video footage or photos from the recent wedding of a no-name model to a super-wealthy—and much older—businessman. Below that was a plea for info on a second-rate musician's run-in with the law a few weeks ago, followed by a solicitation for details on why a social media influencer suddenly sold her California estate well below the asking price.

Jaq clicked on the first prompt and scrolled through the responses, amazed at what she saw. Blurbs about alleged sightings, photos, even a homemade video with the promise of more information should a payout be extended.

She turned off the computer, unable to stomach any more.

CHAPTER 25

ನನನ

Jaq milled around the house, sweeping up the remnants of firewood in her garage, vacuuming the living room carpet, tidying her desk. Any chore she could find to delay the inevitable.

The time to dive into her newfound opportunity was now. She had to eat. But the inner turmoil refused to subside.

She paced the living room and kitchen, thoughts of beating her ex-boss to a pulp bubbling to the surface. She could not be like him, seeking any opportunity to exploit people for personal gain. How could she ever look Ben's mom in the eye if she used his death to further her own well-being?

Cara was the linchpin in all this. She'd start with the woman who had no issue being the center of attention.

Jaq sat down at her computer and connected to the VPN before opening the forum page. It took a minute to decide the best way to word her question, but once she typed it and clicked the button to post, she relaxed. It was out of her hands now. She could do nothing except compile supplemental information for the writers at The Prescott Diaries while she waited.

Jaq clicked on the file that housed all her research on Cara. She scrolled through the first five articles, typing notes into the online workspace for reference. An hour passed.

Her forearms ached from all the typing, and her neck and back were stiff from too much uninterrupted time in her worn-out chair. She rubbed her neck and stood up to stretch, trying to prepare herself for what lay ahead.

A loud ding startled Jaq awake.

She lifted her head, confused. A sticky note hung from her chin, and she yanked it off.

Her eyes focused. The ding was a response to her post. She had fallen asleep while waiting for a response, the chaos of the past few days finally catching up with her.

Jaq opened the message and squinted to read the blurry font.

"For your story," it said. "I took it last week."

Below the text was a username and contact information, along with a video file. Jaq's virus scan gave the all-clear, and she turned up her speakers before clicking the play button.

The scene was chaotic, but the mahogany bar in the background gave away the location—Maxwell's, not far from where Jaq sat both times she was there.

At the center was a table with several women. A waiter walked toward them with a cake covered in white candles and purple rose piping. A buxom brunette with cleavage accentuated by a low-cut blouse sat in the middle, a birthday hat positioned on her head like a dunce cap. The group broke into song, their Happy Birthday tribute more like that of sailors two days into their leave than a chorus of young women.

Jaq paused the video and checked its length. Three minutes and thirty-seven seconds. She pressed the button again, and the footage resumed.

The events played out on screen, nothing more than a group of drunk rich girls out on the town. Was this the sender's way of inserting herself into the story? Mack had warned her some people would do anything for a chance at fame.

Jaq's shoulders drooped. Her first query—one it had taken hours to get up the nerve to post—was a failure.

She dragged her mouse pointer to the edge of the screen, but before she could close the video, Cara's lithe figure appeared in the background.

Jaq froze. She was dressed in black stilettos and a flimsy red dress. The girls continued to wail as Cara raised her wineglass in a mock toast. She turned, and Jaq leaned in for a closer look.

A man sat beside her at the bar, also watching the birthday celebration. Thin, with hair styled in a fashionable updo that could only be Cara's doing, Ben looked nothing like the man Jaq once knew. He held a bourbon glass in one hand, the other clenched at his side, matching the tightness of his jaw.

But his frustrated stance was not what caught Jaq's eye. She paused the video again and panned out as best she could with her limited software capabilities.

Acid stung the back of her throat, and her chest tightened. She gripped the edge of her desk, afraid she might pass out.

Cinched around Cara's tiny waist was a silky black scarf, just like the one wrapped around Ben's neck the night he died.

CHAPTER 26

The video played on, but Jaq barely noticed. It felt like she was in someone else's body. Her hand was frozen in mid-air. Only it wasn't her hand. It was a balloon, large and undefined, like an ill-sketched cartoon.

The focus of the video was the birthday party, of course. But a few seconds after she toasted the celebration, Cara yelled something at Ben and tried to leave. Ben blocked her exit, his shoulders rigid and his back to the camera as the birthday-goers partied on, oblivious to the drama unfolding behind them.

Jaq's hand started working again, and she rewound the scene so she could note the time. She restarted the video, and a few seconds later, Ben took a sharp step backward.

Jaq paused the video once more and zoomed in. Using the controls on her keyboard, she moved frame by frame, following his movements. Cara floated in and out of view, and Ben shifted from left to right as he spoke, his back still to the camera.

Jaq caught the glimmer of crimson liquid in Cara's glass a millisecond before Ben reared his head back. She zoomed out and in again, this time detecting tiny droplets of liquid in the air, just beyond Ben's head.

There was no reason to feel shocked, but she was. Cara, for all her purported sophistication, had thrown her drink in Ben's face.

Jaq resumed the video as Cara stomped away. Ben turned, and Jaq gasped at her first unobstructed view of his face. Gray streaked through his dark locks, threatening to overtake them. Deep wrinkles furrowed his once youthful brow. And his eyes... Once a brilliant steel blue, they were dark. Haunted, almost.

Jaq's anger melted. "What happened?" she asked, tracing the outline of his face on her screen. Tears pooled in her eyes. "I loved you. Why did you leave?"

Grief overtook her, and she put her head on the desk and cried.

Jaq showed up at Sam's doorstep unannounced. "I didn't want to be alone," she said. "Hope you don't mind."

"I'm making dinner. Wanna join me?"

Jaq nodded and followed her to the kitchen.

Sam pointed to the head of lettuce on the counter and turned her attention to a pot of water boiling on the stove. "How's it going with Mack?"

"Okay, I guess." Jaq rinsed the lettuce and set it on the counter to dry. A package of garlic bread lay nearby, and she pulled the pieces out and spread them on a cookie sheet while she waited for the oven to preheat.

"It still amazes me people share stuff on that site but won't talk to us." Sam shook her head and drizzled olive oil in the pot.

Jaq eyed her cousin as she tried to separate the semi-cooked pasta with a plastic spaghetti fork. She had made the mistake of scrolling through the comments, looking for something she could share with the writing team. What she found was down-right malicious... And not just posts about Cara. One user speculated Ben was nothing more than a guy from the wrong side of the tracks using Cara to fund his aspirations. Another questioned how a person with any decency could be involved with someone so clearly damaged. She could not argue with either assessment.

The oven dinged, and Jaq slid the pan inside. "Someone sent me a video today..."

"Through the site?"

Jaq nodded and set the timer. "Of a birthday party at Maxwell's."

Sam glanced her way as she carried the steaming pot to the sink. "What could possibly be interesting about that?" She lifted the colander and hot water spilled out of the holes while the spaghetti stayed nestled inside. "Let me guess. Somebody was trying to make a name for themselves." She transferred the pasta to a large serving bowl and poured red sauce over it before reaching for a pair of tongs. "We get that all the time. Just last week—"

"Cara and Ben were arguing in the background."

Sam dropped the tongs in the bowl and fished them out. "Oh. I see." She looked at Jaq. "Was this the same night as...?"

"Yeah. Same night as his death."

Jaq felt numb. It was almost comforting. She had spent the better part of an hour fast-forwarding and rewinding the video of Ben and Cara, noting timestamps and movements. Her initial plan was to send the information to Mack's writers, but Cara's scarf was a game changer.

Sam sprinkled fresh basil over the pasta and handed her a bowl.

The first bite of food was warm and soothing, like homemade cocoa on a snowy day.

The tension in Jaq's shoulders eased.

"You know, if Ben and Cara *were* fighting," Sam said between mouthfuls, "this video you're talking about gives us a motive."

Jaq ripped the edge off her garlic bread and used it to sop pasta sauce off the side of the bowl. "I was thinking the same thing."

"This whole accidental death thing doesn't sit well with me, just so you know. My dad either." Sam wiped her mouth with a napkin and reached for her wineglass. "This video might just be what we need to demand a meeting with Cara and her father."

"I was hoping you'd say that." Jaq twisted spaghetti around her fork. "I'll send you the file as soon as I get home."

CHAPTER 27

Sam called the next morning, waking Jaq from the most peaceful sleep she'd had in months. "You're not gonna believe this," she said as Jaq sat up, her eyes still clouded and her brain foggy.

"Believe what? Sam, what time is it?"

"Ten after eight. You're still in bed?"

"Not anymore." Jaq threw her legs over the edge of her mattress, trying to ignore the draft that smacked her bare skin.

"Well, wake up! You'll want to hear this."

Jaq shuffled to the kitchen, where the coffeepot sat empty. She muttered under her breath and reached for the carafe.

"So, I showed my dad the video you sent me." Sam's words tumbled out like she might die if she did not get speak them fast enough. "He called Lawrence Worthington first-thing this morning, demanding he bring Cara in for questioning."

Electricity soared through Jaq's veins like a shot of espresso. "Seriously?"

"Uh-huh. He threw out all sorts of protests, too. How it's New Year's Eve. Harassment. You name it."

"Sounds about right."

"He thought he was the one in control, but all he did was piss my dad off. I swear, no one has ever told that man 'no' before."

Jaq's eyes narrowed. "Sam. What are you not telling me?"

Laughter filled the earpiece. "Oh, nothing. Just that he and Cara arrived with Henry about a half-hour ago."

"Henry?"

"Yup. I know he's a Worthington and all, but damn, he's hot. Did you know he had a law degree?"

"I did not." Every day, she learned more about Henry and his involvement in his family's affairs. And none of it was good.

"Listen, Jaq... I've gotta go. Call you later, okay? I just figured you'd want to hear the news."

Sam hung up, leaving Jaq to stare at both a dead phone and an empty coffeepot.

Thirty minutes of restless wandering about the house was all it took. Jaq got dressed, poured coffee into her travel mug, and drove to the Sheriff's Office.

She told herself it was to get more details about Andy's meeting with Cara, but who was she kidding?

She was hoping to run into Henry.

Jaq pulled into the parking lot a little before ten. It was quiet, but that would change soon enough. Every New Year's Eve, without fail, someone celebrated a little too hard and spent the first twenty-four hours of the new year in a holding cell instead of with friends and family.

Jaq parked her car beside Sam's SUV. Before she could shut off the engine, a commotion broke out near the entrance.

Jaq craned her neck to see past Sam's vehicle. Cara stood in front of the building, fighting to light a cigarette. Henry and Lawrence were on opposite sides of her, their arms crossed and their irritation clear.

"You let them ambush me!" Cara stomped her boot on the pavement. "Dammit, Henry! You're supposed to be protecting me."

Jaq lowered herself into the seat and reached for her notebook. As Cara griped between puffs of her cigarette, she supplied ample material to capture. Words like "misdemeanor" and "entrapment" drifted Jaq's way, along with the phrases "criminal investigation" and "suspicious circumstances."

Jaq noted everything, her hand cramping as she tried to keep up.

There was a long pause, and Jaq looked up.

"This is all because of Ben's stupid ex." Cara mashed her cigarette into the sidewalk with her heel. "You know she's related to the Sheriff, right? I looked it up."

Jaq's palms turned sweaty, and she almost dropped her pen.

"Cara, let's go." Lawrence's voice was demanding but still in control. It was how Jaq imagined every powerful businessman sounded. Quite the contrast to Cara's insufferable whining.

He reached for Cara's arm, and she yanked it away.

"I'll go when I'm damn good and ready."

With such a defiant, disrespectful streak, no wonder Cara constantly found herself in trouble.

"Suit yourself." Lawrence's footsteps echoed against the sidewalk and faded to nothingness.

"You can't stay here," Henry said. He sounded irritated, but she also sensed a protective streak—pity, even—for his younger sibling.

Jaq peeked over the edge of her car door, but Sam's vehicle obscured her view.

"Don't worry. I'm leaving," Cara said. "But not before I go back in and tell that nosy Sheriff he can kiss my—"

"You will not do that, Cara. I mean it."

Jaq peeked over the door frame again as Henry took her by the wrist and marched her toward a car idling at the curb. He opened the back door, pushed her in, and tapped the front window. The car pulled away, and Henry headed for the opposite end of the parking lot.

Jaq put her seat in its upright position and grabbed her purse and keys before opening her door.

"Why am I not surprised to see you here?"

Jaq dropped her keys, and they bounced against the asphalt. "Henry! You scared me." Her heart did somersaults, but it had nothing to do with him startling her. Irritated or not, he was gorgeous. Even more so today, the business attire replaced with a nubby pull-over and jeans.

"What are you doing here, Jaq?"

A closer look at his eyes revealed he wasn't angry. Instead, he looked worn down.

Jaq retrieved her keys from under the car and locked the door. "I'm meeting my cousin," she said, fighting to keep her voice even, to not give away the emotions swirling beneath the surface.

"I guess that shouldn't surprise me, either." He shoved his hands in his pockets and turned away.

Jaq stepped in front of him before he could leave. "Henry, don't go. I've been thinking a lot about the other night."

He laughed, but there was no humor in it. He turned on his heel and walked around her.

"I mean it." Jaq didn't know whether to follow him to his car or let him go. She decided the best way to get him to talk was to tell the truth. "Yes, I was at Maxwell's that night, trying to learn more about what happened to Ben. But I wasn't expecting to meet you. I just wanted some answers."

He turned around. "I wasn't expecting to meet you either," he said, walking toward her. "It was nice. Having someone want to know me for something other than my name."

His mouth was inches from hers, and she smelled the faintest whiff of cinnamon. She bit her lip, fighting the urge to ignore their conflict and kiss him right there in the parking lot.

"Guess I was wrong about that, too."

His words were like a splash of ice water to her face. "Henry—"

"Save it." He looked at her once more and shook his head before walking away.

Jaq shoved her keys into her purse and trudged the short distance to the entrance, hoping Sam could somehow keep this trip from being a complete disaster.

CHAPTER 28

ನಾನಾ

"You can't be here," Sam said when Jaq entered her office. She sat with her back pressed against the desk chair, her expression as listless as her voice.

"I don't understand. Did something happen?"

"Not something. Someone." Sam stood and motioned for Jaq to follow her.

A few hours ago, she was bubbling with excitement at the thought of questioning Cara. Now, Sam looked like someone peed in her cornflakes. It was unnerving.

Jaq hurried to keep up, the tips of her boots squeaking against the linoleum hallway.

Sam stopped outside a door labeled "Observation Room" and checked both ends of the hallway.

Jaq raised an eyebrow.

"Just wanna be sure we're alone," Sam said and ushered her through the doorway.

Jaq followed her into the small space and stopped before the large glass opening. She leaned forward, resting her head against the glass as she took in the adjacent room. Three coffee cups sat on the table beside an ashtray with a half-smoked cigarette nestled in one of its grooves. A ring of purplish-red lipstick lined the brown filter.

This was where Andy questioned Cara.

Jaq whipped her head around. "What's going on, Sam? Just a little while ago, I couldn't shut you up!"

"Cara, Henry, and Lawrence were just here." Sam yanked at her ponytail holder, and her hair fell into her face. She brushed it behind her ears in irritation.

Jaq eyed her cousin. Her body language was a mixture of anger and fatigue. "I know they were here. I saw them talking outside."

"You didn't say anything, did you?" Sam stared her down, like she was a suspect.

Jaq studied the smoky interview room, looking for clues as to why Cara was so agitated. Surely, an innocent person wouldn't be so upset over a few simple questions.

Sam paced back and forth in the tiny space. "I swear, Jaq. Your timing couldn't be worse. I never would have called you if I'd known..." She stopped. "Why are you here, anyway?"

Sam's eyes narrowed, fueling Jaq's discomfort. Normally, they were on the same page. But not today.

Jaq tried to control the panic filling her chest, but it still rose from deep in her stomach, threatening to choke the words right out of her. "Sam, what happened? Why are you acting so weird?"

Sam sighed and pointed to the metal chairs stacked against the wall. "Grab one," she said. "And I'll show you."

Sam locked the door and Jaq forced a chair open, trying to ignore the squeal of metal that echoed through the tiny room. She waited for Sam to start the video, her skin prickling in anticipation and her stomach churning.

Sam rewound the recording and queued it partway through the conversation. "Here. This should be okay."

Okay for what? Jaq's instincts were on fire, her synapses in overdrive. She couldn't pinpoint why, but she sensed the days of asking her family for help with crime scene coverage were over.

"You have no reason to summon us," Henry said. He sat opposite Andy, to the right of Cara, as Lawrence towered behind. "We have been nothing but cooperative."

Jaq's stomach did another flip-flop at the sound of Henry's voice, and she struggled to stay focused.

"I demand to know what this is about." Henry clenched his jaw, staring Andy down.

But Andy didn't flinch, his demeanor stiff and official. "For the record, please confirm that you are Ms. Worthington's legal representative."

"Yes. I am the attorney representing Cara Worthington." Henry stared into the glass, aware he was being filmed. "And I would like to know why you read my sister her rights and parked her in this tiny room until we could get here."

Andy shifted in his seat but did not give off an aura of discomfort. He looked quite intimidating sitting there in his police uniform, holding all the power.

Jaq felt sorry for Cara.

Almost.

"We brought your sister in for questioning," Andy said, tapping his notepad as he spoke, "because we have additional information about the death of Benjamin Rutherford. Information we need her to explain."

Cara looked horrified. She opened her mouth, but Henry prevented her from speaking with a firm wave of his hand.

"What kind of information?" he asked, his expression cold and his eyes callous. He was putting on a show, playing a role that did not suit him.

"We received a video yesterday." Andy pointed to Cara. "That shows your client arguing with the decedent at Maxwell's on the evening of December twenty-second."

Cara started to speak, but Henry cut her off again. "You've never gotten into an argument with someone in a public place?" he said. "Please don't tell me you brought us all the way down here for that."

Andy held their attention for at least ten seconds.

Jaq froze, waiting for the kill shot.

Andy pushed a photo Henry's way. "I brought you down here because your client was wearing the scarf we found wrapped around Mr. Rutherford's neck."

Cara gasped and looked like she might cry.

Henry's tan face paled, but he regained his composure. "You're telling me you have definitive proof that this is Cara's?" He pointed to the photo. "That no one else in town has this same scarf?"

"This is ridiculous!" Lawrence's voice boomed, and Jaq jerked her head back in surprise. He slammed a fist on the table, rattling the ashtray in his fury. "I want to know this instant where this evidence came from. Why are you spying on my family?"

Sam stopped the recording.

"Hey! What are you doing?"

"That's all I can share." Sam motioned for Jaq to put her chair away.

"But—"

Sam pointed to the chair again.

Jaq snapped it closed and leaned it against the wall. "I don't understand," she said, trying not to pout as she followed Sam down the hall to the front of the building.

"Not much to understand." Sam spoke in her matter-of-fact tone, normally reserved for irate family members accusing the Sheriff's Office of arresting someone without justification. "Lawrence has insisted we recuse ourselves from the investigation and let the state police take over." She jammed her finger into Jaq's chest. "Because of you."

They passed one of the few officers on duty, pecking at the keys on his keyboard. Jaq recognized his bushy, gray beard. He was at Sam's Christmas party, dressed as Santa.

Was that really just a week ago? Things had gone so awry in such a short amount of time.

"Go home," Sam said, practically pushing her out the door. "And let this go, Jaq. I mean it."

But they both knew she couldn't do that.

The sunlight hit Jaq in the eyes as she exited the station, and she walked to the car with her head down. Lawrence could make all the demands he wanted. Now was not the time to give up. It was the time to put her skills to use and get the answers no one else was willing to pursue.

CHAPTER 29

Jaq drove home, a dark cloud of confusion and anxiety hanging over her.

Henry, Ben, Cara.

The scarf.

It was too much to process.

She dropped her keys on the countertop and dug the leftover chicken salad sandwich from her fridge. The lettuce was wilted, the bread soggy. She picked at bits of chicken before giving up and tossing the entire thing in the trash.

Surely, Maxwell's would have quite the spread planned for tonight. At least a special or two to celebrate the new year... Maybe even an eligible bachelor with nothing better to do.

Jaq reached for her phone. On the restaurant's website was an animated announcement with fireworks and Auld Lang Syne streaming in the background. Details followed, including a list of meals available for one night only. She dialed the main number, and it rang and rang. Jaq searched the website for information on to-go orders and tried that number instead.

"Maxwell's Steakhouse."

Glassware rattled in the background, and Jaq envisioned the same bartender from the other night preparing for the celebration.

"Can you tell me if there are any reservations available?" she asked.

"Don't know. Call the main line. This number's for to-go orders only."

He hung up, and she stared at the phone, thinking.

Tenacity wasn't Jaq's only trait. She was also crafty, knowing where to be and when. At ten after eight, she placed a to-go order.

"It'll be ready in about an hour," the bartender said. He hung up as celebratory cries filled the background.

Jaq slipped into a creamy blouse, black slacks, and her favorite heels. The same outfit she had worn to the paper's end-of-the-year budget meeting.

She pushed tiny diamond studs into her earlobes. What a colossal waste of time that was. Ethan hadn't even shown up until halfway through their discussion about annual expense limits.

It seemed like a lifetime ago.

Jaq cranked up the car radio and sang along as she drove to the restaurant. There would be no negative thoughts tonight.

The line at Maxwell's extended down the block, and Jaq parked several streets away instead of waiting for a curbside spot. Her heels were worn just enough to make the walk manageable.

She scooted her way through the patrons crowding the waiting area and informed the host she was there to pick up a to-go order. He handed a stack of menus to the server and called the next party's name before waving her on.

Jaq walked the short distance to the bar, a route she was getting to know all too well. No barstools were available, so she scooted beside two older gentlemen. They glanced her way, and she ignored them, small talk not part of her agenda tonight. "I have a to-go order for Darcy," she said to the bartender.

He nodded and held up a finger while he finished another customer's drink request.

Jaq scanned the room. The restaurant overflowed with guests, making it unlikely the people waiting at the entrance would make it inside before the new year arrived. Large parties clustered near the back, eating, laughing, and clanking their glasses together in semi-toasts.

"Miss Darcy?" the bartender said, and Jaq turned around. "We're running about an hour behind. Get you a drink while you wait?"

She ordered a cranberry vodka, and he poured it for her before setting it on a cocktail napkin. She reached for her wallet, but he shook his head and pointed behind her. She turned as Henry appeared.

He gave the bartender a wave and tugged at her arm.

She covered her glass to prevent the liquid from sloshing out.

"Why am I not surprised to see you here?" he asked.

The light at the bar was dim, but Jaq could still detect the twinkle in his eye.

"Truce?" he said, his hands up.

"That depends." Jaq smiled and took a sip of her drink, hoping it would calm her nerves. "Where's your sister?"

Henry shrugged. "With friends, I guess." He looked around the crowded room. "Not here."

He sipped his drink while Jaq eyed his toned forearms and chest, noticeable even beneath the pin-striped dress shirt. She wiped a hand across her forehead, unsure if it was the drink making her flush or the man keeping her company.

She tilted her glass for another sip. Maybe it was both.

Someone bumped her from behind, and juice splashed across her face and chest.

"Sorry," the man said in a slurred voice. He pushed past her and disappeared into the throng of people at the other end of the bar.

Jaq held the dripping glass away from her blouse, and Henry leaned over the bar to grab a towel. He reached out to pat her blouse before catching himself.

"Here," he said and tossed the towel at her as his cheeks glowed a pinkish red.

Jaq dabbed at the liquid splashed across her chest and tried to squelch a smile.

Henry took another drink, and when Jaq looked back up, he cast his eyes elsewhere.

She smiled without reservation this time, his actions revealing everything she needed to know.

They stood to the side of the bar, out of the fray as they talked and shared cocktails. Jaq was on her second refill, the to-go order all but forgotten, when the bartender called her name.

"You're not staying?" Henry asked.

"Wasn't planning on it." Jaq took the bill from the bartender and gave Henry her best smile as she reached for her wallet. "But I can be convinced otherwise."

He covered her purse with his hand. "Put it on my tab," he said, ignoring Jaq's protest. "And go ahead and close me out, if you will. I'll settle up later."

The bartender nodded and handed Jaq the bag with her food as Henry leaned over the bar and tossed the towel into a receptacle. His slacks formed against his athletic build, and he smiled at her when he turned back around.

Maybe it was the vodka, but Jaq no longer cared if Henry sensed her attraction to him.

"Want to get out of here?" he asked.

"Sure," she said, her mouth mere inches from his. "What'd you have in mind?"

CHAPTER 30

ನುನು

Jaq and Henry pushed through the crowd gathered at the restaurant's entry and made their way to the riverfront. The silence between them felt comfortable, like they had known each other for years.

They passed through the part of town most popular in the spring and summer, when baked goodness from the cultural street festivals and the shouts of fair rides carried as far as Jaq's neighborhood. Tonight, it was all but empty, only a few stragglers daring to venture into the chilly night air. One of them lit a cigarette as Jaq and Henry walked by, the orange flame giving way to the distinct scent of tobacco.

Jaq shoved thoughts of Sam from her mind and eyed Henry as they stopped at a bench just shy of the bridge connecting downtown to new residential buildings with condos and apartments. Another Worthington investment.

"I'm not sure how I feel about your connection to Benjamin," Henry said. He thrust his hands in his pockets and blocked the breeze from hitting Jaq as they looked out over the water.

"I wasn't trying to cause you any problems, Henry. I swear."

Noisemakers and cheers carried down-river from Maxwell's. Jaq peered up at the clear, star-filled sky, trying not to shiver. Her pants afforded little protection against the wind, and her feet felt like blocks of ice against the frozen pavement. Even her knee-length dress coat did little to ward off the chill. But it didn't matter. She'd gladly stay—become a human icicle—if it meant spending more time with Henry.

He tapped her arm and gestured ahead. Jaq scooted closer as they walked, the scent of sandalwood and vanilla warming her.

"My sister... Well, I love her, and all. But it's no mystery she's a bit of a drama queen."

Jaq laughed. "I guess you could say I learned that the hard way."

Puffs of breath filled the bitter air as they walked on. Blood flowed to Jaq's extremities, making her fingers and toes tingle, then burn. She didn't care. Her attraction to Henry was intoxicating.

Still, there was one issue she had to address.

"Have you ever heard of The Prescott Diaries?" she asked.

Henry shot her a curious glance. "Mack Lundgren's website?"

"You know Mack?"

"We went to law school together. For a brief time, anyway."

They stopped at the edge of the bridge. A group of teenagers huddled nearby, their voices high-pitched as they discussed the annual New Year's Eve fireworks show hosted by a neighboring county.

Jaq frowned. Ben was supposed to bring her to see the fireworks last year but was called into work at the last minute. She ended up watching the display with Sam instead.

Henry put a hand on her shoulder and guided her forward. "Mack's a decent guy. Had several classes with him until he dropped out. Something to do with his brother being killed... A random attack on the subway, I think." He shrugged. "I don't remember all the details."

So Mack's own tragedy *had* precipitated his creation of The Prescott Diaries. Jaq felt a little better about her decision to work for him.

"How do you know Mack?"

Henry stopped, and Jaq grabbed his arm to steady herself.

He frowned, the wrinkles at the crease of his mouth deepening. "You're the one who gave the Sheriff the video."

"Yes. But hear me out, Henry. Please."

He stiffened but did not leave.

"My cousin Sam—you met her at the station—she's the one who put me in touch with Mack." Jaq stared at Henry, trying to gauge his thoughts, but his expression was unreadable. "Your sister called my boss after I helped you get her home. Told him I was harassing you."

Henry raised an eyebrow.

"He suspended me." Jaq's hands were at her sides, and she fought the urge to clench her fists. "This job—with Mack—it's just to make ends meet. Until this whole mess with your sister dies down." She shared the details of her arrangement as a contractor but avoided further discussion about her financial situation. Henry would find out soon enough just how different their worlds were.

"Someone just randomly sent you the video?"

Jaq stared at the scuffs crisscrossing the ends of her shoes.

"What are you not telling me?"

She looked up, no longer able to deflect his gaze. "I posted a request on the site, asking for information related to Ben's death. The video was from the girl who filmed the birthday party."

Henry turned his back to her and stared at the water.

Jaq waited, not sure what else to say. He had to know the truth.

"You don't think Benjamin's death was an accident."

"No. I'm sorry. I don't."

Henry turned around. "Why? What makes you say that?"

"A hunch. Plus, you didn't know Ben like I did." Jaq's eyes brimmed with tears.

He touched her chin as two women passed by. The shorter one wore a hot pink puff jacket with the hood pulled up over her bright blond hair. She looked younger than the woman she was with, dressed in all black.

They stopped when they saw Henry.

"Is that who I think it is?" the woman in pink asked, her voice muffled as she spoke behind a gloved hand.

The woman in black stared at Jaq. "Can't be. She's nobody."

Jaq glared back, and the woman's eyes widened. Her friend tugged at her coat sleeve and urged her to keep moving.

Jaq shivered, and she and Henry resumed their walk along the river, their heads down as the wind picked up. She stumbled on a crack in the pavement, and Henry caught her before she could fall.

He was so close, his hands so warm and strong, she was certain he could hear her heart thumping against her chest.

She pulled back, mindful of the remnants of cranberry and vodka on her breath.

Henry looked hurt but let go of her arm.

She cleared her throat, and they walked on. The number of people outdoors increased as they neared the residential part of town. Groups gathered near the waterfront, bundled in thick coats and winter hats.

Jaq and Henry passed a large white banner strung across the front of an apartment complex, advertising the fireworks show.

As if on cue, a large pop exploded overhead, followed by bright, colorful sparkles that filled the sky.

Henry stopped in front of a three-story brick building. "This is one of our buildings. Want to go up for a better view?" He pointed to the roof, and Jaq nodded.

He flipped down the alarm box cover and typed in a key code. The alarm beeped, and he grabbed her hand, squeezing so hard he mashed her fingers together.

Jaq looked at him in surprise.

He stared past her, and she turned around. The two women were marching their way with a man the size of a linebacker. They did not look happy.

"Come on," he said and shoved her through the door. He locked it as the group neared the building.

The man yanked on the door handle as Henry and Jaq stayed hidden in the shadows. He put his hands up to the glass, trying to peer inside. "I know you're in there!" he said, banging his fists against the door. It rattled, and Jaq flinched.

"Is this because of me?" she asked, her voice barely audible.

"Nah, I get it all the time."

They waited until the banging stopped. Henry peeked his head out before leading Jaq down the hall to the stairwell. "People don't seem to understand I have no interest in being a celebrity," he said. "Cara's the one who thrives on the attention. Not me."

The mention of Cara was an unwelcome splash of reality.

Jaq stopped short of the stairs "I meant it when I said I don't want to cause you any problems. I know your sister hates me."

Henry smiled a sweet smile that made her feel all toasty inside. For a moment, she forgot she was freezing her ass off in an empty building on New Year's Eve with the brother of her nemesis.

"She doesn't hate you," he said. "She hates herself. It's just easier to take it out on everybody else."

He opened the door to the stairwell and waved Jaq through. It closed behind them, and Jaq turned around. Henry was so close, she felt light-headed.

What was this man doing to her?

Fireworks boomed overhead, but their electricity paled next to the excitement Jaq felt as Henry tucked a strand of hair behind her ear.

He grazed her neck, his fingers like fire against her skin.

It seemed like an eternity before he leaned in and kissed her. Gentle at first, then with an intensity Jaq never expected from someone so refined.

CHAPTER 31

नननन

Henry and Jaq lost all track of time, neither the echo of fireworks nor the dankness of the stairwell able to separate them from one another.

But the cold concrete steps could not be ignored forever. Henry ushered Jaq out of the building and down the street to the only eatery still open. They ate and talked, and she had never felt more comfortable with someone she barely knew.

As the sun peeked over the horizon, he stood outside her car, waiting with her while it warmed up. "Call you later?" he asked through the cracked window.

Jaq nodded and drove away. She tried not to focus on the dingy streets guiding her home, the trek somehow longer than when she drove into town last night. As she neared her house, she passed the run-down savings mart and two gas stations, one of which closed last year, while the other was partially boarded up and barely drew any customers. Even the nearest fast-food places had shuttered over the last few years. What was once a vibrant part of town sat desolate, the victim of neglect and apathy.

Jaq pulled into her driveway and groaned at the sight of Mr. Wilson's gaudy decorations. Last year, they hadn't come down until Easter. Bringing Henry to her place was intimidating enough. *If* she invited him over, the focus needed to be on her manicured cottage, not the junk threatening to overtake it.

She smiled as she shoved her key into the lock. A sneak attack on Mr. Wilson's inflatable decorations might just do the trick.

Frigid air hit her like a jackhammer. She hadn't turned up the thermostat before leaving for Maxwell's, and the temperatures had dipped near freezing again.

She kicked it up a notch and walked from room to room, checking her faucets. Her phone vibrated in her pocket, and she grabbed it, her heart fluttering at the thought of talking to Henry again.

"Where you been?" Sam asked, the familiar noise of the police station resonating in the background.

Jaq tried to mask her disappointment. "I thought you were off."

"One of our guys called in sick, so I told my dad I'd help out."

Jaq turned on her bathroom faucet and eyed the flow.

"I've been calling you," Sam said. "See any fireworks last night?"

"Lots of them." Jaq walked to the kitchen, unwilling to divulge her whereabouts just yet.

There was a loud crash in the background, followed by someone hollering for help.

"Crap, I gotta go," Sam said. "I'll stop by later, and we can have our own celebration. Okay?"

Celebration in Sam-speak meant drinking until you did something stupid or passed out on the couch. Not exactly Jaq's idea of fun, but she couldn't sit around and wait for Henry to call either.

"Sure," she said, snapping her kitchen faucet off. "But my house is freezing."

"We'll figure something out. Call you when I'm headed out." There was more commotion in the background, and Sam hung up.

Jaq sank onto the couch and reached for the throw blanket hanging off the back. She missed Henry already.

Jaq felt like a popsicle when she woke up. She grabbed warm clothes while she waited for the shower to heat up. The water felt as delicious as Henry's lips against hers. She lathered and rinsed, savoring the memory of his hands on her flesh.

She threw on an oversized sweater and comfy athletic pants and brewed a pot of coffee while she waited for her computer to boot up. Several messages awaited her on The Prescott Diaries. The first had nothing to do with Ben's death, just someone trying to get his name in front of her for a potential payday.

Jaq tapped her pen against her notepad. Even though Henry knew about her partnership with Mack, it still felt like she was betraying him.

She reached for the power button as another message appeared in her inbox along with three photos. Curious, Jaq downloaded the files. Prior to their dinner at Maxwell's the night Ben died, he and Cara attended a concert at the music hall. According to the sender's message, Cara was intoxicated and the owner asked them to leave.

Jaq logged this information and scanned the remaining messages. Before she knew it, she had a series of notes, with places to research and people to contact. An outline formed in her head, and she transcribed her thoughts as the sun passed overhead and began its downward journey.

CHAPTER 32

A knock at the door startled Jaq. She looked up from her computer screen, confused.

"Coming!" she called, trying to shake the fog from her head. She glanced at her watch and was surprised to see she had been hunched over her computer for almost two hours. No wonder she hurt all over.

She twisted her neck from side to side, trying to loosen it up as she made her way to the front door. She flung it open, hoping Sam had stopped for food on the way over. "You were supposed to call..."

Her voice trailed off.

Henry stood on her front porch, a paper sack in one hand and roses in the other. He looked as handsome as ever in jeans and a thick pull-over.

Jaq forced the look of surprise off her face and ushered him in. She smoothed her sweater and covered her mouth with the back of her hand, trying to hide the stench of stale coffee on her breath.

Henry leaned over and kissed her cheek before offering her the bouquet of roses.

She blushed. Henry Worthington was a romantic. Who would have ever guessed?

"You don't like roses," he said with a frown.

Jaq plucked them from his hand. "Of course I do. You just caught me off guard, that's all." She smoothed her hair with her free hand, wishing she had thought to put makeup on when she got out of the shower.

"I think you look great," he said and pulled her close.

Jaq stepped back. "What would your sister think?" she asked, taking in every feature of his handsome face. She wanted to kiss him—more than she had ever wanted anything—but Cara's eventual retribution could not be overlooked.

"Don't know," Henry said. He pulled her toward him once more. "And I don't care."

He kissed her, and Jaq sank into his embrace, all concern over her appearance and stinky breath forgotten. When they separated, she led him down the short hallway to the kitchen, scanning the room as they entered. Thankfully, the sink was dish-free, the only thing out of place the coffeepot, still warm from its latest brew.

Henry situated the bags on the counter as the spicy scent of Chinese food filled the small space. "I took a chance," he said, lifting cardboard boxes out of the bag while Jaq retrieved a vase from beneath the sink.

"I love Chinese food," she said, running water over the flowers as she trimmed the stems. She arranged the bouquet in the vase and filled it with tap water before adding the packet of flower food. "But you haven't told me how you found me."

"You're not the only one with sources."

A romantic with a sense of humor. Jaq smiled and handed him two plates.

Henry set them on the counter next to the food. "If I'm being honest," he said, his breath warm in her ear. "I couldn't stay away."

She didn't resist. Heat flowed between them as he planted his lips on hers and ran his hands along her back.

"Our food's gonna get cold," she said. His touch lingered on her skin as she heaped food from each box onto their plates and carried them to the small, round kitchen table.

Henry eyed her before taking a seat. He unwrapped a pack of chopsticks and gathered a blend of peppery chicken and noodles. "You lived here long?" he asked between bites.

"In this house?" Jaq scrunched her nose as she tried to manipulate her chopsticks around a piece of shrimp. Henry smiled and slid a pack of plastic utensils her way. He gathered another bite as she tugged on the edge of the wrapper. It gave way, and the fork and knife skittered across the table and onto the floor.

At this rate, she'd never eat! Jaq shot Henry an exasperated look and grabbed silverware from the drawer. She sat back down and stabbed at the food on her plate, trying to hide her embarrassment.

Henry laughed and rubbed her knee with his hand. "I meant, how long have you lived in Prescott?"

Jaq looked up in surprise, her food woes forgotten. Did he really not know about his dad's takeover of the farm?

"I grew up about two hours from here."

"Really? I figured you lived up north."

Henry reached for an egg roll and shrugged. "Some of our family lives in New York. But I don't care much for the city. I only go up there with my dad on business. Or with Cara, when she wants to see a show." Jaq bristled, and he cleared his throat. "I used to spend summers up there as a kid, though. At my grandparents' farm."

Jaq almost choked on her food.

"A horse ranch, actually. You ride?"

She found her composure and shook her head.

He leaned back in his chair and smiled. "It's something everyone should experience. At least once. I know a great place to—"

A loud knock at the front door interrupted him.

Jaq jumped up before Henry could react and rushed out of the kitchen. She cracked open the front door just enough to make out Sam's cheeks, bright pink against her white coat.

"I stopped and got us food," Sam said, brushing past Jaq. "You wouldn't believe the day I've had..." She stopped just short of the kitchen and looked over her shoulder. "Hey, did you see that car parked on your street? Fancy! Normally, I don't like those foreign jobs, but—"

She froze at the sight of Henry sitting at the kitchen table. The bag she was carrying slipped from her grip, and a small white box tumbled to the floor.

Bits of orange chicken stuck to the flap, and Jaq laughed. "What are the odds?" She wiped off the edge of the box before setting it on the table.

For once, Sam was speechless.

Henry stood up and extended his hand. "Hello again, Miss..."

"Thomas," Sam said, finding her voice. "But call me Sam." She stood in the middle of the kitchen, looking more than a little uncomfortable. "I'm sorry. I didn't realize Jaq had company."

Ever the gentleman, Henry pulled out a chair. "Care to join us?"

"The more the merrier!" Jaq said, and Sam stared at her like she had lost her mind. She cleared her throat and pulled another plate from the cabinet.

Sam hesitated before sitting down, a puzzled expression clouding her face.

CHAPTER 33

"So, you're telling me," Sam said with a loud hiccup as the three of them sat in Jaq's living room after dinner. "You've never been out of the country? I don't believe it."

The corner of Henry's lip shot up in a crooked but adorable way. "I'm quite serious. Never been outside the good ole U. S. of A."

"Not even Mexico?" Sam stared at Jaq in disbelief. She bent a hand forward like she was showing an underling her fingers adorned with jewels. "I thought anyone who's *anyone* vacationed in Cabo."

Jaq couldn't suppress her giggle at their running joke about the rich and famous, although she could no longer be sure it applied to everyone in the upper echelon. Certainly not the man sitting in her dingy living room drinking from a two-dollar wineglass.

Henry ran his finger over the rim, too polite to request clarification. Jaq couldn't remember what sparked this conversation, but thankfully, Sam was keeping her obnoxiousness at a manageable level. Tact had never been her strong suit, but so far, so good.

Jaq relaxed the longer they sat in her living room, chatting like old friends. She'd pay for it later—the inevitable prying from

Sam about what she was doing with Henry while Cara was under investigation for Ben's death—but none of that mattered right now. If Sam and Henry were willing to put the legal conversation aside for the time being, that was good enough for her.

She would answer all of Sam's questions later... But, first, she had to figure out the answers herself.

"Not even Canada?" Sam asked with another hiccup. Or maybe it was a burp. So much for controlling herself.

Henry shook his head again. "Nope. Sorry to disappoint."

"Wow." Sam leaned back in the chair. "That is so hard to believe..."

"Maybe so, but it's the truth." Henry's arm brushed against Jaq's, and she smiled. "I've never been anywhere outside the states. I've always wanted to see Tahiti, though. I hear it's gorgeous."

"But your sister... She's been all over the globe, right?"

And there it was.

Jaq shot Sam a dirty look. Why did she have to ruin everything by bringing up Cara?

Henry didn't seem to notice. "Cara has always been... Well, let's just say, more open to adventure."

"That's putting it nicely."

Jaq choked on her drink.

"You okay?" Henry asked, glancing her way.

She nodded and got her coughing under control. She glared at Sam again. This time, her cousin held up a hand as if to say she understood.

They sipped their drinks in silence.

Jaq spoke first. "Henry works with the local children's foundation, Sam. Did you know that?" She turned slightly to assess his profile. It was quickly becoming a familiar view, but it still stirred something inside her. "Sam's dad—my uncle—hosts a fundraiser for them every year."

Henry nodded. "We've made several donations over the years. But I'd never met the Sheriff. Until...." His hand was resting on Jaq's leg, but he pulled it away as his expression shifted.

"Is this always going to be a wall between us?"

Sam announced she had to use the bathroom and disappeared down the hallway.

Jaq touched Henry's arm.

His jaw was stonelike, his mouth turned down. He jumped up, knocking over his empty wineglass. "She's my sister," he said, walking back and forth in the small space. He glanced at Jaq, and his expression softened before the stony, walled-off Henry resurfaced. "I know I said earlier I didn't care what she thought, but I do when it might hurt her." He paused, his back to Jaq. "I *want* to be okay with this. But..."

"But what?" Sam would be back any moment now, but Jaq didn't care. The pull to be with Henry was too strong to dismiss because of family entanglements. They weren't Romeo and Juliet, for heaven's sake. They were two adults, perfectly capable of being together if they wanted. Jaq stood up and caught his arm as he passed by. "Henry," she said, forcing him to stop. "But what?"

His shoulders sagged as a dark expression overtook his features. "But my family. If my dad finds out..." He waved toward the hallway where Sam had retreated, like she would somehow announce their private rendezvous to the whole town.

"That's what you're worried about? Your father?" Jaq's lips were millimeters from Henry's, and she touched his cheek with the back of her hand. He stared into her eyes, and she tickled his ear with her lips. "Because I have zero concern for what anyone thinks."

Neither noticed when Sam grabbed her purse from the kitchen and exited through the garage door.

Jaq's phone buzzed on the living room floor the next morning. She squinted at the sunlight streaming through her windows and shifted her eyes to the blank screen on her TV.

She and Henry must have fallen asleep while watching the movie. What time was it? She fumbled around with one hand, trying to find her device on the floor without disturbing Henry.

She grazed the phone's edge and glanced at the caller ID as she pulled it to her ear. "Hello?" she said in a low whisper.

"Jaq! I'm so glad you picked up."

"Sam? What's going on?"

She didn't answer right away, and Jaq checked her phone to be sure they hadn't been disconnected.

"Jaq..."

Sam was never this subdued unless something was terribly wrong.

Jaq's heart raced in terror. "Sam, what is it? Did something happen to Andy?"

"No. Not him." Sam's breathing was erratic, like she was running on adrenaline. Or fear.

"Sam—"

"It's Cara, Jaq. Cara is dead."

Jaq dropped the phone, and it bounced off Henry's arm.

"Ow!" he said, opening one eye. "I've had some rude wake-up calls, but that's a first..." He laughed, then noticed the expression on Jaq's face. He shot upright, concerned. "Jaq, what is it? What's wrong?"

"I'll call you back." Jaq gripped the phone in her hand and hung up as she avoided Henry's gaze.

"Jaq?"

"Gimme a minute," she said and slid off the couch.

Once in the hallway, she raced to the bathroom. She tried calling Sam back, but it went to voicemail. Before she could convince herself it was a bad idea, she tapped Dahlia's name in her list of contacts.

"Happy New Year, Miss Darcy! Please tell me you're calling to say you're back. I could really use some help."

A blend of street noise and officers calling to one another filled the line. Jaq knew the sounds well, and it hurt not to be there. This was the biggest story Prescott had ever seen, yet...

"Jaq?" Henry was outside the bathroom door. "Everything okay?"

Jaq covered her phone and eyed the shadow beneath the door. "Be out in a sec," she said. "Will you start the coffee for me?"

There was a brief pause before Henry disappeared.

"Miss Darcy? Hello?"

Jaq's head throbbed. "I'm not back yet," she said. "But I just heard the news."

"It's insane! I've never seen anything like it. Reporters from other *states* are here..."

Sam hadn't said where they found Cara—or who found her—but if Jaq's instincts were to be trusted, she knew exactly where the body was. "You're at The Cornelia, right?"

Dahlia hesitated, and that was all Jaq needed for confirmation. She hung up as the distinct aroma of fresh coffee wafted through the door.

Jaq took several deep breaths, determined to stave off an anxiety attack. She had spoken with her share of grieving loved ones over the years, but she had never been there at the exact moment the news was delivered.

She made her way to the kitchen, trying to prepare herself for what might be the hardest conversation of her life.

CHAPTER 34

സയസ

"I don't understand, Jaq. This makes no sense."

It was the third time Henry spoke those words, the confusion on his face unmistakable. He walked over to the kitchen window and watched as squirrels scampered through the trees in the backyard, taking advantage of the break in weather to scavenge for any remaining nuts. "I spoke to her yesterday," he said. "She was headed out with friends."

"Henry, I get this is hard..." Jaq reached for him, but he was having none of it.

He paced around the kitchen, his words flying at Jaq like darts. "I told her not to go out. To stay in for a change, but she wouldn't listen. She was upset"—he waved a hand in the air—"about everything."

Jaq looked at her feet and pursed her lips. Now was not the time to defend herself.

"I told her to let it go. That we would..." Henry's voice caught in his throat as he struggled to continue. "That we would figure it out. I mean, the police have nothing tying her to the scene the night Benjamin died."

Under normal circumstances, Jaq suspected Henry would be sensitive to how he addressed Ben's death. But grief wiped away all pretenses. Its fog enveloped you, a nightmare from which you could never wake. And it was more than just the sense of loss. It was the pain of not getting to say goodbye.

The notion she was an expert on the grieving process was laughable. She never felt the need to mourn her dad—how could she when he was someone she never even met?—but her childhood was filled with incidents the year after her mom's death.

And how she handled the loss of Ben could be classified as anything but "well."

Henry stopped, hands clenched at his sides like he was fighting with himself about something. "I need to go," he said.

Jaq followed him into the living room. "Henry, wait."

He bent down to search under the couch for his shoes. He slipped them on and Jaq followed him to the kitchen, where he grabbed his wallet and keys off the counter. He fumbled with the key fob for a moment, and his engine roared to life in her driveway.

"I'll call you when I can," he said. He grazed her forehead with his lips as he brushed past.

The front door slammed before Jaq could respond.

She peered through the living room blinds as Henry climbed into his car and tore down the street. A puff of exhaust lingered behind.

Jaq shook, her emotions unchecked as her mind raced. So much had happened since that first night at The Cornelia.

Was Cara's death related to Ben's passing? If deemed a suicide, it was possible.

Jaq frowned. If Ben's death wasn't an accident, Cara's might not be either.

Was the penthouse cursed?

Was Cara?

These questions, along with Henry's warning about his dad, bounced around in her head like pinballs.

Jaq watched as the sun turned Henry's tire tracks into slush. Her confusion lingered, a squatter refusing to leave.

When the sun got high enough to blind her, she stepped away. But even the vivid rays streaming warmth into her living room could not reach the darkest recesses of her mind.

CHAPTER 35

The news was annoyingly quiet about what might be the biggest story to ever hit Prescott.

Sam refused to answer both her work and personal lines, so Jaq finally sent a text message, asking her to call as soon as she could. She tried Henry's phone, too, but it went straight to voicemail. Her heart fluttered at the sound of his voice, but she couldn't leave a message because his mailbox was full.

Stupid technology!

She shoved the phone in her pocket and searched the kitchen for a distraction. Dishes were piled in the sink, and the trashcan overflowed with takeout boxes. No time like the present to give her house a little love. She grabbed a tote of cleaning products and moved from room to room, scrubbing, dusting, and tidying up. Finally, with the main rooms clean, she plopped into her desk chair. The notes she had shoved to the side when Henry dropped by were still where she left them.

Jaq pulled the stack toward her and lifted a folded-up page from the top of the pile—the timeline she crafted of Cara's past.

She stared at the dates and notes on the paper.

Cara was dead. How much of the story was there left to tell?

She tossed the timeline on her desk and leaned back in the chair. The photo of her mom on the bookshelf caught her eye, and she fought back tears. It was times like this when she missed her mom's strength the most. She would know what to do.

Jaq looked away as an image of Mrs. Rutherford struggling to keep it together as Ben's body was lowered into the ground filled her mind.

This was no longer about her feelings. She owed it to Ben's mom to figure out what happened the night he died.

Jaq opened The Prescott Diaries website, not surprised to see it alive with activity. New posts appeared on the front page like firecrackers. Pop, pop, pop. One after the other.

"Looks like Cara's exploits caught up to her," one said.

"Guess that's what you get when you live life like it's a never-ending party," noted another.

The few people who dared take a humanitarian approach were blasted with negative counter-remarks.

The crease in Jaq's brow deepened. The ease with which people judged one another behind their anonymous personas was depressing. Even Cara deserved better.

A red number flashed near the top of the page. Over five hundred posts were yet to be viewed. As Jaq watched, the number jumped to six hundred. Within seconds, it was at a thousand.

She turned off the monitor and wandered through the house. Now was not the time to get lost in other people's opinions. It was the time to focus on the things she could control...

But Henry's presence was unavoidable. The scent of his cologne lingered in the air, providing both a sense of comfort and sadness.

She sat on the couch and ran her hand over the nubby material. Lying there with Henry was the warmest she had felt in months.

"Dammit," she said, no longer able to ignore the emptiness in her soul.

Her tears fell to the carpet, leaving a large, wet spot at her feet.

CHAPTER 36

Jaq tried calling Sam and Henry again but got nowhere with her inquiries. On a whim, she tried Dahlia, but she, too, was occupied.

Had everyone in this town forgotten how to use their phone?

Jaq slammed her device onto the table. The napkin holder rattled in response, frustrating her even more.

"Fine, then!" She yanked her coat off the rack and marched to her car. If no one would answer her calls, she would force them to talk in person.

Her first stop was The Cornelia. The police had blocked off the street in front of the hotel. Even the mass of reporters was farther away this time than the night of Ben's death.

The realization they regarded Cara as more important than Ben soured Jaq's mood further. Unable to pass along the main road, she drove to the next street and pulled into a parking lot about two blocks from the hotel. She had no plan as she exited the car, but being here was better than sitting at home waiting for Sam or Henry to return her call.

A police officer stopped her as she exited the lot.

"Just curious what's going on," Jaq said with a wave toward the hotel. The officer was young, and, unfortunately, not someone she recognized.

"I can't divulge that information, ma'am."

Jaq pulled her press badge from her coat pocket.

"No one but law enforcement allowed," the officer said. She pointed toward the lot. "I've got orders."

Jaq pivoted on one foot and headed for her car. She stopped when she saw a dark green wagon parked a few spots down.

Dahlia was there, somewhere amid the chaos.

Didn't the officer say law enforcement only? Jaq debated whether to march over and demand she be let through, but logic won out. There was nothing to gain by raising hell. She was already in enough trouble.

Jaq stomped to her car, more irritated than when she began this journey.

Her engine idled as lukewarm air spit through the vents. She could try Maxwell's, but doubted she'd get far. Knowing Lawrence, this entire section of town was shut down. If he wanted to keep the events surrounding Cara's death private, it was likely no one in Prescott would ever know the truth about what happened.

As for Henry... What if he was inside right now, tending to his sister's affairs? The last thing he needed was her forcing her way into what might very well be the worst day of his life.

She couldn't do that to him.

Jaq's engine hiccupped as the gas gauge hovered just above empty. This day just kept throwing her curve balls.

She yanked the shifter into reverse as Dahlia appeared in the rearview mirror, her bright red coat shining in the afternoon sun. Jaq put her car in park and turned the engine off.

Dahlia was loading equipment into the back of her car when Jaq said hello. She jumped and looked up, her cheeks red and chapped. "Good grief, Ms. Darcy," she said and slammed the hatch shut. "You scared the crap out of me!"

"Sorry." Jaq touched her arm. "I was hoping you'd tell me a little more about what happened here. To Cara."

Dahlia squinted in the sunlight as she eyed Jaq. "Thank goodness Ethan brought you back! This story. I'm definitely going to need your help. I was telling Ethan just yesterday—"

"He doesn't know I'm here."

"Oh." A confused look crossed Dahlia's face. She tried to squeeze by, but Jaq didn't budge. "Ms. Darcy, come on. If you aren't back, you know I can't talk about any of this with you."

"But—"

Dahlia opened the driver's side door and crawled in before Jaq could argue her case. She started the car and let it run while she buckled her seat belt and checked the mirrors.

Jaq stepped to the side as Dahlia reversed out of the parking spot. She shivered beneath the deceptively sunny sky.

Dahlia stopped the car. She hesitated before cracking her window. "I heard the housekeeper found Cara this morning," she said over the whine of her engine. "Rumors are it was an overdose." She ran her hands up and down her arms as a cloud of breath filled the car's interior. "Now, go home, Ms. Darcy. Please. It's cold as shit out here."

Dahlia pulled away as Jaq's mind fed on the information like a ravenous animal. Where was Cara when she overdosed? And was it intentional or accidental?

She hurried to her car. If she went to Sam's and waited for her to get home, maybe she could get the answers she needed.

Jaq turned the key in her ignition and was greeted, not by the engine rumbling to life, but by a red "E" blinking on her dash.

"Son of a bitch!" Jaq slammed her fists into the steering wheel and snapped the engine off. She tried Sam again, but it went to voicemail. She hung up and dialed the main number for the Sheriff's Office.

"Deputy Collins," a deep voice said after the third ring. "How can I direct your call?"

Jaq's head pounded. The sun was sliding in the sky. The longer she sat in her uncooperative car, the colder it got. She explained who she was and asked the deputy to get Sam on the phone.

"I'm sorry, but Miss Thomas is unavailable. Can she call you back?"

Jaq hung up, her frustration the only thing keeping her warm. She sat in her car until she couldn't stand it any longer and walked over to the officer standing guard. "I'm sorry," she said, shuffling her feet both in embarrassment and to warm them. She pointed to her car. "I've run out of gas and can't get anyone on the phone. Can you help?"

The officer looked her over with suspicion. An uncomfortable silence filled the air before she reached for the radio on her shoulder.

Jaq waited, her fingers turning as numb as her toes. Her gloves were sitting in the alcove by the front door, and the tennis shoes she had thrown on offered minimal protection against the chilled sidewalk. What was she thinking, leaving her house without winter gear?

"Help's coming," the officer said. "But it'll be awhile." She glanced at Jaq's attire and retrieved a business card from her pocket. She pointed to the hotel entry. "Give this to the doorman. He'll let you wait inside."

A wall of heat greeted Jaq as she entered The Cornelia. The doorman glanced at the business card and escorted her to the lobby.

Holiday decorations still hung from the ceiling as the twinkling Christmas tree welcomed guests. It looked just as it had the night she and Henry sat on the leather couch, drinking Irish coffee.

Jaq walked over to the window. Police moved about out front, bundled in thick coats and gloves. She glanced at her watch, wondering how long she would have to wait for help to arrive.

"Jaq?"

She turned around in surprise. "Henry!"

He looked too tired to care about much of anything, let alone why she was there.

Jaq reached for him, but he stepped back.

"You shouldn't be here," he said, looking past her.

Jaq turned. Lawrence was at the opposite end of the lobby, addressing a group of well-dressed men. He signaled in their direction.

Henry gave Jaq a look she could not decipher before making his way to the group.

Lawrence put an arm around his shoulder and guided him toward the elevators.

Jaq stared out the window again, the chaos outside nothing compared to the turmoil within.

CHAPTER 37

ཉཉཉཉ

Sam didn't call Jaq until well after the moon shone high in the sky. And she was rushed, unable to talk for more than a minute.

"Can't you tell me anything about Cara? Anything at all?" Jaq hated pleading for information, but being in the dark was far worse.

"Only that her death is under investigation."

"But she died of a drug overdose."

"We haven't determined the official cause of death yet." Sam lowered her voice. "Did Henry tell you that's how she died?"

Jaq leaned back in her chair and rubbed her eyes. She had been staring at her monitor far too long with no break. Post after post aligned with Dahlia's Intel, and it wasn't exactly a secret Cara was a troubled soul. "Henry didn't tell me anything," she said. "He was with his dad."

"Oh." The line was silent for a moment. "I'll stop by later, okay?"

Another call came in before Jaq could set her phone down.

"Jacqueline Darcy?"

The voice on the other end was deep and unrecognizable. "Yes," Jaq said. "Who's this?"

The caller was silent.

"Hello?"

No response.

Jaq pulled the phone away from her ear and glanced at the number. The area code was not local, and the caller ID offered no further information. She tossed the phone onto her desk.

A few minutes later, it dinged, and a notification appeared on her lock screen. Jaq ignored it, too focused on the notes she was gathering to care about trivial distractions.

The more Jaq flipped through her files—now with comments and other media shared through The Prescott Diaries—the faster she wrote. Spending time with Henry had numbed her journalistic instincts, but they roared back to life as she scanned file after file, her fingers flying so fast her spell checker turned the screen red from all the typos.

Ben's last moments on earth screamed foul play. And now Cara's death had to be factored in, as well. Jaq hadn't decided whether she'd share any of the information she uncovered with Mack's writers. Right now, she just wanted the truth.

She pored through her collection of files, jumping from paper copies to digital versions as she scoured each reference. Even the most innocuous details could not be overlooked. Something bigger was at play. She could feel it.

Her fingers ached from typing. She scribbled a few notes on a legal pad before getting up to stretch. It was after midnight. She looked around the living room, debating whether to continue.

Papers were scattered everywhere. Snack bags and gum wrappers lined the carpeted area around her desk. It was organized chaos, and how she did her best work. Just like when she was a kid. Tromping through the mud. Observing butterflies as they hovered near vibrant flowers. Listening to birds call for their partners. These simple beauties opened her mind and her soul, an unexpected blessing in the chaos of death. For good or bad, life's tragedies formed the path she would take.

Jaq picked up the trash and neatened the files on her desk. The rest she stacked in a pile beside her chair. She put her computer into sleep mode and turned off the desk lamp. Whatever clues remained buried in her files would have to wait until tomorrow for discovery.

She yawned as she reached for her phone and tapped the text message icon. Sam had promised she would stop by, but clearly those plans had changed. No telling what lame excuse she sent for her absence.

But the text wasn't from Sam. It was from the same unknown number that called earlier. "For your eyes only," it said.

Jaq pulled her phone closer. A video file accompanied the cryptic text. She turned her computer back on and fumbled in her desk drawer, looking for a USB cable. When she connected the phone, her anti-virus software confirmed no threats, so she downloaded the file and turned on her speakers.

The Christmas tree in the lobby and Frank milling around the front desk immediately gave away the location. But this wasn't just some random video taken at The Cornelia. Henry was standing near the entry, speaking to a man in a bright blue suit with slicked-back hair.

Jaq paused the playback and leaned forward. Was this man with Lawrence earlier, when she ran into Henry? She couldn't be sure.

She restarted the video. The man wagged a long finger in the air, and his diamond-encrusted ring glimmered in the lights of the

Christmas tree. He said something, but his voice was too low to make out the words.

Henry fidgeted like he had just consumed a double espresso. "Derek, I mean it," he said. "This can't wait. It has to be addressed. Today."

They walked away. Exited stage left, Jaq thought, even though there was nothing remotely amusing about the situation. She stared at the screen as bystanders entered and exited the lobby. The video could have been taken any time during the holiday season. She right-clicked the file name on her computer drive and was not at all surprised to discover the metadata had been wiped clean.

Jaq zoomed out, looking for anything that could serve as a marker. For all she knew, this video could have been filmed weeks ago... Perhaps while Ben was still alive.

She blinked several times in rapid succession, trying to rid herself of the temptation to cry. There was no time for that. She had to focus. Confirm the date, so she could narrow down whatever it was Henry had ordered Derek to do.

Jaq watched the footage at a slower speed. An old man and woman passed by, their heavy winter coats cinched tight. A younger woman appeared soon after, the elegant silk of her evening gown flowing to her strappy black heels. Her partner was dressed in a tuxedo with no overcoat. They sure weren't walking anywhere dressed like that.

Jaq tapped her fingers against the desktop, thinking. Every year, the mayor hosted an event between Christmas and New Year's. Marcus would never let something so important pass without ample coverage.

She did a quick search of *The Gazette's* Society page as the video played in the background. The mayor's event was on December 28.

Jaq jotted this information on her notepad and reached for her mouse. But before she could stop the video, Cara appeared with a young man. His curly brown hair was gathered in a loose bun, and he wore a bomber jacket, skinny jeans, and casual shoes. Cara had on a short black dress and thigh-high boots.

Jaq maneuvered the video one frame at a time. The man guided Cara to the entry and signaled to the doorman. Her coat grazed the floor as she swayed from side to side.

Jaq snorted in disgust. They hadn't even left the hotel, and Cara's partying was already underway.

Headlights bathed the entrance. Cara dropped her purse, and her date bent over to retrieve it.

Jaq gasped and fumbled for the playback controls.

She rewound the video and played it again, this time at full speed.

The signal to the doorman.

Headlights, presumably from the car pulling in to pick them up.

Cara dropping her purse.

Jaq paused the clip as the mystery man bent down. She zoomed in. The glint of gold around his neck was but a flash. Had she not watched the video in slow motion, she would have missed it.

The herringbone design was distinct, as were the kinks where Ben wrapped it around his wrist.

The chain should have gone to Ben's mom after his death. Instead, Cara's flavor-of-the-month was wearing it around his neck.

Henry's veiled conversation no longer mattered. The only thing of importance now was this man... And where he was the night Cara died.

CHAPTER 38

ನವನವ

Jaq awoke at her desk, the rude scraping of Mr. Wilson's shovel disturbing her slumber.

She opened an eye and groaned. The front yard was visible without even lifting her head. Gray skies loomed as flurries swirled in the breeze before collapsing to the earth.

She pulled herself up and groaned again as pain shot through her joints. She stretched, lifting her hands to the ceiling before twisting her neck from side to side, trying to secure the desired pop. Her efforts were unrewarded.

She shuffled to the window. The ground glimmered with fresh snow, as tiny fragments of sun peeked through the overcast sky. She shivered and looked down at her cold, pale hands. A blanket was draped over the living room chair, and she wrapped herself in it before returning to the window.

Mr. Wilson's shovel screeched as he dragged it back and forth, trying to dislodge a block of icy filth from his driveway.

Jaq bristled at the intrusion. Or maybe it was the dampness seeping through her floor that made her shiver.

She made a beeline for the shower, where she lingered beneath the spray. Steam enveloped her as she kept the handle turned as far left as she could tolerate. Droplets danced across her forehead, and she reached for the hair clip nestled in her shower caddy. The last thing she needed this morning was a wet head.

Jaq stepped out of the spray and yanked her hair up. Her bath scrunchie fell to the floor and tickled her toes as she twisted her hair into a bun. She secured the ends in the clip's teeth and bent over to retrieve her scrunchie.

She held the bun in place to prevent her hair from coming dislodged. Her thoughts drifted to the man in the video with Cara. Who he was. How long they had known one another.

She needed a clear image of his face. Then she could search online for other photos. Figure out who he was before she shared the video with Sam or Andy.

Jaq rinsed soap suds from her skin and exited the shower, her body damp as the steam hovering in the bathroom tickled her nose. The haze was comforting, like the blanket she nestled in earlier.

But then her heart rate quickened.

She couldn't see.

Couldn't breathe.

What was happening?

Jaq choked as she tried to get air to her lungs. Panic consumed her as steam from the shower filled her pores. She stared at the ceiling, pleading for help.

The overhead light flickered, and Jaq grabbed for the towel rack. Cold metal soothed her hot flesh. As quickly as it began, her heart rate slowed, and her breathing turned steady.

Jaq stared at her patchy reflection in the mirror. Dark eyes, with even darker circles beneath, stared back, offering no explanation.

A drop of water plopped against the sink basin with a loud ping.

The faucet dripped again, and Jaq finessed the handle until the drip stopped. If only she could do the same for the flood of emotion.

There was a knock at the door as Jaq reached for her coffee tin.

She took her time filling the reservoir and scooping grounds into the basket. Sam had ignored every text and call, and Jaq had half a mind to let her freeze on the front porch.

Another knock, more urgent this time, rattled the doorframe.

Jaq growled and headed down the hallway. She flung open the door, prepared to let her cousin have it.

But it wasn't Sam at her doorstep. It was Henry, looking cold and disoriented.

Jaq fought to regain her composure and ushered him inside.

His eyes were drawn, his listless expression one of someone who could not remember the last time he slept. He followed Jaq to the kitchen and tossed his coat over a chair. It slid to the floor, and he stared at it, as if he could not muster up the energy to care.

The coffeemaker gurgled and hissed as hot water dripped through the grounds and into the carafe. Jaq reached into the cabinet and pulled out another coffee cup, her eyes never leaving Henry. "I've been worried about you," she said. "Are you okay?"

"I've been better."

He ran a hand through his hair, and Jaq fought the urge to pull him close and tell him everything would be okay.

"We met with the funeral director today." His frown deepened, but his eyes remained wide without fixing on any one thing.

Memories of her mom on medication—a shell of herself near the end—resembled the state Henry was in. If anyone understood what it meant to deal with the ramifications of losing someone you loved, Jaq did. Yet she couldn't move. She stayed where she was, unsure of what to say or how to comfort him.

He noticed her staring at him. "The doctor gave me something to help with my anxiety," he said and shrugged.

Seeing him so vulnerable hurt Jaq's heart. Henry always acted so together. Not the type of person you would expect to suffer from an anxiety disorder. But then again, how well did she really know him?

Jaq poured the coffee, and they made their way to the living room. Henry took a seat in the side chair while she sat on the couch, trying to balance her cup as she sank into the cushions.

The steaming liquid soothed her throat. And her nerves. She waited for Henry to speak.

He gave her a half-smile and cradled the cup in his hands as he stared into the space between them. His eyes were glazed, his posture stooped.

The silence was maddening. Jaq had to say something. "When will the service be?" she asked.

"Sometime later this week, I guess. The police"—he gave her a sideways glance—"won't release the body until the medical examiner signs off."

Jaq gripped the coffee cup. Her chill was back, but it had nothing to do with the temperature of her house. "Were those the family lawyers with your dad yesterday?"

"Yes and no. One of them—Derek—he's our head of security."

Jaq kept the look of surprise off her face as her mind contemplated this information. What security issue could Henry possibly be concerned about?

She sipped her drink, more convinced than ever something was amiss. The question now was just how deep Henry was involved.

She frowned. Was this why he didn't want her to meet his dad?

Henry touched her leg, and she looked up in surprise.

He leaned in, as if to kiss her, and Jaq reared back.

Henry sat back in the chair, visibly hurt.

Jaq set her cup on the coffee table and shoved aside all thoughts of Derek and family entanglements. "Henry, why are you here?" she asked. "Really."

His face turned red, and he squirmed in his seat.

"Don't get me wrong." She sank into the couch cushions again. "I'm glad you are. It's just... Yesterday, you made it pretty clear you didn't want me around."

She stared at her hands, folded in her lap. No matter how she spun it, how much she tried to pretend it didn't matter, his actions cut deep.

"This is all so overwhelming," Henry said, his voice taking on that broken, detached quality so typical of pharmaceutical intervention. "Funeral arrangements, decisions about my sister's affairs. Stuff I never thought I'd have to deal with. And my dad? Best you don't meet him until things settle down."

Jaq wanted to ask when that would be, but kept her mouth shut.

"Anyway, I came here to apologize. In person. I didn't mean to hurt you, Jaq. You have to believe that."

His expression was one of deep regret, and Jaq forgave him on the spot. "It gets easier," she said, sliding into the chair beside him. "I promise."

Henry wrapped his arms around her and held her tight, like she was the only person on earth he could trust.

CHAPTER 39

❧❧❧❧

"Henry, wait. You don't understand!"

Jaq didn't care that she was standing in the doorway with only a thin t-shirt and leggings between her and the bitter air.

Henry couldn't leave. Not like this.

"I do understand!" Henry's voice grew louder as he marched her way. "You're no different from everyone else in this town."

"Henry—"

"Don't bother." He thrust a finger toward her desk. "And, to think. I believed you cared about me." He shook his head. "What a fool I am."

Jaq couldn't run after him, her feet bare and the ground frozen. She could only stand there, helpless as he climbed in his car and sped away, narrowly missing Mr. Wilson's trashcans at the curb.

A blast of frigid air slapped her cheeks, and Jaq shut the door as the tears fell, hot against her cool skin.

Why hadn't she considered the possibility Henry would pass by her desk? That he would see the words "overdose" and "questionable circumstances" scrawled across the notepad?

Even worse, she had doodled his name and a question mark in block letters as she watched the video of him and Derek.

Jaq flopped onto the couch. Fire filled her stomach, threatening to spit back what remained of her last meal.

She tucked her legs into her chest and closed her eyes. Images of Henry filled the darkness. They were on the beach, the sky a crystal blue as they chased each other through the surf. Laughter filled the air as waves crashed around their feet, threatening to topple them.

Henry reached for her, his hand gentle against her cheek as he grazed her face. She waited, her lips parting as he leaned in to kiss her...

A low vibration startled her to her senses. Jaq opened an eye and stared at her phone rattling against the coffee table. She shook the cobwebs from her head and reached for the phone. "Hello?"

"Miss Darcy?"

Dahlia. As if things weren't bad enough.

Jaq scowled. "Yes, Dahlia. It's me."

"Oh, good," Dahlia said and giggled. "For a second there, I dialed someone else."

Jaq waited.

Dahlia cleared her throat. "Um, Ethan asked me to call. We need you at the VFW fundraiser tonight."

Adrenaline surged through Jaq's body, dissolving the last of her mental fog. She sat up as a sensation of warmth filled her veins. "He really said that?" she asked.

"Yeah. We need you there by six. I'd go, but Marcus is out of town. Ethan's letting me cover a reception at Cadbury Farms! Can you believe it?"

Dahlia was still squealing her delight as Jaq hung up. Her initial excitement was suffocated by the return of the gnawing feeling in the pit of her stomach. Cadbury Farms was *the* spot for notable events. Dahlia had no business being there. She could barely work a camera.

"What a load of crap," Jaq said and stomped to the shower.

She wasn't being asked to return to work. She was being punished.

"I need a favor."

"Oh, yeah? What's that?" Sam asked with a loud crunch.

"Wait... Are you eating carrots?"

Even as a kid, when vegetables were fresh from the garden, Sam turned up her nose and fed them to the dog. Eating carrots now meant one thing—Sam was trying to mask her cigarette cravings.

Jaq cupped her forehead with her palm. Just what she needed... Another obstacle.

"What do you want, Jaq?" A referee whistle blared in the background, followed by the sound of a jeering crowd. "I'm kinda in the middle of something here."

"Can you go to the VFW tonight and take a few photos?"

Sam's photography skills were nothing to brag on, but the annual fundraiser wasn't exactly noteworthy.

"What for?" Sam stopped her crunching. "Don't tell me... You're back at work now that Cara bit the dust? Talk about shithouse luck."

Yep, Sam was in a mood. Just like every other time she tried to quit smoking.

Jaq massaged the bridge of her nose. She should have known better than to ask her cousin for help.

"C'mon, you idiots. Catch the damn ball!"

There was a loud noise, followed by rustling.

Jaq walked to her desk and flipped her notepad over, not wanting to be reminded of Henry's unpleasant departure.

"So, you gonna tell me what's up or not?"

Jaq left the memories of Henry at her desk and walked to the living room window. "Ethan wants me to handle the fundraiser while Dahlia covers some wedding reception," she said as she peered through the curtains. Tiny icicles hung from the eaves, the perfect depiction of nature frozen in time.

"So why you need me?"

"Because I don't trust his intentions."

Sam's crunching filled the void. "Whose wedding you crashing?" she finally asked.

"Does it matter?"

"If you want me to cover for you, it does."

Sam could be so irritating, but she was Jaq's only hope. "I don't know," she said. "But the reception's at Cadbury Farms, if that tells you anything."

"You're hoping to run into Henry, aren't you?"

Jaq didn't respond. The less Sam knew, the better.

"You honestly think he's gonna go? After what just happened?"

"Knowing how Lawrence operates... Yeah."

Another whistle punctuated the air, this time followed by cheers.

Sam chomped louder in Jaq's ear. "And exactly how do you plan on avoiding Dahlia?"

Jaq had an idea, but there was no time to share it. "Look, are you gonna help me out or not? I'm on a tight schedule here."

"I guess. The game's over, no thanks to these stupid refs." Sam's footsteps echoed as she walked to her bedroom. The rustle of hangers drifted through the phone. "Hey! You think that cute bartender will be working tonight?"

CHAPTER 40

ನಾನಾ

Jaq pulled her hair into a ponytail and clasped it with a silver clip. She looked in the mirror and made one quick adjustment before spraying her hair into place. She could not afford to be late.

She exited her house around the time the Society page said the nuptials were scheduled to begin. The drive along the winding, isolated roads to Cadbury Farms was beautiful but treacherous, the occasional slick spot threatening to spin her car out of control.

Jaq pulled through the main gates and drove another half-mile or so until the old barn popped into view. It wasn't much to brag on from the outside—its red paint peeling and its roof in dire need of an overhaul—but the venue was booked all-year round.

She parked far enough away to avoid the valet attendants, but not out of walking distance. She buttoned her dress coat and gripped her camera bag as she ventured into the chilled air.

The flowers alongside the walking path were crushed, their vibrant beauty buried beneath patches of snow. Just six months ago, she had been here, snapping photos of an engaged couple whose parents were members of the city council. The flowers were a lush purple, pink, and yellow, complemented by a grove of trees blooming with crisp green foliage. The perfect backdrop for a young couple's wedding memories. Unlike tonight, when open-door views of the sunset would be replaced with portable interior heaters and an outdoor firepit for the rare guest seeking to embrace the crisp air or step away for a smoke.

Jaq maneuvered around pockets of snow as she made her way along the gravel road. As tempting as it was to veer into the grass, the threat of meeting a critter or breaking an ankle in a hole they burrowed to prepare for winter was enough to keep her on the path.

She fidgeted with the press badge in her pocket as she neared the entrance, but no one was waiting to check her credentials. She had succeeded in being one of the first guests to arrive, well ahead of the wedding party.

Jaq entered the barn and took a quick left, slipping into the shadows of the large, vaulted space. She pulled a collapsible tripod from her bag, adjusted it, and attached her camera to the head.

A middle-aged woman dressed in formal wear far too tight to be strutting around in, shuffled by, a large binder in one hand and a cell phone in the other. She stopped when she spotted Jaq. She lifted a hand, as if to signal her over, but the ringing of the phone interrupted her.

"Dammit, Molly! I told you to give me at least thirty minutes' notice." The woman glanced Jaq's way once more before turning on her heel and heading for the entry.

Jaq chuckled. Whoever this Molly was, she was in for a rough night.

A group of workers in black pants and crisp white shirts clustered near the makeshift stage. Caterers set up the fresh fruit tower, caviar station, and a champagne fountain on tables behind them as an older gentleman in a bow tie eyed the spread. He checked his clipboard as three more helpers passed by, balancing the oversized wedding cake on a large tray. They made their way to the center table lined with white silk.

The wedding planner walked over to the man in the bow tie and pointed at her watch. A young girl followed behind, her cheeks laden and her shoulders stooped as she tugged a large rolling cart filled with silver dishes and crystal. The infamous Molly had arrived.

Jaq adjusted her camera lens, using the wait staff as test subjects. She leaned over and checked the viewfinder, moving it around until she settled on two young men struggling to position a heater in the exact location the wedding planner noted.

A blast of air warmed Jaq's legs as she waited for the festivities to begin.

CHAPTER 41

ನಯನ

Live music rang in Jaq's ears as she hid in the shadows. Guests piled in, a few dropped off at the entry by limousine, while others exited from high-end SUVs and sports cars. Jaq counted over sixty arrivals, many of them heading straight for the bar as the band performed 80s music on the stage.

The lead singer tapped the top of the microphone and asked for everyone's attention. The guests turned toward the entry, and he welcomed the bride and groom as they entered the barn in a horse-drawn carriage.

The bride's father, an anchor from the evening news, helped her down and gave her hand to the groom, who led her to the area cleared for dancing. Her off-white dress shimmered in the spotlight as her wedding train floated along the ground. The bridesmaids, dressed in burgundy gowns with intricate lace overlays, were too busy with the groomsmen to notice.

The couple danced their first dance as man and wife, and Jaq's cynicism ballooned as she eyed them in her viewfinder. The entire world before them, they had no sense of death or loss or anything "normal" people had to contend with. This marriage would be like so many others. Done in a year or two. Three tops. And the cycle would inevitably start over again.

Guests in luxurious attire made small talk and sipped their high-end drinks. One, sitting at a nearby table, complained about the quality of her steak while another rambled to a bored-looking date about his latest real estate purchase in Key West.

Jaq scowled. She could pay off her house with what these people wasted on an evening that would soon be forgotten by everyone except the person writing the checks.

Irritated, she shifted her viewfinder away from the happy couple and panned the crowded space. Dahlia was at the opposite end of the barn, her curls bouncing as she moved her camera from one focal point to another. Ethan stood nearby, directing her as the flash went off, pop after pop.

Jaq squinted. The camera lens was larger than the one Dahlia normally used. She zoomed in as Dahlia fiddled with the same lens Ethan refused to pay for months ago. "What the—?"

Someone tapped her shoulder. "Miss?"

Jaq looked up in surprise. She had intentionally avoided using a flash, her camera serving no purpose but to cover her true intentions.

The older gentleman in the bow tie stood before her, unamused. He was a foot taller, his high hairdo making him the size of a giant, even next to her three-inch heels.

"Miss, the photographers are supposed to be over there." He pointed to the area where Dahlia and Ethan stood.

"My apologies." Jaq gathered her equipment.

The man eyed her with suspicion. "Let me see your invitation," he said. He shifted the clipboard to one hand and retrieved his walkie-talkie from his belt.

Jaq patted her coat before opening her camera bag. "I know it's here somewhere." She shoved her lens in the front pocket as she pretended to search for the nonexistent piece of paper.

The man pressed the button on his walkie-talkie as the band fired up a fast-paced dance tune. He turned away from the speakers.

Jaq grabbed her bag and bolted toward the front of the barn.

Inebriated groomsmen clustered near a heater, eyeing the bridesmaids cutting up on the dance floor. Jaq ducked between them, scrunching her nose as the smell of cigars and booze hit her dead-on. She squeezed through, her head down and her camera bag tucked against her chest, as the man in the bow tie hollered at her from behind.

A pair of black leather dress shoes blocked her path.

She darted her eyes back and forth, frantic to find another route of escape.

A man's hand gripped her arm, and she looked up as Henry pulled her out of the fray.

"Jaq? What are you doing here?"

She gave him her most pitiful look as the man in the bow tie caught up to them.

"You." He wheezed and pointed a finger at her as he struggled to get his words out. "I don't know what you think you're doing, but—"

"Help!" Jaq mouthed to Henry. She couldn't afford another confrontation. Not with Ethan there.

Henry stepped forward. "It's okay," he said. "She's with me."

"She can't have that camera." The man tapped his clipboard. "Approved photographers only."

Jaq wanted to ask if he was a drill sergeant in everyday life but held her tongue.

"Understood." Henry took the camera bag and slung it over his shoulder. He pointed Jaq toward the entry. "I'll take care of it."

The man hesitated before retreating into the crowd.

Jaq shook her head. "What a tool."

"Come with me."

She tried to dislodge the lump in her throat as Henry marched her out of the barn.

"I'm taking you home," he said and waved to the valet.

Jaq dug her heels into the dirt and yanked her arm away. "No!"

The valet froze, and Henry stared at her like she was insane.

A crowd gathered near the barn's entrance. The groomsmen stumbled over one another, fighting for the best view.

"Last I checked, we weren't together, Henry. You don't get to tell me what to do."

"He may not," a booming voice said. "But I sure as hell can."

Jaq turned to find a red-faced Lawrence standing behind her. Steam seeped from his pores as the winter air met his fiery temperament. He grabbed Jaq's wrist, squeezing so tight she feared he might snap it in two.

Henry tried to separate them.

"Don't try to protect her! Hasn't she caused our family enough trouble?" Lawrence released his iron grip on Jaq and gestured toward the crowd. "I can't believe you're okay with this. Look at the scene she's caused."

"She's allowed to be here, Dad. It's called the first amendment."

"No, son. It's trespassing." He stared at Jaq with a hatred she did not expect. "And I have half a mind to call the state police and have her permanently removed from this venue."

"How is this trespassing? You invited her paper to cover the event."

"Let's just see about that, shall we?"

The band had stopped playing, and at least half the wedding party was crowded around them, like rubberneckers unable to drive past a wreck without gawking.

Jaq rubbed her hand as Lawrence motioned toward the crowd.

Ethan appeared, and Lawrence put an arm around his shoulders. "Mr. Richards. So nice to see you this evening."

Her boss looked like a lost puppy in Lawrence's grasp. "How can I help you, Mr. Worthington?"

"Now, Ethan." Lawrence looked down his nose at the man standing before him, like he had no business being there any more than Jaq did. "I expected more from you when I asked the paper to cover this wedding…"

Ethan shuffled his feet as Lawrence went on about what a privilege it was to be invited to such a well-to-do affair. How he thought they had an understanding.

Jaq could not hide her surprise. Exactly how many stories involving the Worthingtons had been buried?

Ethan shifted his beady eyes her way before returning his attention to Lawrence. "I'm truly sorry," he said. "She doesn't work for me anymore." He flicked a hand in her direction, like he was shooing away a nagging mosquito. "I don't even know why she's here."

Lawrence nodded, patted Ethan on the back, and called an attendant over. "Escort her off the property," he said, giving her one last look of disdain. "If she tries to return, have her arrested."

The attendant reached for her wrist, and Jaq yanked it away. If they expected her to slip into the night without having her say, they had sorely underestimated her resolve.

Ethan tried to leave, but she stepped in front of him. "I always knew you were a drunk," she said, unable to control the sneer that crossed her face. "But I never took you as a coward, too. I guess that's what happens when you're bought and paid for."

Ethan's face turned purple, and Lawrence shoved him to the side. "Now, you listen here," he said, jamming a finger into her chest.

It hurt, but Jaq did not flinch. She refused to be intimidated. And she sure wasn't going down without a fight.

She clenched her fists.

Henry had been quiet this entire time, but now he stepped between them. "Enough!"

A murmur rippled through the crowd.

"Henry—"

"Don't 'Henry' me, Dad." He shooed the attendants away and jerked a thumb in Jaq's direction. "This is preposterous. She's not hurting anyone! You want to talk about *her* not needing to be here? We shouldn't be here either. We should be at home, thinking about how to honor Cara's memory. Not putting on a show"—he waved to the crowd—"for people we barely know."

Lawrence remained stone-faced. "Don't you see what she's doing, son? She's trying to put a wall between us. Like she did with Cara and Benjamin. Don't tell me you're falling for it."

"You are an asshole," Henry said and reached for Jaq's hand. "No wonder Cara hated you so much."

The expression on Lawrence's face was priceless, and Jaq could not suppress her grin. Oh, how she wished her camera was in hand. *This* was a moment worth capturing.

Henry led her through the stunned crowd. "You drove, right?"

Jaq pointed down the long road leading to the gated entrance.

"Perfect." He clasped her hand tight. "I could really use the air."

They walked to her car without another word, even the night creatures silent in a world gone awry.

CHAPTER 42

"I am so sorry, Henry. This was not how I wanted things to go tonight."

Henry backed Jaq's car out of her impromptu parking space. Without a word, he drove toward the entrance and turned onto the main road.

"I needed to talk to you," she continued. "And I didn't know how else to do it."

Henry kept his eyes forward as the lights of a passing car bathed the front seat. He flicked the headlights, and the driver turned off his brights, but Jaq still saw spots as they made their way through the next curve.

She felt for his leg. "Henry..."

He glanced her way. "It's all right," he said, his voice flat but strong. "That's been a long time coming, I can tell you that."

Jaq giggled.

"What's so funny?"

"The look on your dad's face. I can't imagine anyone has ever stood up to him like that. Especially with so many people around."

Henry suppressed a grin.

"And Ethan! What a scumbag he turned out to be."

"You really didn't know my dad was paying him to control what was reported about our family?"

Jaq shrugged as she envisioned Ethan's fancy dinners with out-of-town celebrities and politicians. Dinners that seemed increasingly frequent, taking him away from the office and giving him an excuse to deflect responsibility to people like Dahlia, who had no business managing anything. "Maybe I should have, but no. I didn't know."

Now it was Henry's turn to chuckle. "You aren't much of a journalist, are you? I mean, everyone in Prescott knows Ethan Richards is morally conflicted."

"I can't help it if I try to see the good in people." Jaq playfully punched his arm. "And 'morally conflicted'? What the hell is that? Lawyer-speak for being your dad's lackey?"

"Well, he's not the only one..."

Jaq raised an eyebrow.

"Surely, you've heard the stories."

"I haven't heard anything."

"You will, working for that website." Henry clenched his jaw and refused to look her way.

Jaq touched his leg. "Please. Let me explain." She rushed to get the words out before he could shut her down again. "I received another video this week from an anonymous sender."

Henry shot her a sideways glance.

"Of you and Derek. At The Cornelia."

They were nearing a yellow stoplight and Henry tapped the brakes a little too hard. The sudden change in motion snapped Jaq's head forward.

"Ow!" she said as stars sprinkled her vision.

He looked appalled. "Oh, Jaq. I'm sorry." The light changed, and he pulled onto a side street. "Are you okay?"

She rubbed her neck. "What'd you tell Derek to take care of?"

Henry's face turned a deep red. "That's what you're worried about? And here I was, thinking I'd hurt you."

He mashed the gas pedal, and the car lurched forward.

"Good grief, Henry. Are you trying to kill me?"

They drove in silence, Henry sitting upright, with the driver's seat as far back as it would go. He gripped the wheel, keeping his hands firmly at ten and two.

Jaq laughed, and Henry demanded to know what was so funny.

"You," she said, struggling to catch her breath. The pain in her neck no longer seemed important. "You look like my grandma."

Henry glanced down and relaxed his grip on the steering wheel, but the more Jaq tried to control her laughter, the worse it got. He shot her a sideways glance, his jaw firm, but broke into laughter himself as the intensity of the events at the reception faded.

He reached for her hand. They neared the turnoff, and Jaq held her breath, waiting to see which way he would go. Left would take them downtown; right would lead to her house. She wasn't ready to go home.

Henry turned on the left blinker and pulled through the intersection. "You don't have any place to be, do you?" He massaged the spot just above her knee.

"Just with you," she said, placing her hand over his.

They crossed the river and pulled up in front of a three-story brick building about a quarter mile from the water's edge. The city lights were coming to life, and she looked over her shoulder as Henry pulled into the building's garage. The city seemed alive somehow, even though few dared mingle in the night air.

The lobby was bright, with a nook off the front door. A Christmas tree sat nestled in the corner, cotton snow, glimmering packages, and stuffed reindeer filling every inch of space beneath it.

"Our property manager loves the holidays," Henry said. He put his hand on Jaq's back and guided her toward the elevator at the end of the hall. "I bet it'll be Valentine's Day before she takes all this down."

"Sounds like my neighbor."

They made the brief trip from the lobby to Henry's condo on the top floor. Were it not for the enormous windows overlooking the riverfront and the sounds of traffic in the distance, Jaq would have believed he whisked her away to a cabin, not a condo in the heart of downtown. Off the entryway was the kitchen. Rich cherry cabinets and stone countertops evoked a feeling of warmth, as a fireplace split the dining area and living room, its see-through glass affording a 360-degree view of the logs nestled inside.

The thought of being buffered from the world and all its drama was an intoxicating proposition. She reached for Henry's hand as he gave her a tour.

Frames lined his navy walls, but they passed too quickly for her to note the contents. Henry stopped at the first room. Champagne-colored bedding contrasted with the dark, queen-sized headboard, and a mahogany writing desk sat beneath windows overlooking the river. A closed laptop sat perpendicular in the center of the desk, with several law journals stacked to the side.

"How do you get anything done?" Jaq asked. She leaned against the desk and watched as a small boat cruised along, its lights shimmering atop the water. "If it were me, I'd sit here all day, staring out the window."

"There are days I do." Henry pointed down-river. "See that boat? It's my dad's. I take it out sometimes. Float wherever the water takes me."

Jaq could feel the heat of his body so close to hers. She cleared her throat and took a step back.

Henry squeezed her hand and guided her down the hall, past the bathroom to his bedroom. She took it all in. The thick masculine bedding and oversized headboard, perfectly centered lamps on both nightstands, the flawless placement of books and decorative items on his floating shelves.

Not a trace of dirt or dust was visible, and she blushed at the state of her house when Henry visited.

"My housekeeper came today," he said as if he could read her mind. He shrugged and flashed his irresistible half-smile. "I don't advertise it, but I'm something of a slob."

"I highly doubt that."

He wrapped his arms around her waist, his touch stirring something deep within. She had never felt this way about anyone. Not even Ben, who, until now, she considered the love of her life.

"Henry..."

He pulled her tight, his lips finding hers as he slid his fingers through her hair. He pulled back and stared into her eyes.

The furnace kicked on and blew warm air in their faces.

Jaq tucked her head into Henry's chest, certain she could stay there forever, listening to the steady, comforting sound of his heartbeat.

CHAPTER 43

ଊଊଊ

Ever the gentleman, Henry guided Jaq to the guest bedroom around two. She slipped on one of his t-shirts and crawled under the covers, the soft mattress and exhaustion of the day no match for her excitement over their developing relationship.

She awoke to an angry Henry talking on his phone at the other end of the condo. She made her way to the kitchen, the hardwood floors chilling her toes.

Henry stood in front of the window, staring at the water. His shoulders were rigid as he clenched and unclenched his hands.

The floor creaked, and he turned as she entered the living room. "You're up," he said. No emotion, just the facts. Like he was delivering an opening argument at trial.

Jaq hugged him, and he softened his stance. She snuggled as tight as she could, wishing for one more moment of tranquility.

Henry granted it, holding her close as the smell of roasted coffee filled the air. The pot beeped three times, and he pulled away. "That was my dad," he said, tossing his phone on the kitchen counter. "In case you hadn't already figured that out."

Jaq stared out the window. The sun was peeking above the horizon, hazy against the river's edge. It had to be seven o'clock. Maybe eight. The sun splayed orange and yellow rays across the water, making it sparkle like crystal despite the murkiness. "I take it he's mad?" she said.

"That would be an understatement."

The sun climbed higher in the sky, burning Jaq's eyes. She turned as Henry slid a tray her way. He watched as she added sugar and a splash of silky cream to her coffee.

She sat on one of his high barstools and gripped the coffee cup for warmth, the stone harsh against her bare arms.

"You must be freezing." Henry was already dressed, but she had nothing to change into. He grabbed a sweatshirt from the coat closet. "See if this fits," he said before disappearing down the hallway. He returned with black leggings and a pair of boot socks.

"Ex-girlfriend?" Jaq asked with a smirk.

Henry's eyes widened, and he looked like he had been slapped.

Jaq turned the leggings over in her hands. They were a name brand and hardly worn. "These were Cara's?" she asked, her voice catching in her throat.

Henry nodded, wrinkles blemishing his otherwise boyish face. "She stayed here sometimes. When she needed to get away—"

"From your dad." Jaq slipped into the oversized leggings and pulled on the socks as Henry refilled their coffee cups.

They sat on the sofa. Even with the thick leggings, the leather cushions were cold. She took another sip of the rich coffee, pleased it was the same creamy shade and sweetness as before. Henry had paid attention. It was the most romantic thing anyone had ever done for her.

"Tell me more," she said, scooting closer.

He reached over with his free hand and ran it through her hair. "About Cara? Or my dad."

"Either. Both. I don't care."

"What can I say? When it came to my sister... He was vicious. There's no other word for it." Henry took a drink as anger consumed his features. "In high school, Cara brought home a note saying she needed help, or she wouldn't make it to the next grade. Instead of working with her—trying to figure out the problem—he just yelled at her. Called her lazy and worthless and stupid. Forced her to stay in her room and study until she got her grades up." Henry drank the rest of his coffee in one gulp, oblivious to the temperature. "Turns out, she was dyslexic. All those years, and no one would listen."

He paused and shifted his eyes upward, the tension in his jaw easing. "I used to sneak her food, though, you know? Did what any big brother would." He swallowed hard. "I guess I won't get that chance anymore."

"I'm so sorry, Henry," Jaq said. She was no fan of Cara's, but this depiction at least explained some of why she acted the way she did. She tucked her head into his chest, wishing she could bring him some comfort as he moved through the inevitable dark days ahead.

CHAPTER 44

The clouds turned gray on the horizon as snow sprinkled from above. White powder settled on the riverbank and coated the cars parked on the street below.

Jaq leaned against Henry's large windows, mesmerized as the flakes landed atop the water and struggled for survival. Her breath frosted the windows, and she wiped it away with the sleeve of her borrowed sweatshirt.

The snow tapered off, and Jaq returned to her spot beside Henry on the couch. "There's just something about the snow," she said, scooting closer. "It's so mesmerizing."

"You ever ski?"

"Sam and I talked about going but never found the time."

"Cara and I go once a year. Breckenridge is her favorite..." Henry's voice trailed off as he realized this tradition was no more.

"We used to take annual trips, too," Jaq said, hoping to shift his attention to the present. "Mostly places within an hour's drive. But Andy surprised me and my mom one year with a deep-sea fishing expedition in Clearwater."

"Do you still spend time with your parents?"

Jaq shook her head and stared at her hands. "My mom had cancer... When I was little. And my dad died before I was born."

Henry pulled her close. "I'm sorry."

Jaq nestled in the crook of his arm. "What about your mom?" she asked. "You don't talk about her much."

Henry stiffened. "She died when I was young. In an automobile accident on the way to pick us up from school."

Jaq sat up and touched the side of his cheek. She stared into his eyes, sensing the depth of his pain. "I can't imagine losing someone so special without having a chance to say goodbye."

He nodded and looked away.

They finished their coffee in silence.

Jaq put her cup on the end table and massaged the base of her neck. Henry's mattress was softer than hers, and the jarring at the stoplights hadn't done her any favors.

He motioned for her to turn around. "Tell me more about your mom," he said, kneading her tight shoulders.

Jaq closed her eyes. "She was something else. And did she love to fish! That trip to Clearwater? We caught so much, we had to throw them back. Certainly more than we ever caught fishing at my grandparent's farm..."

Her voice faltered. She could still feel the hot breeze as they sat on the dock, poles in hand.

Henry dug his thumbs into her neck. Jaq winced, but the sensation put things in perspective. Now was not the time to broach the subject of her family's land. There was already enough drama.

Henry patted her shoulder and stood up. "Believe it or not, I used to dream about building a house outside the city. There's something very appealing about the simple life."

"What's stopping you?"

"What do you think?" He walked to the spot where Jaq had just watched the snow fall and glanced at her over his shoulder. "There's no way my dad would let me and my sister just leave the life he's worked so hard to build."

"Is that why Cara took over The Cornelia? To please your dad?" It never occurred to Jaq it might be anything other than a way to corral her poor behavior.

"Some of it." Henry stared at the water for a moment before facing her. "But mostly it was to keep her out of trouble. She had no female role models after my mom died. No one to steer her down the right path."

Shoplifting as a teen, partying all night with adults while she was still underage, getting pulled over for driving under the influence... Jaq was already familiar with Cara's discretions, but she let Henry tell his version anyway, without interruption.

"Despite it all," he said, his voice laced with pain, "I loved her. She had a good heart."

Jaq gave him a funny look.

"Well, she used to, anyway. Before my dad ruined her. My dad ruins everyone, you know."

"I guess I shouldn't be stunned by Ethan's behavior, then," Jaq said with a scowl. "But I am."

"Yeah, well. That's what working for my dad does to people."

"Is that why you started your own practice?"

"That was the plan. But you know how it is with family. You can't refuse them when they need help." He shrugged. "That's how I ended up at the Sheriff's station, defending Cara."

The ticking of the wall clock seemed extra loud as the silence between them grew.

"She didn't kill him, Jaq. Cara did not kill Benjamin."

She stared at him in surprise.

Henry twisted his hands as he spoke. "You didn't know her like I did. She had her issues, sure. But she's not capable of that sort of violence."

Jaq's mind raced. The possibility Cara killed Ben did seem far-fetched the more she learned about her. The only one she seemed violent toward was herself... And there was no way she was strong enough to hang Ben's body from that beam.

Just how far would a big brother go to help his troubled sister?

Jaq eyed Henry as he walked toward the couch. "Is it possible Cara's death was not intentional?" she asked.

He froze, like the deer she passed on the way to The Cornelia the night Ben died. "Surely, you don't mean murder." He sat down, leaving a sizeable gap between them. "After all that she's been through? I don't know how anyone could blame her... You know. For taking matters into her own hands."

Suicide might seem probable on the surface, but Cara's actions screamed otherwise. Several posts on The Prescott Diaries had detailed her activities in the days leading up to her death. From shopping binges to partying with friends, if Cara were grieving, only she knew it.

Henry was staring at her, waiting for her to respond.

Jaq took a deep breath. "I don't think Cara killed herself."

"That's ridiculous!" Henry slapped the leather cushion between them. "I mean, who would want my sister dead?"

Jaq crossed her legs and tucked her feet beneath her. "Think about it, Henry. What reason did she have to be reckless? I mean, the video my uncle has is circumstantial. And even if Cara were guilty of something, knowing your dad, he'd get the charges negotiated down." Her mind was in hyper-drive, and she couldn't stop herself if she wanted to. "Remember that video I told you about... The one of you and Derek? Cara was there, too. With someone I didn't recognize. A man with curly hair pulled into a bun. I think we need to consider the possibility—"

"Unbelievable!" Henry shook his head. "You just don't quit, do you?"

Jaq pursed her lips. "You just said Cara caused all sorts of trouble. Isn't it possible her actions finally caught up to her?"

"What kind of trouble?" Henry said with a sneer. "The kind that involved your ex-boyfriend?"

"That's not what I meant." Jaq's icy tone matched his expression. "I wasn't talking about Ben. But yes, that's a possibility."

Disbelief clouded Henry's face. "You think this is all her fault, don't you? Benjamin's death. Hers."

"I don't know what to think anymore, Henry. And I don't think you do, either." Jaq's eyes narrowed. Her entire livelihood revolved around trusting her instincts. He was keeping something from her.

Henry stood up as something occurred to Jaq. She got up and forced her way into his line of sight.

"You were worried about her! *That's* who you were talking to Derek about. You wanted Cara to have protection." She ran her hand through her hair as he stared at her, his expression a blend of skepticism and suspicion. "What I can't figure out, though, is whether you were protecting her from herself or from someone else."

Henry's frown deepened. "I can't talk about this anymore," he said and turned toward the entryway. "I think you should leave."

"Henry, wait." Jaq touched the side of his arm—a half-hearted attempt to diffuse a situation she could no longer control—but he shrugged off the gesture and walked to the door.

He snatched her coat from the nearby rack and waited.

Jaq retrieved her phone and dress from the guestroom, trying to ignore the many thoughts tumbling through her mind.

"You can get the clothes to me later," he said when she returned, neither his face nor his voice revealing any emotion.

Jaq fumbled to remove Cara's socks. The hard tile against the soles of her feet sent a shiver through her body. Or maybe it was Henry's anger.

She pulled on her coat and reached for her heels. "I'm sorry I offended you," she said, trying to keep the emotion from her voice. "But these are questions you need to answer. If not for your benefit, then for Cara's."

He looked exhausted in the harsh entryway light, the bags under his eyes overshadowed only by the deep creases in his forehead. She kissed him on the cheek and said she'd call him later. The door locked behind her as she headed for the elevator, her dress tucked between her right arm and her chest.

The ride to the parking garage felt like an eternity. A thin layer of snow covered her car, the concrete walls of the garage affording little protection against the elements.

Jaq swept some of the precipitation from her windshield before huddling in the front seat while the engine warmed.

If she had learned nothing else from her attempts to talk to Ben after he broke things off, it was the importance of giving people their space.

She put her car in reverse and backed out of the parking spot.

Henry would come around in time.

He had to.

She could not afford to think otherwise.

CHAPTER 45

ᚾᚢᚾᚢ

"About time you called me back," Sam said. "I was getting worried."

"Sorry," Jaq said. Her phone was in her purse, and she didn't notice the missed calls until she got home.

Sam chuckled. "You stayed at Mr. Moneybags' place, didn't you?"

Jaq avoided the question. Her head pounded like a hangover, even though she'd had nothing to drink. She poured water in the coffeepot's reservoir. "Listen, can you stop by today? I need your help with something."

"Fending off old farts last night wasn't enough? One of 'em got a little handsy, you know."

"Sam—"

"While you were hobnobbing, I spent my evening trying to get a few decent shots. And this is the thanks I get..."

The pain in Jaq's head intensified. "It doesn't matter anymore."

"What do you mean 'It doesn't matter'?"

Liquid hissed as it spilled onto the hot burner, and Jaq tapped the carafe to center it beneath the spigot. "It means I'm out of a job."

"What? What the hell happened at that reception, Jaq?"

"Look, just get over here as soon as you can, okay? I'll explain everything then."

She hung up, feeling even worse than before.

Sam leaned over Jaq's shoulder, looking at the files pulled up on the computer screen. She still wore her coat and gloves, the house as cold as a Minnesota fishing shanty in February. "What makes you think Cara's death is a murder?" she asked.

Her breath smelled like stale cigarettes, and Jaq crinkled her nose. So much for New Year's resolutions.

Sam took a seat on the couch, and Jaq reached for the stack of papers she had printed while waiting for her to arrive. The pages were divided in two, one stack turned sideways atop the other.

Jaq swiveled in her chair and passed the top stack to Sam. "These are from Mack's site. Not the salacious stuff. General info about the renovation at The Cornelia, Lawrence's business acquisitions, you name it." She handed Sam the second stack. "And these are from the papers."

Sam thumbed through the pages. "What am I supposed to be looking for here?"

"It's what's *not* there."

"Okay?"

Jaq pointed to an article from *The Beacon*. "The basic info between this and the other papers is the same. They make it sound like Lawrence did us a favor acquiring the farm."

Sam smacked her forehead with her hand. "Neither of us needs to relive that," she said.

Jaq nodded. "I know. But I learned last night that Ethan's been covering for Lawrence. Only printing what he approves. And

Henry says he's not the only one running interference." She faced the monitor, trying to hide her disgust. She opened another tab for The Prescott Diaries and pointed to the third paragraph. Where the papers read like a marketing catalog, highlighting the tax revenue and tourism benefits, Mack's writers questioned the personal impact the Worthington's takeover would have on the people of Prescott.

"Jaq, I'm hungry. Please tell me there's a point to this."

"The *point* is Lawrence has done an excellent job containing the traditional methods of communication." Jaq spun her chair around. "But he didn't count on a site like Mack's that he can't control. Aside from the typical concerns of defamation or slander"—Jaq waved a hand in the air—"The Prescott Diaries does not have the same journalistic constraints newspapers do. And it certainly doesn't matter whether Lawrence approves of the coverage. It's probably better for business that he doesn't."

Sam looked mildly interested. "Okay. So, you found someone not willing to capitulate to the Worthington's demands. So what?"

"Do you know anything about Denise Worthington?"

Sam looked baffled.

"Henry and Cara's mom." Jaq moved to the couch and flipped through the printouts from The Prescott Diaries until she found what she needed. "She died years ago. In a car accident."

Sam took the paper from Jaq and eyed the text. "It says here the medical examiner determined cause of death the same day?" She scrunched her nose. "That's odd. It takes us several days, at least."

"Uh-huh. And that's where I need your help."

"You want me to dig up the case files for you."

Jaq nodded. "It happened too long ago for me to find anything useful online." She pointed to the article. "Even this is pretty vague, which tells me not much is out there."

"Why don't you just ask Henry?"

"He was just a kid when she died," she said, averting Sam's gaze. "You're the only one who can find this information for me."

Sam pointed to a sentence halfway down the page. "This quote is from the Tate County Sheriff's Office. That's, like, two hours away."

"Surely, you can get someone to answer a few questions..."

Sam tossed the papers to the side and stood up. "Jaq, how much further are you going to take this? You just lost your job, for heaven's sake. And you can dodge the conversation about Henry all you want, but I get the sense he's not too happy with you, either. Where does this end?"

Jaq clenched her jaw. "It ends when I get to the truth."

Sam sat down again and touched her knee. "I know you want closure. But how much more can you afford to lose?"

Jaq brushed her hand away. "I don't have anything left to lose, Sam. Can't you see that?"

She returned to her desk, determined not to let her tears fall.

Sam sighed. "How much of your future are you willing to risk for someone in your past?"

Jaq's shoulders stiffened. "It's not just about Ben, Sam. Not anymore." She wiggled the mouse and her monitor lit up. She kept her eyes on the screen. "Look, are you going to help me or not?"

Sam retrieved the printouts and flopped onto the couch. "If you turn up the damn heat and get me some food, I will."

CHAPTER 46

Twenty-four hours went by with no word from Sam or Henry. Not even The Prescott Diaries offered anything legitimate, the forums serving as nothing more than a platform for revenge posting. Every comment was a tirade about the rich. How socialites like Cara deserved their comeuppance.

What they failed to acknowledge was their own complicity in skyrocketing Cara to fame... And how they were just as bad now, seeking notoriety in her death. It was a sad commentary on the state of social media, if not Prescott in general.

Jaq could only take so much. She shut her computer off and wandered through the house, seeking a distraction. She started a load of laundry, but even the act of hauling clothes from her bedroom to the tiny closet off the kitchen did nothing to ease her restless energy. If anything, it only fueled the need to be laser-focused on something outside herself.

She was a journalist without a purpose, and it sucked.

Jaq's phone buzzed, and she jumped. She snatched it from the countertop and groaned.

It wasn't Sam or Henry. It was Dahlia.

Jaq stared at the phone like she had never received a call before. It buzzed three more times, and she held her breath, waiting to see if Dahlia would leave a message.

A minute passed, and the phone buzzed again.

Jaq sensed an anxiety attack hovering at the periphery. She forced herself to take a few deep breaths before picking up.

"Miss Darcy, hi." Dahlia sounded nervous, and Jaq waited for her to continue. "Um, listen. Ethan asked me to call. Says you have some of our equipment?"

Any concern over an anxiety attack went to the wayside.

The nerve!

"Ethan knows damn well all the camera equipment I use is my own," Jaq said through gritted teeth. It occurred to her Dahlia might not be alone. "Why are you doing his dirty work?" she asked. "The last place you want to be is under that prick's thumb."

"I don't want to get in the middle of things," Dahlia said with a nervous giggle. "Even if the camera and lens are yours, you have other stuff that belongs to the paper. Passwords, office keys, photos..."

The pictures Jaq took at the wedding reception were garbage, but they didn't know that. "What photos?" she asked.

"Anything you've captured onsite. It's all property of the paper."

Jaq's eyes narrowed. If Ethan was trying to rattle her with this call, he was a moron. "Look, Dahlia. I know Ethan's there with you. Tell him he can have whatever he thinks I owe him when he has the balls to contact me himself."

"There's no need to make this ugly..."

"Condescension is not your friend here, Dahlia. And neither is Ethan. I'd remember that."

"Just drop off everything at the office this week, Miss Darcy, and we can put all this behind us. Okay?"

"How about you contact my lawyer instead?"

The line was quiet, and Jaq hoped Ethan was turning a lovely shade of green. Confrontation had never been his thing. It's how people like Lawrence manipulated him into doing whatever they wanted.

"Fine," Dahlia said. "If that's how you want to handle this. Who should we contact?"

"Henry Worthington, Esquire."

There was an audible gasp on Dahlia's end, followed by a hushed conversation in the background.

"That's right," Jaq said. "You tell Ethan he can contact Henry if he wants to discuss anything about this unlawful termination. I'm done. With the both of you."

Hanging up on a cell phone was not as satisfying as slamming a receiver, but it sufficed. Jaq smiled as she imagined the look of horror on Ethan's face.

He would get what was coming to him. She'd see to it.

"My dad and I will be there in a few," Sam said when she called Jaq later that afternoon. "Got a pizza preference?"

The heads-up only exacerbated Jaq's anxiety. She gathered the files and papers on her desk, forming a neat enough stack to shove everything in a drawer.

She was tidying pillows on the couch when her phone buzzed. She glanced at the caller ID, disappointed it was not Henry. "Mack? Everything okay?" she asked, cradling the phone between her ear and shoulder as she moved about the living room.

"Better than it is with you, I take it."

Jaq slumped to the couch. Of course things were not okay. What did she expect? Mack ran a gossip site, and when it came to the Worthingtons, the jackals kicked into over-drive, no matter how small the connection was.

The front door opened, and Andy carried in two pizza boxes and a large paper sack. Sam followed behind, her arms filled with files.

Jaq put a hand over the phone and indicated she needed a minute.

"I saw the notes you sent over on Benjamin Rutherford's death," Mack said. "I think there's a deeper story there. And I want you to be the one to write about it."

Jaq was confused. Surely, he had heard about the fiasco at the wedding reception. And what happened to handing her work off to the existing team of writers?

"I heard about this weekend," Mack said when she did not respond. "Sounds like things got pretty ugly with your boss."

The mere mention of Ethan fueled Jaq's feelings of anger and disappointment. She wanted to believe people were decent. Why was everyone so determined to prove her wrong?

"Former boss," she said as Sam grabbed plates and napkins from the kitchen and Andy cleared the coffee table. He set the pizza boxes on top and pulled a six-pack of beer from the paper sack.

The tiny space felt cramped with so much activity.

"I don't think he understood your potential," Mack said. "But I do." A child's cry filled the earpiece. "Listen, I've gotta run. But let's talk tomorrow about expanding your role, okay?"

Jaq hung up, and Sam handed her a plate. She sank into the chair beside the couch, her mind racing. The first bite of warm dough soothed her nerves and lessened her desire to kick Ethan in his capped teeth. Somewhat.

The folders Sam carried in were stacked at the edge of the coffee table. Jaq polished off her slice of pizza and reached for the first file. Ben's full name was printed on the label.

The pizza felt like cement in her gut, and she slid the folder to the side. The second one was dedicated to Cara and twice as thick as the others. Jaq thumbed through the contents, nothing she read a surprise.

Andy popped a beer from the plastic ring and held it in the air. "Want one?" he asked.

Jaq declined, opting for a breadstick to settle her stomach. Garlic butter dribbled down her chin, and she reached for a napkin.

A piece of paper sticking out of a light blue folder caught her eye. The file was thinner than the others, only housing a few pieces of paper.

Jaq leaned in for a better look and almost dropped her breadstick.

Across the top, in Sam's handwriting, was the name Jacqueline Marie Darcy.

CHAPTER 47

"I'm a person of interest? Are you kidding me?"

"Don't be silly." Sam plucked the folder from Jaq's hand and pulled out a sheet of paper. "Your name came up in our research, though."

Jaq's read the text and her surprise morphed into a raw, seething heat. The kind of anger that simmers in one's veins until it finally demands release.

Her hands shook as she dropped the paper to the coffee table.

"Forget all that." Andy tapped his index finger on a green folder with Denise's name on the label. The glass tabletop rattled in response. "*This* is what you need to see."

Jaq flipped the folder open and scanned the first page.

"Remember my buddy, Malcolm?" Andy asked. "He used to invite us over for cookouts when you two were little..."

Jaq and Sam looked at each other, and Sam raised her shoulders in a half-shrug.

Andy dismissed the question with a wave of his hand. "Anyway, Malcolm was working at the Sheriff's Office when Denise was killed. Said Lawrence raised all kinds of hell, demanding they release her body immediately. Threatened to sue everyone involved, from the cops to the clean-up crew."

"Like being an asshole was going to get him anywhere." Sam chuckled, and Jaq shot her a sideways glance. She cleared her throat before taking a swig of her beer. "I mean, you'd think someone in his position—someone who deals with lawyers every freaking day—would know better."

"Right?" Andy shook his head. "Our old pal Lawrence was worried about the press showing up and taking pictures without permission. Kept going on about Henry and Cara. How he wanted to be the one to tell them. Didn't want what happened to their mom to be splashed all over the news. Pretty much any excuse he could come up with, Malcolm said." Andy leaned against the couch cushions and stared up at the ceiling. "I mean, everyone knows what Lawrence Worthington cares about, and it sure as hell ain't the kids."

The receptors in Jaq's brain lit up like firecrackers. Try as she might, she could not get away from the Worthingtons. First, it was the family farm. Then Ben. Now Ethan and her entire livelihood.

What was she thinking, getting involved with Henry?

She jumped up, too irritated to remain seated.

Sam watched as she paced the living room. "Jaq, sit down," she said, patting the chair. "C'mon. You're making me antsy."

Jaq returned to the folders splayed across the table but did not sit. "So, what then?" she asked, retrieving the autopsy information from Denise's file. "Lawrence had someone in the Medical Examiner's Office rush this?"

Stamped less than six hours after they pulled Denise from her mangled SUV, the death certificate confirmed the speed of the coroner's findings. Even in a small town like Prescott, bodies were held for several days to give the police time to gather evidence or take statements from any witnesses...

"Jaq?" Sam said.

She quit thumbing through the report and laid it atop Denise's folder. "Sorry, what was that?"

Sam eyed her before continuing. "I said the coroner died of a massive stroke about a month after Denise's wreck. So, no one knows why he rushed the findings or released the body so fast." She shoved the autopsy report to the side and pointed to stapled papers with "Forensic Toxicology Results" stamped in bold across the top. "According to this, though, Denise was drinking around the time of the accident."

Jaq reached for the report. "Says here her blood alcohol level was point one-oh. That's awfully high for a lunch outing."

"Here's the weird part," Andy said from his perch on the couch. "Malcolm questioned the restaurant owner and the server working the day of the accident. They swore up and down Denise drank club soda. Even found a receipt on her person, supporting those claims."

"And the police still didn't believe them?"

"Malcolm couldn't rule out the possibility she paid for the drinks in cash. You know, so Lawrence wouldn't know she was off the wagon." He frowned and took a drink. "No telling what they kept from each other."

Jaq ignored the reference to her uncle's failed marriage and searched for the photocopy of the lunch receipt, noting the timestamp. "Says here Denise ran her car into the utility pole just before two. About twenty minutes after she paid her bill." She glanced at the accident report again. "Nothing here indicates there was alcohol at the scene." She looked up. "Did anyone mention a drinking problem?"

Sam shook her head and reached around Jaq. She fumbled through the remaining pages in Denise's file and brought the list of witness statements to the forefront. "According to several people at the school, Denise picked Henry and Cara up every day after lunch, without fail. Was real involved, too. Stayed in contact with the teachers, volunteered her time to help out. You name it. Not a word about her being an alcoholic."

Jaq read through the statements. Malcolm was thorough, talking not only to the kids' teachers but also to the principal and office staff. He interviewed fifteen individuals, and they all spoke highly of Denise.

"What did Lawrence say?"

Andy finished his beer. "Nothing. Just demanded they turn the body over to him." He stretched his legs, and his feet bumped the coffee table.

Jaq caught a stack of papers before it could fall to the floor.

Andy stood and gathered the empty beer cans. "You got anything else to drink around here?" he asked over his shoulder as he headed for the kitchen.

"Second cabinet to the left."

Sam wagged her finger at the folders sitting on the end of the coffee table. "If you check out the records from Cara's childhood, you'll see she needed extra attention with her schoolwork. Dyslexia, I think."

Henry said they weren't aware of Cara's learning disability until high school. Was he lying, or had Denise chosen to keep this information to herself? Jaq rubbed her temples. She didn't know what was the truth anymore.

Sam gathered the dirty dishes and trash into a pile as Jaq picked up Denise's folder and took it to the couch. She flipped to the toxicology report and ran her finger down the list of findings. "What's this?" she said, pointing to a name near the bottom.

Sam leaned in. Garlic and beer coated her breath, but it smelled far better than stale cigarettes. She spelled out the name and shrugged before flopping backward into the cushions. "I don't know why they can't use normal names for that stuff."

Jaq scanned the other items on the list, recognizing a pharmaceutical-grade allergy medicine and an over-the-counter anti-inflammatory. The report also showed traces of elevated vitamin levels, specifically vitamins C, D, and calcium. Denise's protein levels were elevated, too, but the autopsy showed she was in good health overall.

Andy returned, trying to balance three glasses. "You need more vodka," he said, handing Sam and Jaq their drinks before settling into the chair. "Oh, and you're low on cranberry juice, too."

Jaq nodded, too distracted to care. She walked over to her desk and pulled up a browser on the computer. She ran several searches before spinning around in the desk chair. "I don't think Denise was drinking the day she died," she said.

Sam nursed her drink, waiting for Jaq to continue.

Andy's eyes were closed, his glass already empty. He looked up and motioned toward Jaq's drink, sitting untouched at the edge of her desk. She handed it over, debating—not for the first time— whether to take her uncle to an AA meeting. But that was a problem for another day.

She turned sideways and pointed to the computer screen. "One of the medications in her system is a fertility drug. Denise was trying to get pregnant."

"And drinking was off the table completely?" Andy sipped his beverage, as if to console himself this could ever be a possibility.

Jaq nodded. "There's a greater chance of miscarriage or an ectopic pregnancy if you drink while taking it."

Sam looked puzzled, and Jaq explained how serious the complications were for both the baby and the mother.

"Makes sense she'd stay away from the booze then," Sam said and set her glass down on the coffee table with a loud clink. "So, if Denise wasn't drinking... Then how the hell did she wind up with a blood alcohol content of point one-oh?"

"That's a damn good question," Andy said and hiccupped.

"I'm driving home. Just so you know." Sam took his glass along with hers to the kitchen.

Jaq chewed on the end of her pen, ignoring them both.

Fertility drugs, an inexplicable blood alcohol content, Cara's overdose. Even Ben's so-called accident. Too many odd things had happened in the Worthington realm.

The incidents had to be related.

But how?

CHAPTER 48

ದಂದಃ

Jaq's house was quiet that evening once Sam and Andy left. She cleaned up the mess of paper plates and other items tossed to the side, still struggling to make sense of the many questions surrounding Denise Worthington's death.

An empty vodka bottle sat on the kitchen countertop, Andy's reminder to buy more.

Jaq swept it into the trash bin, irritated. She could use something strong right about now, the gnawing, nagging feeling in her gut refusing to relinquish its grasp.

She reached for the phone. Her heart pounded as she waited for the call to connect.

Secretly, she hoped it would go to voicemail, but Henry answered on the third ring. Glasses clinked in the background against the murmur of people chatting.

He was out on the town while her life was falling apart.

Jaq contemplated hanging up. Was the fight really worth all this? Maybe she just needed to cut her losses and move on.

"Jaq? Hello?"

Henry's voice was refreshing, like going from the scorching sun to crisp water when she jumped in the lake. She couldn't give up just yet.

"Henry, hi," she said. "I'm not sure if anyone from *The Gazette* has been in touch with you, but—"

"Someone from the legal team left me a voicemail this afternoon."

The connection was poor, and their relationship was too new to judge his emotions, but he did not sound upset. Jaq took that as a good sign. "I'm sorry I pulled you into this mess without talking to you first. Ethan caught me off-guard, and your name just popped out."

"It's okay." There was a pause as music blared through the earpiece.

"Listen, I need to go. But I can meet with you tomorrow. Stop by my office around nine?"

Jaq agreed and hung up, feeling worse than before she called.

The prospect of seeing Henry made her feel ill, not excited. He was in full lawyer-mode. His willingness to help had nothing to do with his feelings for her.

Jaq headed to bed, where she tried to ignore her anxiety over their meeting. It might just cost her more than she could afford.

Henry's office was quiet as Jaq entered the next day.

Quiet and small. Only a ficus tree and a metal receptionist desk filled what could barely be considered a lobby.

Henry appeared in the lone doorway and motioned for her to enter.

Despite its constrictive size, his office was filled with rich décor. Awards sat strategically placed alongside decorative vases and legal tomes on dark, molded bookshelves. Two diplomas hung on the wall opposite the entry.

Henry gestured toward the chairs facing his cherry desk. Jaq took a seat as he scooted past, nearly catching his hip on the corner.

"I'd kill myself in here," she said, regretting the words as soon as they escaped. What a terrible thing to joke about.

But Henry seemed unaffected. "I told Cara the desk was too big, but she insisted. She was trying her hand at interior design, you know."

A frown crossed his face, and Jaq struggled to keep her emotions in check. She wanted nothing more than to walk around the desk and press her body against his, but the status of their relationship was still questionable.

Henry sat in the desk chair and slid a stack of papers her way.

Jaq leaned forward.

"I need you to sign these," he said and handed her a pen. "Doing so makes our lawyer-client relationship official."

Jaq signed the first two pages, only skimming the terms. Her eyes widened when she reached the table with the breakdown of his fees.

Henry pointed to a box at the bottom of the page with his initials. "This specifies I'm taking your case pro bono. I'll only charge for any extraordinary expenses."

Jaq put the pen down. "Henry, I can't let you do that. I know how important it is to get paid for your time."

"I want to. And not because..." He blushed. "Look, I think it's important to make Ethan answer for what he's done. People have a right to know what's going on in their community. The unfiltered version. Not what my dad says is okay to print."

"Are you sure?"

"I am. But know there's a strong likelihood I'll be forced to recuse myself." He leaned back in his chair. "Either way, I'll get things going."

"Henry—"

"This is bigger than you and me. I can see that now."

Jaq signed the documents and handed Henry the pen. He counter-signed the pages and stacked them near the edge of his desk.

"I'll make you a copy before you leave," he said and pulled a leather-bound notebook out of a side drawer. "But right now, I need you to tell me everything you can about Ethan and his management of *The Gazette*."

He flipped to a clean page, and Jaq touched his hand. He looked up, his brow furrowed.

"Henry, I want nothing more than to see Ethan pay for what he's done. But that's not why I'm here."

Henry blinked and pulled his hand away. "I don't understand. I thought you wanted my help."

"I want *you*." Jaq squeezed into the small space between Henry and the desk and kissed him before he could react.

He resisted at first, then pulled her toward him.

"There's something else we need to talk about," she said, her voice muffled against his chest as they cuddled in the chair.

Henry cast his eyes downward. "Not my sister again..."

She looked away.

"Jaq?" Henry pulled back. "What are you keeping from me?"

Her instincts told her his office was not the safest place for a discussion about his family. She stood up and motioned for him to follow. He walked with her to the reception area and leaned against the metal desk.

"There's something you need to know," Jaq said and clasped her hands together. "I asked Sam and Andy to help me..."

Henry bristled, and Jaq touched his arm.

"If there's one thing you can count on, Henry, it's my gut. Call it journalistic instinct. Whatever you want. But I'm telling you, there's more going on here than you realize. So much more."

Henry eyed her and crossed his arms.

"I asked Sam and Andy for help," Jaq continued. "And they dug up a ton of information. About Ben, Cara. Of course, most of it was stuff we already knew."

"What's your point?" Henry's eyes narrowed. "Let me guess. They were looking for stuff on me, too."

"Not exactly..."

"Jaq, what the hell is going on?"

She stared into the eyes of the man she was certain she was falling for. It pained her to think of hurting him, but he deserved the truth.

"They looked into your mom's death," she said. "And we uncovered something no one can explain."

CHAPTER 49

ನಲನಲ

Henry uncrossed his arms and tilted forward. "My mom's off the table, Jaq," he said, his voice strained with emotion. "You better have a damn good reason for bringing her into this."

She had crossed a line, but he needed to understand what they were up against. "I do, Henry. I promise."

He leaned against the desk, visibly calmer this time. "Okay," he said, as if his legal side had kicked in and he was focused on the facts now, not his emotions. "Tell me whatever it is you think I should know."

Jaq retrieved her purse from Henry's office. He watched as she pulled out copies of the files Sam and Andy had gathered.

She rolled the chair from beneath the desk and motioned for him to sit. "I need you to look at these"—she handed him the files—"and tell me what you see."

He shuffled through the first few pages and looked up in frustration. "Jaq, I'm not a cop. I've only represented one traffic case... My sister's." He thrust a finger toward the accident report. "What am I supposed to be looking at here?"

Jaq pointed to the blood alcohol level. "If you represented Cara in her DUI case, then you know this is well past the legal limit."

Henry stared at the paper, his eyes wide. "This can't be right," he said as he reached up to massage his left temple. "My mom didn't drink, Jaq. Ever."

She flipped to the toxicology report and pointed to the list of medications. "I know she didn't. At least, not while taking this."

Henry glanced at the prescription and looked confused.

"It's a fertility drug," Jaq said. "Your mom was trying to get pregnant."

He remained silent, devoid of all facial expression, but Jaq could tell by the rapid movement of his eyes he was thinking things over.

"It doesn't surprise me she wanted more kids," he finally said. "Every Christmas, she looked forward to the gatherings more than anything." Pain tugged at the corners of his mouth. "A full house was the best gift of all, she used to tell me."

Jaq touched his arm.

"Of course, I was just a kid. No telling how good my memory is." His shoulders hardened as he resumed his examination of the papers. "But I know for a fact she didn't drink. My dad will never admit it, but he's an alcoholic. They used to fight all the time about it." Henry's eyes darkened as more memories surfaced.

"If it makes you feel any better, the police questioned the workers at the restaurant, and they swore she wasn't drinking either."

"I'd probably say whatever I needed to cover my ass, too." Henry attempted a smile but it fell flat. "Even back then, there'd be some liability if they let her drive drunk."

"The cop investigating the accident said the owner and bartender were reputable witnesses." Jaq pointed to a copy of the receipt. "Plus, your mom had this in her purse."

Henry stared at the itemized receipt before looking up. "This receipt is from a lunch for two, Jaq. Did the police confirm who my mom was with that day?"

Jaq stared at him in surprise and shook her head. "We just assumed it was your dad. The bartender said they usually met for lunch before she picked you and Cara up from school."

Henry frowned. "Not that year. My dad was out of town when..." His voice caught and he set the papers down on the desk beside him. "I'm sorry," he said, sounding like a forced version of himself. "This is just a lot for me to absorb."

The nerves in Jaq's spine crackled. Henry had clarified something Malcolm's team missed: Denise was with someone other than her husband the day she died.

CHAPTER 50

ನಾನಾಲ

The sun was starting its descent, and the crisp mountain breeze took Jaq's breath away as they exited Henry's warm office. Spring needed to get here already.

"You really can't remember who your mom met for lunch that day?" she asked Henry as they walked to her car.

"I was eight." He gave her a knowing look, and she giggled.

"Not Mister Superstar Lawyer? Oh, wait! That wasn't until you were *nine*, right?"

He laughed, too, and for a moment, the seriousness of the situation faded into the background.

Jaq tucker her arm through his.

"All I can say is it wasn't my dad. He was gone that entire week. I know because he missed our Christmas play. I had lines and everything."

Jaq smiled at the boyish way in which Henry described an important moment from his childhood. They stopped by her car, and she fumbled in her purse for the keys. A gust of wind blew hair into her face, and Henry reached over and tucked it behind her ear.

Their lips met as another gust blew against them, and they huddled together for warmth.

"Why don't we leave your car here?" Henry said as his lips found hers.

Jaq put forth no argument.

"So, you never really said whether you asked your uncle to dig up dirt on me."

They were in Henry's living room, their takeout food sitting half-eaten on the coffee table as they snuggled before the fireplace.

Jaq snuggled closer, her eyes closed as she cherished her current state of contentment. "What's the matter? You worried they'll find something?"

Henry chuckled. "Of course not. But I must admit, I'm curious."

"Can't we talk about this later?" Jaq asked, tickling his neck with her lips.

"We can," Henry said, rubbing his hands down her back. "But I'm going to expect one hell of an answer if you make me wait."

Jaq sat up. "No one has ever made you wait for anything, Henry Worthington. Maybe it's time you learned some patience."

He laughed again and leaned against the cushion.

"I didn't ask them to look you up. Promise." Jaq settled into the crook of his arm. "I didn't ask them to look up anything on me, either."

Henry propped himself up on one arm. "Why would there be anything on you?"

"Because your dad started the process of filing a restraining order against me. After I helped you get Cara home that night."

Henry didn't respond.

Jaq stared at his handsome face. "I know, I know. It seems so stupid now." She rested her head on Henry's chest. "Not that it matters now. I mean, Ethan got what he wanted…"

Henry shifted abruptly and Jaq's head flopped to the couch.

"Hey!" she said. "What are you doing?"

"I just thought of something. Be right back." His feet smacked against the hardwood floors as he headed for the bedroom.

Jaq curled up with a throw pillow, trying not to miss his warmth. "Ouch!"

Jaq peered down the dark hallway. "You okay?"

Henry appeared behind the couch. "I stubbed my toe," he said, and she shifted positions as he took a seat on the couch. He had his cell phone in hand, and he unlocked the device. "Listen," he said, tapping the speaker icon and holding the phone between them.

"Henry." An older gentleman's voice permeated the air.

"Your dad?" Jaq whispered.

Henry shook his head. "Geoffrey Winters."

"Oh." Jaq recalled the older gentleman dining with Henry her first trip to Maxwell's. Lawrence's go-to legal advisor.

"Henry," Geoffrey said, his voice insistent, like he was trying to convince a child to eat his peas at dinner. "As I told you before, you need to stay out of this. And stay away from… That woman."

Jaq pointed to her chest, and Henry grinned.

Geoffrey continued. "Your father has requested I reach out to our friends at the Sheriff's office and *The Gazette*. I need you to stand down in the meantime, you hear? That's an order. Direct from your dad."

Henry stopped the recording and set his phone between them.

"He seriously said. 'Stand down'?" Jaq's mind raced. "And what did he mean 'our friends' at the Sheriff's office?"

"He's former military. But, yeah, that was my question, too."

"When was this?" Jaq leaned over to see if she could make out the date of the message, but the phone was locked.

Henry held the device up to his face, but it did not respond. He typed 1227 on the keypad and handed it to her. As suspected, Geoffrey left the message not long before Ethan suspended her.

But none of that mattered at this particular moment.

Jaq's heart felt like it would burst. The PIN to open Henry's phone was the date they met.

She pulled him toward her without another word.

CHAPTER 51

"Where'd the restraining order come from?"

"What do you mean?"

Sam ushered Jaq inside. The TV blared from the living room as the announcers talked over one another, offering their input on a penalty call.

"Late night?" Sam pointed to her improperly buttoned shirt.

Jaq blushed and hung her coat over the couch arm. She had headed to Sam's place as soon as Henry dropped her off at her car.

Sam eyed the TV. "So, what is it you're going on about?"

"I asked where—"

Sam held up her hand as a wide receiver broke loose and ran down the field. "Go!" she screamed, jumping up and down as he crossed the finish line and the clock ran out. She slumped in her recliner and snapped the TV off. "Whew! I had a hundred bucks riding on that game. Bet Morales they couldn't lose, they're on such a streak."

Sam was a sports fanatic, but this whole betting thing was new. An uneasy feeling settled in as Jaq eyed the large television mounted over the fireplace. "New toy?" she asked.

Sam stared at her like she was off her rocker. "From my dad. At Christmas, remember? You watched me open it." She stood up. "What has gotten into you?"

Jaq followed Sam to the kitchen. She poured two drinks, and they sat down at the kitchen table.

Jaq stirred the ice in her glass with a finger. Had things really gotten so bad she actually thought her cousin was consorting with the enemy?

She lifted the glass to take a drink and envisioned Denise Worthington leaving the restaurant, unaware it was the last drive she would ever make. Her stomach churned, and she shoved the beverage to the side.

Sam snapped her fingers. "Yoo-hoo."

Jaq blinked. "I asked how you came about a copy of the restraining order. Since it was never processed."

Sam shrugged and sipped her drink.

Jaq eyed her. "Someone at the station is helping Lawrence."

Sam looked genuinely surprised. "You're mistaken. My dad handpicked everyone there. Some of those guys have been with him since the beginning!"

Jaq nodded. Saying it aloud didn't make her feel any better. But Sam's defensiveness didn't make it any less true.

Sam slammed her glass to the table

Jaq looked up, startled.

"Start talking," Sam said. "I want to know what makes you think any of my dad's guys would betray him."

Jaq cleared her throat. "The Worthington's lawyer left Henry a voicemail the same day Ethan suspended me. Told Henry he'd work with their friends at the paper and the Sheriff's office to make sure I wasn't a problem."

Sam furrowed her brow.

"Anyone there seem extra-friendly lately?" Jaq asked. "Have some extra cash to throw around...?"

She didn't finish, her eyes meeting Sam's.

"Morales!" they said in unison.

Sam jumped up. "I'm calling my dad."

CHAPTER 52

"Morales? I've had my suspicions," Andy said that evening as they stood in his kitchen while he made pot roast.

"Anything tying him to the Worthingtons?" Jaq asked. "Or Ben?"

"Excellent questions. And something I'll investigate first thing tomorrow." He bent down to check the oven, and for the first time, she noticed his hair thinning in all the wrong places.

Jaq bit her lip. Who was she to judge the weight of another's burden? Little time had passed since Ben's death, yet it felt like eons. Wrinkles that once deepened her forehead only when she laughed had taken up permanent residence. She could hardly blame Andy for the toll his divorce had taken.

Sam hugged her from the side. "It'll all be okay," she said.

Jaq nodded and fought back tears. "I just need it to end."

Andy wrapped his arms around them both. "It will, Muffin. That I can promise you."

The timer dinged, and Andy opened the oven door. The smell of bay leaves, onion, and beef broth filled the kitchen as he grabbed a pair of oven mitts and transferred the sizzling pot to the cooktop.

Jaq reached for a paper towel to dry her eyes.

Andy pulled a large fork from the utensil holder. "I don't know about you knuckleheads," he said, transferring the contents to a serving dish. "But I'm starving."

Henry was in the shower the next morning when Jaq's phone rang. She grabbed it off the nightstand and tiptoed down the hall. "Sam?"

"You won't believe what just happened."

Jaq pulled the phone from her ear and glanced at the time. It was five after nine. She rubbed her eyes and made her way to the kitchen in search of coffee.

"We got to the office early this morning. Just like my dad said… To see if we could find anything incriminating on Morales."

"Sam, slow down. I haven't had my coffee yet."

But Sam was too excited to pay her any mind. "You'll never guess what we found! Morales. At my dad's desk, searching his computer."

Jaq almost dropped the coffee cup she pulled from the cabinet. "Seriously?"

"Busted him cold. I've never seen my dad so mad! He yanked him out of his chair and practically dragged him down the hall."

Morales was no small man, but neither was Andy. Jaq grinned at the thought of her uncle manhandling the rat. Brute force was more than appropriate for the trouble he had caused.

"Where's Morales now?" she asked.

Henry appeared in the kitchen, looking confused and wearing nothing but a pair of navy boxers. Droplets of water glistened on his chest and shoulders.

Jaq pointed to the coffeepot, and he brushed past her.

"In holding," Sam said. "Look, I gotta go. But I wanted to tell you before it hit the news. There's gonna be hell to pay."

"No doubt. Call me later."

Henry finished filling the coffeemaker. "What was that about?" he asked with a quick glance over his shoulder.

Jaq walked toward him, feeling more playful than she had in ages. "Oh, nothing. They just identified one of your dad's sources, that's all."

Henry looked surprised. "Who?" he asked.

"Doesn't matter," Jaq said and reached for him as the coffeepot sizzled in the background.

CHAPTER 53

తుతుతు

"You need to leave."

Henry's voice was insistent as Jaq rolled over and peered at him from beneath the covers. The hall light hit her in the eye, and she squinted as she fought off a yawn. "What time is it?"

"Jaq, I'm serious. You've got to get out of here."

He yanked the covers off.

"What is the matter with you?" Jaq scrambled to grab a pillow, the sudden change in temperature taking her breath away.

"My dad." Henry's voice was part-whisper, part-hiss. "He just called from his car. You can't be here when he shows up."

"Really?" Jaq's eyes watered from the sudden exposure to light. Or was it the sting of Henry's rejection? She wasn't sure.

Henry touched her shoulder. "It's not how it sounds," he said, shifting his tone as he stroked her arm. "I don't *want* you to go. But my dad... You've seen how he operates. The less he knows about us right now, the better."

She wiped away the dampness brimming at her lashes, unable to contain her smile.

There was an "us."

How wonderful such a simple word sounded.

Henry rushed Jaq down the hallway toward the emergency exit.

Her shoelaces flapped against the hardwoods, and she nearly stumbled. "Henry, slow down!"

He turned as the elevator doors dinged.

Jaq slid into the stairwell a second before Lawrence emerged. The door latched behind her, and she ducked below the small glass window, out of sight.

She pressed her ear against the door, listening.

"What are you doing out here in the hallway, son?" Lawrence said, sounding less like a dictator than she remembered.

"I assumed this would be a quick visit."

Jaq peeked through the tiny opening as Henry checked his watch and glanced her way.

"It's almost nine," he said, shifting his focus back to his dad. "I'm surprised you aren't at the office."

"I could say the same about you."

Lawrence whipped his head around, and Jaq ducked at the last moment. She remained hunched behind the door, her heart racing like she had just finished a marathon.

The sudden weight of a body against the door frame startled her, and she scolded herself for being so jumpy. She raised her head for another peek, but her view was obstructed as Henry and Lawrence spoke in muffled voices.

Was he protecting her from his dad? Or their topic of conversation? She wanted to believe it was the former, but this was family, after all. Anything was possible.

Jaq put her ear to the door again, trying to hear something—anything—that would tell her what was so important Lawrence felt compelled to rush over in the middle of the workweek to speak with his son. But he had chosen now of all times to tone down his booming voice, and she could not make out his words.

Henry's voice was clear, however, as he mentioned Cara and her memorial service. Jaq stayed in a crouched position, ignoring the ache in her legs, until the elevator dinged.

She stood up and counted to five before grasping the door handle. Her eyes adjusted to the light as a muscular man with a shaved head stared at her in surprise.

It wasn't Henry obstructing her view. It was the man who escorted Cara from The Cornelia the night Ben died.

CHAPTER 54

Henry shot a hand between the elevator doors, halting them in their tracks. "You can get out of the way, Travis. She's not a threat."

The man stepped to the side, and Jaq sized him up. He was tall. Solid, too, his tailored shirt and pants clinging to well-defined muscles. Not as bulging as Cara's security detail, but fit enough to make anyone think twice about confronting him.

Jaq refused to be intimidated, however. "Yeah, Travis," she said, oozing sarcasm. "There's nothing to worry about with little ole me. Except the fact that I'm not Cara. You can't control me."

Henry fought off a smirk, and Travis looked at Lawrence like a dog seeking permission from his master before he could act.

Lawrence's face turned a deep shade of red. He looked even angrier than when Henry called him out at the wedding reception.

"I don't know who you think you are, Miss—"

"You know who I am." Jaq took a few steps in his direction but stopped as Travis inched closer. "Clearly, you think you run this town and everyone in it. But not everyone who lives here is willing to sell their souls."

Lawrence clenched his jaw but remained silent, sizing her up.

Jaq steeled herself. People like Lawrence Worthington didn't get voted most successful businessman in the state multiple years running without good reason. His ability to evaluate opponents and seize upon their weaknesses was legendary. But she knew he was nothing but a bully, and the best way to handle someone like that was to stand her ground. The day she popped Lauren MacDonald in the nose for teasing her about the dress she wore—her mom's favorite, it so happened—was the day things changed for the better. Lawrence was no different. He just needed someone to put him in his place.

He stepped forward, and for the first time, Jaq noticed the stiffness in his movements. Like he had to think about every step. But his physical weakness was not a deterrent. "You really don't want to try your luck with me, young lady," he said, staring through her with eyes as cold as death.

Henry tried to step between them, but Lawrence brushed him aside, his eyes never leaving hers.

Jaq clenched her fists in preparation for the next blow. "Let's deal with this right here, right now," she said and took a step in his direction for emphasis. "I've got nothing left to lose. You made sure of that."

They traded death glares as they gauged each other's weaknesses.

"You've got a lot of nerve." Lawrence puffed out his chest, his aging frame more an inconvenience now than a hindrance. "Didn't your parents teach you any manners?" He turned to Henry. "I thought you had better taste than this, son."

Henry raised a finger. "Now wait just one minute—"

"This isn't about me and him, Larry." Jaq smiled as the nickname visibly irritated Lawrence. "It's about me and you. Did you honestly think I'd forget about my grandparent's farm? How you stole it from us?"

Henry's head snapped back. "Wait. What? Dad, what's she talking about?"

Lawrence gnashed his teeth like a cornered dog.

"You told me the family that lived there was more than happy to sell for a hefty profit."

Jaq snorted. "Hefty profit, my ass! He left us with nothing, Henry. Stole my Grampa's land while Andy was completing the paperwork."

Lawrence's eyes flashed and his face contorted as he drew his shoulders back. Spit formed at the edge of his mouth. Jaq could see why so many people gave into his demands. He was nothing but evil, clothed in a tailored suit and fancy shoes.

There was movement behind her, and Jaq caught a whiff of Travis' aftershave. She stepped sideways, avoiding his grasp.

The four of them stood in a near-circle, waiting.

Henry spoke first. "Dad—"

"Not now, Henry. She doesn't know what she's talking about." Lawrence looked Jaq up and down, his leering glance reminiscent of her first face-to-face encounter with Cara.

Jaq felt wobbly and dug her heels into the carpet to steady herself. But Lawrence's next shot was not directed at her.

He faced Henry. "It's this... *Tart*," he said. "Or your family."

Henry shifted his eyes between Jaq and his dad. Back and forth, assessing the situation like any trained lawyer would.

Jaq held her breath as Henry brushed his dad aside.

"I'm truly sorry about what happened with your family," he said, his voice barely a whisper. "But my dad's right, Jaq. You'd better leave."

"You heard him, Miss Darcy."

Jaq looked at Lawrence then Henry.

She wanted to speak. To ask Henry why he didn't fight for her.

For them.

But she couldn't.

She couldn't say a word.

Travis reached for her arm, and she yanked it away.

With a final glance Henry's way, she turned on her heel and exited through the stairwell, unwilling to remain in his presence any longer.

Her footsteps pounded against the concrete stairs, echoing the emptiness in her heart. What a fool she had been to expect Henry to choose her over his family.

But she *did* expect it. After everything they had been through, the relationship they were building, his actions were a kick in the gut she did not see coming.

When she said she had nothing to lose, she was mistaken.

More important than finding the truth about Ben's death or salvaging the family farm, she had gambled on a relationship with the man she loved.

And she had lost it all.

CHAPTER 55

A day passed.

Then two, with no word from Henry.

No apology or explanation for his decision.

Nothing but silence.

Shame hovered over Jaq like a dark rain cloud. If Henry couldn't stand up for her—wasn't willing to fight for their relationship—how much could she have meant to him, anyway?

She paced the house, agitated and depressed.

First Ben, and now Henry. What was wrong with the men in this town?

Sam called to check on her, but Jaq didn't feel like being sociable. When she called Mack later to accept his offer of full-time employment, it was not because she was excited about doing so. It was because she had to pay the bills until she figured out her next move. Even if that move meant leaving Prescott altogether.

Mack set up a meeting for the following week and gave her a few assignments to complete. She didn't feel like doing much, but at least she could mope in private and still earn some money.

Jaq forced herself to pull up the website's forum pages and scrolled through the posts quickly, weeding out relevant tips from the garbage. Within an hour, she had enough information to craft a thousand-word post on the break-up of two prominent school board members. She reread what she had drafted and sent it to the editors for approval.

Her next task was to gather information about two musicians spotted in Prescott over the holidays without their well-known spouses. Jaq clicked through several postings and comments until she landed on a photo snapped by a bystander. The musicians were nestled together in a corner, against a backdrop of dark walls and low-hanging bar lights. The surroundings looked familiar, but she couldn't place the location. She zoomed in, but the image blurred further, making it impossible to identify the venue.

Stupid cell phone cameras. Jaq shoved her mouse to the side. Everyone envisioned themselves as the paparazzi, grabbing snapshots for fortune or fame. Not that long ago, the focus was on gathering the truth, not exploiting someone because they were famous.

She frowned. Being Becca Allen was akin to playing dress-up. And it didn't make her any better than the people online. She, too, was feeding the gossip machine for no reason other than to earn a paycheck...

A knock at the front door interrupted her mental tirade.

Jaq made her way to the peephole. An older gentleman stood outside her door, his coat collar turned up and his hat pulled down. Neither could mask his sharp features and silvery hair. Geoffrey Winters looked cold and more than a little out of place as his maroon luxury car idled at the curb.

Jaq opened the door just wide enough to acknowledge his presence.

"Jacqueline Darcy?" he asked, his face as rigid as Stonehenge.

She nodded.

He thrust a thick envelope into her hand. "This is for you," he said, his expression listless. "Good day."

A blast of air swept across Jaq's bare arms, and she stepped backward as Geoffrey climbed into his car and drove off. The breeze slammed her front door shut.

She shook as she made her way to the living room, but not from the outside temperature. The envelope, stamped with a gold-embossed seal from Geoffrey's law firm, crinkled in her tight grip.

Whenever legal issues arose at the paper, their in-house legal counsel took care of it. She had no one to help with whatever this was. Not even Henry.

Her heart thumping against her chest, Jaq ripped off the top of the envelope and pulled out a stack of papers. She scanned the first page, her eyes wide with disbelief.

Lawrence was suing her for personal damages. Demanding reparations for "emotional distress and slanderous acts intended to cause damage to the Worthington brand," the cover letter said.

Jaq flipped to the next page, horrified but unable to look away. A table detailed activities to support the lawsuit. The snapshots she took of Cara and Henry outside his office were noted first, followed by a claim she forced her way into Cara's penthouse after Ben died. Other malfeasance included capturing photos at "a Worthington-sponsored event for personal gain," acting "belligerent" in multiple confrontations with Lawrence before his peers, and promoting "salacious, unfounded accusations" about Cara's involvement in Ben's death and Lawrence's takeover of the farm. Ethan and Henry were listed on the last page as witnesses to these acts, along with the bodyguard that chased her down the street.

The allegations were complete nonsense, but Lawrence was demanding millions in reparations, and she had no way to fight it.

Jaq threw the documents against the dining room wall. They fluttered and scattered to the floor. She didn't know whether to laugh at the absurdity of it all or cry.

She headed for the kitchen and flung open the cabinets, searching for anything on-hand to drink. She came up empty, Andy's reminder to restock her supply filling her mind.

There was no escaping the reality of her situation. Her fate had been sealed. She had no choice now but to take Mack up on his offer, even though it went against everything she believed in. And, even then, whatever money she earned would not touch the cost of doing battle with the wealthiest, most powerful man around.

Jaq's throat was on fire and her stomach churned. She raced to the sink, where she threw up nothing but bile. She held her mouth under the faucet, gulping cool water until the bitter taste faded.

She steadied herself and stared out the window. Sam was right. She never should have picked a fight she could not win.

Movement caught Jaq's eye, and she instinctively ducked down. Someone was in her backyard!

She raised her eyes just above the wooden ledge of the windowsill. It was someone tall, that much she could tell. The figure passed in front of Mr. Wilson's back patio, still aglow with Christmas lights, and she made out the bulging silhouette and bald head.

The hair on the back of her neck stood at attention as tiny beads of sweat formed on her chest and brow. Lawrence's hired hand sneaking around her yard only meant one thing. And it wasn't good.

Jaq fumbled in her pocket, searching for her phone.

Dammit! She left it on her desk when Geoffrey knocked. Distracted by the legal papers, she had walked right past it.

Jaq turned toward the living room, calculating the time it would take to get from where she stood to her desk.

About ten seconds, she guessed. But even if she made it there before the man got inside, what good would it do? Her family lived too far away to be of any help.

She was on her own.

The realization struck her like a prizefighter delivering a fatal blow. Jaq swallowed, trying to rid her throat of the acid bubbling up from her stomach. In a crouched position, she tiptoed to the living room, her heart pounding with every touch of the floor.

A loud noise echoed through the hallway, and she froze.

Every muscle twitched in anticipation. Something in her brain connected as the man—Travis, her brain pulled from the ether, his name was Travis—entered the house.

In a moment of clarity, Jaq pictured Cara, of all people. She wasn't alone when she died. Of this, she was certain.

Jaq shook her head furiously, trying to dislodge the distraction from her mind.

Her phone. Her desk. That was her mission.

A loud thud shook the floorboards. Travis was inside.

Jaq felt around the desktop with her left hand, searching for her phone. She grasped it as she heard the creak of the bathroom door. She unlocked her screen as the file directory on her monitor caught her eye.

Everything she had gathered since Ben died was saved in a zip file on her hard drive and a stand-alone backup. If something happened to her, that information would surely be destroyed.

Jaq looked at her phone and back at her monitor as she heard Travis lumbering down the hall.

She knew what she had to do.

CHAPTER 56

Jaq grabbed the poker from the hearth and braced herself.

Her phone lay on the floor nearby, just out of reach. Out of the corner of her eye, she could see the green upload meter creeping along. Sixty percent remained.

Travis sneered at Jaq's weapon of choice, and she sneered back. Her only option now was to distract.

She gripped the poker so hard blood vessels ruptured in her hands. She moved around the room, drawing Travis this way and that, doing her best to keep his attention away from her computer screen. "I won't be as easy to handle as Cara," she said, swiping the poker in his direction. "It's Travis, right?"

His confident expression displayed a crack of uncertainty.

"So, you're a bully *and* a coward." Jaq forced herself to laugh, even though she was terrified. Travis was twice her size, at least. Cara had to be as outmatched as she was. Was Ben?

Jaq blinked.

Travis took a step forward, and she gripped the poker with every ounce of her strength.

He lunged, and Jaq reared back, narrowly missing the coffee table. She teetered before righting herself.

Travis grinned. "You're in over your head," he said, pushing the sleeves of his jacket up his beefy forearms.

"You go right on thinking that."

Jaq hoisted the poker in the air.

Travis swayed back and forth, watching and waiting.

With one rapid movement, she smashed the poker into the coffee table. Hundreds of shards filled the air between them.

Travis stepped back in surprise, and Jaq raised the poker over her head. This might not be a fight she could win, but it sure wouldn't go unnoticed.

Travis found his footing and lunged toward her.

Jaq moved out of the way at the last second, and his momentum carried him forward.

Unable to get his hands up in time, he careened face-first into a pile of glass. He yowled as Jaq stumbled backward.

She glanced at her monitor.

The file had finished uploading. Now came the real test.

She braced herself, her back against the desk as an injured and angry Travis teetered to his feet.

He stumbled, his movements clumsy and without purpose. A large gash ran from his jaw to his chin, and a fragment of glass protruded from his left eye.

Jaq calculated the best way to use his injuries to her advantage. With one hand still gripping the poker, she reached behind and felt along the desktop. Her hand brushed cold metal, and she grasped the shears with her fist.

Travis plucked the shard from his eye and tossed it to the side with a grunt. He pounced, and she swung the poker with every bit of strength she could summon. His skin gave way as the tip plunged into his arm.

He howled again. But this time, like a bear under attack, the pain only stoked his anger. He snarled and threw himself toward her, knocking her off her feet.

Jaq's head slammed hard against the floor. She willed her arms to move, to offer some protection, but her efforts were futile. She could do nothing but lie there, watching as Travis leaned over her, his breath reeking of onions and cigarettes.

He straddled her chest and retrieved something from his back pocket. It shimmered in the light as he dangled it above her head.

Jaq's knees were close enough to his crotch to do some damage. She struggled to move, but he sensed her intention and squeezed his legs tighter around her waist.

"Travis." Jaq choked as his weight crushed her airway. "You... Don't have to do this."

He ignored her.

She struggled but her body refused to cooperate. Talking to him was her best hope. "Henry told you to leave me alone. Remember?"

Travis flinched at the mention of Henry's name but continued to wind the sash around his wrists. The material was lightweight, and he made quick work of getting it around her neck.

The perfect choice to prevent immediate bruising, Jaq recalled for some odd reason, having learned of such a thing at a forensics seminar her senior year in college.

Travis' blood spilled onto Jaq's skin as he tightened the sash around her neck. "I'm taking my time with you," he said, pulling on the ends and releasing them just enough to allow the promise of oxygen. He chuckled as she struggled to breathe. "Guess you don't have anything smart to say now, huh?"

Jaq willed herself to focus on his wounds, not the constriction of her airway.

She wriggled her fingers. A warm sensation flooded the tips as her hand came back to life.

Part of her arm was pinned against her lower back, but she wrenched it free. The sudden shift caught Travis by surprise, and he wobbled.

She sucked in as much air as she could before he reapplied pressure once again to her neck.

She fought off the terror creeping through her chest. Drool formed at her lips as her efforts to preserve the last of her breath floundered.

The opportunity to save herself was fading fast.

Frantically, Jaq felt around for the shears. She grazed the cold metal handle and clasped it with her hand.

Travis tightened the sash and leaned forward. "You ain't so bad to look at," he said in her ear. "Maybe I'll take advantage once you're gone."

He lifted himself up, shifting just enough to loosen the weight on her shoulders. Jaq summoned the last of her strength and jammed the shears into his neck.

Flesh gave way to muscle, and she drove the steel blades in harder.

Travis screamed and fell backward.

Jaq gulped in fresh air and rolled away as he flailed about.

The shears fell to the floor with a thud. Travis lifted a bloody hand to his face, stunned.

Jaq's phone had been kicked aside in the commotion. She grabbed it as Travis shook off his surprise and reached for the shears lying nearby.

CHAPTER 57

Travis tried to get up as the blood from his wounds coated the floor, staining the carpet a red so deep even the strongest cleaning product would not get it out. He gripped the shears with one hand and the sash with the other, finally righting himself.

Red liquid seeped from his neck and face. He stumbled, slamming his knee into the metal part of Jaq's coffee table with a loud crack.

"For such a big guy, you sure are a pussy." Jaq grabbed for the poker to her left and wielded it once more. She swung it through the air and connected with his skull.

Seeing his eyes wide—pupils the size of half-dollars—only spurred Jaq on. She raised the poker and whacked Travis across the face.

Bones gave way as blood spurted from his nose.

Whack. She hit him across the temple.

Whack. The poker cracked the back of his skull.

"For Ben," she said in a state of hyper-awareness. She delivered another blow, this one to the top of his head. "For Cara, too."

She kept swinging, each hit carrying less force than the last, laying blow after blow upon him as her super-strength waned.

Travis lay motionless on the ground, his efforts to protect himself fading with each gush of his blood.

Jaq looked down at the reddish liquid pooling near her feet and collapsed.

The poker fell to her side as the front door crashed open and Henry rushed in.

"No, no, no!"

Henry's voice floated toward her. Was she dreaming?

She looked up, her vision hazy and her muscles so spent she could not lift her head.

"Henry?" she said, her voice scratchy. It hurt to talk, to breathe. Was she dying?

Henry wrapped his arms around her and lifted her towards him. "I've got you," he said, holding her tight.

The rhythmic thumping of his chest was soothing.

She closed her eyes.

"Jaq? Wake up, Jaq."

She looked up, even as the lights above stung her eyes, and stared at the man holding her in his arms. "What are you doing here?" she asked, stringing her words together like Sam after a bottle of the good stuff.

"You texted me. Don't you remember?"

Jaq lifted her hand and stared at the dark creases in her palm. Blood was everywhere. On her skin, gushing from a cut on her wrist, streaming down her face. Was this her blood, or had it come from Travis?

"I need help right away," Henry said into his phone.

Jaq blinked as he relayed her address to the person on the other end. He sounded like someone at the end of a tunnel. She cast her eyes around the living room, a stranger in her own home.

"Henry," she mouthed, struggling to stay awake.

He peered into her eyes, his face bathed with concern. "Help's on the way, Jaq. Hold on, baby. Hold on."

She coughed and wiped at her mouth, but her hands didn't feel like they belonged to her body.

Henry pulled her close and rocked her back and forth. "I am so sorry."

"I know," she said, and the world turned black.

CHAPTER 58

"You sure you're ready for this?" Sam asked. She stopped the car just short of Jaq's driveway and waited.

Jaq nodded and gripped her keys in her right hand, hoping Sam wouldn't notice the shaking. It came and went, just like her panic attacks. Only this time, she wasn't just imagining something ominous. Evil had reared its ugly self in this very place and had nearly killed her.

Sam put the car in park and reached for the door handle. Jaq touched her arm, and she leaned back in the seat. "Take all the time you need," she said.

Jaq nodded, her jaw clenched as she tried to prevent another onslaught of tears. She hadn't cried this much since her mom passed.

Gray clouds filled the horizon, and she noticed for the first time the dullness of her cousin's normally vibrant hair. Sam and Andy had both worked overtime to declare her actions self-defense.

Just a few hours ago, Andy had been waiting in her hospital room while they prepared her for discharge. "You're in the clear, Muffin," he said, making his way to her bedside.

"And Henry?" she asked with a croak, the swelling in her neck still irritating her vocal cords.

Andy nodded and refilled her cup from the pitcher beside the bed. "We've determined he had no involvement in any of his dad's dealings. Certainly not the decision to send Travis."

Jaq sipped the cool water, her pain easing. The doctors insisted she would heal, but the physical scars weren't the ones she was worried about.

Andy leaned over to fluff her pillows, and Jaq reached for his arm. "Thank you," she said, her eyes misting as she took in the face of the man who had protected her since she was a child.

He smiled. "You can thank me once both those bastards go away for a very long time."

Sam arrived not long after, and Jaq insisted she take her home. But now, sitting in the driveway beneath clouds ominous against the dark sky, she had second thoughts.

"Have you spoken to him?" Sam asked.

Jaq shook her head. "Figured it best to take this one step at a time, you know?"

Sam patted her on the knee. "It'll be okay."

Jaq nodded and unbuckled her seat belt. No amount of stalling could prepare her for the emotional roller coaster ahead.

She followed Sam up the walkway, her eyes cast downward. Less than a week ago, the paramedics had guided her to the ambulance using this very path. She recalled little about the ride. Just Henry holding her hand and talking to her as the paramedics monitored her vital signs.

The week apart seemed like both an eternity and a single day, as if time sped up and stood still in the same instant. While Jaq recovered in a hospital bed, surrounded by gift baskets and well wishes from Marcus, Mack, and even Veronica, Henry stayed away under Andy's orders. She was forced to endure question after question—to relive the entire ordeal in excruciating detail—without him by her side. And she was miserable.

Sam guided her to the porch but stopped short of the steps.

Jaq looked up in surprise. "You're not coming in?"

She shook her head as Henry appeared in the doorway. He pulled Jaq close, and the scent of his cologne tickled her senses. For the first time in a week, she managed a smile.

He pulled back and stared into her eyes. "I've missed you," he said. "Please tell me you're okay."

Jaq studied his face, filled with love and concern. "I am now."

He kissed her forehead and escorted her inside.

Jaq hung her coat on the rack by the door before hesitating in the entryway. At the end of the hall was the kitchen window, where she first noticed Travis lurking in the backyard. If she entered the bathroom, she'd see first-hand where he breached the exterior.

But to her right was where the main event had taken place. The smell of deodorizer was faint but still detectable. Sam had arranged for a clean-up crew to replace the coffee table and scrub the blood-soaked carpet until every fiber sparkled like new. But it didn't change anything. What was once Jaq's sanctuary would forever be the place Lawrence tried to have her killed.

Henry guided her past the living room and into the kitchen. Sitting on the table were three boxes from Maxwell's. "Best steakburgers in town," he said and slid a box her way.

Jaq eyed the burger and thick, basil-seasoned fries, taking in the intoxicating smoky and savory undertones. She wanted to taste the simple feel of food against her tongue, but the lingering pain in her throat, dulled only by the thick fog of medication, made eating a struggle.

"I told you it was too soon."

"I know, I know," Sam said, sounding exhausted. "But it's what she wanted."

Jaq willed the mental cobwebs away. "Guys, I'm okay. Stop talking about me like I'm not here."

She reached for a fry and dipped it in a pool of ketchup. It was warm and salty in her mouth, with the perfect amount of crispness around the edges. She took her time chewing and swallowed carefully before reaching for another.

Sam pulled her coat off as Henry took a seat.

"I don't need you to worry about me," Jaq said between bites. "What I need are some answers."

Henry opened his box of food and laid a napkin across his lap. "Let's eat first," he said. "Then I'll tell you whatever you want to know."

CHAPTER 59

"You'll be happy to learn Ethan has been officially relieved of his duties," Henry said. They sipped cups of freshly brewed coffee around the kitchen table, the living room a precipice Jaq was not ready to cross yet.

Jaq felt like a kid at Christmas. "Seriously? What happened? And don't you dare spare any details."

Henry smiled. "It didn't take much. I shared some not-so-nice things with the owner about the way he was conducting business. To say she was appalled would be an understatement. Ethan was fired that day without severance."

"Wow." Jaq didn't even try to fight off her grin. Forgiveness would come later. She only wished she could have been there to see Ethan finally get what he deserved.

"The owner was so grateful"—Henry nodded in her direction—"she offered to give you your old job back. With back pay."

Jaq patted Henry on the leg. "I appreciate it. But I've had a lot of time to think about what I want. And it's not a return to *The Gazette*."

Henry shrugged.

"Who'd they put in charge?" Sam asked.

"Marcus somebody..."

"Good choice." Jaq's eyes narrowed. "But Ethan got off pretty easy for someone being paid to look the other way, don't you think? There's no telling how much crap he covered up."

"A civil suit is still an option, you know." Henry clasped her hand in his. "Suppressing the voice of a journalist... Not to mention the reputational damage from his actions."

"You do what you want," Sam said. "But just because we haven't pursued criminal charges against Ethan doesn't mean we won't. Gotta land the big fish first."

"My dad will call in every favor he has..."

"Won't matter." Sam leaned back in her chair, a smug look on her face. "With three murders, and what happened to Jaq—"

"*Three* murders?" Henry looked like he might throw up the meal he just ate.

Sam sat up, startled. "Oh, shit," she said, shifting uncomfortably in her seat. "You don't know."

"Know what?" Henry closed his eyes and rubbed the area near the bridge of his nose. "What did you find?"

"A charm bracelet that belonged to your mom?"

The blood drained from Henry's face. "I went with him to pick it out for Mother's Day. Not long before she died." Darkness overtook his features. "He really is a monster."

"Turns out our boy Travis has a fetish for keeping things. We found Cara's journal and Denise's bracelet at his place. Ben's necklace, too."

"How's that possible?" Jaq asked. "I saw someone wearing it before Cara died."

Sam motioned to the top of her head. "Man bun?"

Jaq nodded.

"Nate?" Henry shoved his chair back and jumped up. "What the hell? He's involved, too?"

"You know him?" Jaq asked.

"He was one of Cara's friends."

"Not much of one, apparently. His was the first name Travis gave up. Said Lawrence paid him to make sure Cara was high the night she died." Sam scowled. "Of course, man bun's claiming he didn't know *why* Lawrence wanted him to do that. Just that he went along with it because he needed the cash. Sold Ben's necklace to Travis for the same reason." She shook her head. "Guess he didn't know what a sicko that guy was."

Henry looked ill. "I overheard my dad telling Travis to take care of the problem... I thought he was talking about work. A real estate deal gone bad or something." He ran a hand through his hair. "I am such a fool. You and Cara needed my protection, and I failed you both."

"Henry, it's not your fault." Jaq pulled his chair toward the table and patted the seat.

He sat down but did not look happy about it. "Did he say why he killed my mom?" His voice cracked as he addressed Sam.

She shook her head. "There's no doubt Travis is involved, though. He's been your dad's henchman for quite some time."

The loud thud of metal whacking against bone as the poker crushed Travis' skull echoed in Jaq's ears. She clenched her hands and tried to ignore the racing of her heart.

"But if I had to take a guess, I'd say it had something to do with money." Sam snorted. "I mean, doesn't it always?"

Henry remained stone-faced, and Jaq kicked her under the table.

"Ow!" she said, rubbing her leg. But she stopped talking and fiddled with her coffee cup instead.

"What about the medication?" Jaq asked.

"Lawrence claims he didn't know Denise was trying to get pregnant. But he's made it clear he'll do whatever it takes to protect his own interests, so I don't buy that for a minute. If you ask me, he didn't want to share another piece of the pie." She stood up and stretched. "Did you know your mom set up a trust for you and Cara?" she asked Henry. "Something your dad couldn't touch."

Henry frowned. "I had no idea."

"Yeah. And from what my dad says, it's pretty sizeable, too."

Henry remained silent.

"So, Cara's death wasn't an overdose?" Jaq asked.

"Doesn't appear to be. Her journal offered a pretty detailed account of Denise's"—Sam formed air quotes with her fingers—"accident, along with several threats Lawrence made. Cara was scared but seemed to believe he wouldn't hurt his children." She snorted again. "Guess she didn't know about all his shady business deals. It was a major miscalculation on her part."

Jaq glanced at Henry. Had she not fought back, Travis might have come for him, too.

Sam got up and walked to the cabinet where Jaq normally kept the liquor. She glanced at the empty shelves, sighed, and returned to the table to retrieve her coffee cup.

Jaq slid hers Sam's way. "Do you have any forensic proof? On Cara?"

"Uh-huh. My dad put a hold on her body but kept it quiet because he suspected someone was leaking information to Lawrence."

Ah, yes. Morales.

A bitter taste filled Jaq's mouth.

"The coroner found strangulation marks on Cara's neck similar to Ben's," Sam said, her back turned as she filled their cups. "The marks were subtle but undeniable."

Jaq instinctively raised a hand to her neck. "The sash."

Sam nodded and grabbed the creamer from the refrigerator. She poured until Jaq motioned it was enough. "My dad's working with the Tate County Sheriff to instigate formal charges for Denise's death." She handed Jaq her cup before sitting down. "Who knows how many other people Lawrence harmed? I mean, Travis' safe was filled with trinkets. Some of them are pretty old."

Jaq raised an eyebrow as Henry stared at the table, anger and sadness clouding his features. "One thing I don't understand," she said with a quick sip of the hot beverage. "Why serve me legal papers if he was planning to take me out, anyway?"

Sam shrugged. "Covering his tracks? He did the same with Denise. Used Travis to spike her drink—"

"So, he was the one with my mom that day at lunch."

"From what we've gathered, yes."

Jaq's head hurt. "But Malcolm's report said she was alone..."

"My guess? Lawrence paid someone to say that." Sam rolled her coffee cup with her fingers as she spoke. "I heard a deputy up there disappeared"—she thrust a thumb toward the living room—"around the time all this happened. Just packed up and left." She shook her head. "Deep pockets can hide a lot of sins."

Jaq frowned. Would Lawrence ever accept responsibility for his actions? Or would they find him one day, hanging in a cell from his own strip of cloth? These were questions she would never ask, because to do so would hurt Henry.

Her eyes met his and the pained expression on his face waned as a darker emotion—anger—took over. "I can't believe what I'm hearing," he said and slammed a fist against the table, rattling the coffee cups. "Did you know he's been trying to reach me? Calling every day. Like I would *ever* help him after all that he's done."

Jaq hated to see him so upset, but she understood. How awful it must be to realize your father—your own flesh and blood—commissioned the deaths of both your sister and mother.

"He's desperate," Sam said. "That's why I'm not worried about his so-called friends in high places. We've done a cursory view of his books, and he's flat broke." She glanced at Jaq. "I think that's how this whole mess started. Cara said in her journal she thought Ben was going to leave her. She went to Lawrence, but he didn't have the funds to help her start a restaurant. Or to pay for Ben's silence. I guess he figured it was easier to eliminate the problem."

As sad as the story was, Ben was no longer Jaq's concern. She scooted closer to Henry.

He looked into her eyes and his anger disappeared. He reached for her hand, tracing the lines of her palm as he spoke. "I pushed you away to protect you. Like I should have protected Cara." His shoulders slumped. "I was hoping if I cut ties, my dad would no longer see you as a threat."

He pulled her toward him, and Jaq did not resist. She tucked her head into his chest. The tears fell, but she did not fight them this time. They were tears of relief, not sadness.

Sam cleared her throat and made an excuse to leave the room.

Henry lifted Jaq's chin and their eyes connected. "I'm sorry for everything," he said, his voice laced with emotion. "I love you, Jaq. I've been in love with you this whole time. I just didn't know what that meant until now."

They kissed, the gentle touch of two people in love, finding their way back together after too much time apart.

He pulled her tight.

"I love you, too," she said, her own feelings of fear and confusion fading in his embrace.

She finally had the answers she needed to leave the past behind and pursue a future with the man holding her like he would never let go.

EPILOGUE

∽∾∽∾

The sun glistened against the lake as the perfect summer afternoon enveloped Jaq.

She stretched her legs atop the thin blanket, her shifting weight crushing the blades of grass beneath. "I really missed this place," she said and turned to find Henry asleep beside her.

She pulled herself from a seated position, trying not to disturb him. With a quick glance over her shoulder, she tiptoed to the shoreline.

The crisp water kissed her skin as she stood atop the smooth, worn pebbles. She held a hand over her eyes and scanned the horizon. In the distance, she could make out the Worthington mansion. It sat empty now, waiting to be sold along with The Cornelia as Henry consolidated the family estate.

A gentle breeze shuffled the grove of trees to her left. Just beyond was a clearing where construction on their future home had begun. Jaq was staying with Sam in the interim, her house also up for sale.

Birds soared past, speaking in a language only they understood.

Jaq could still hear the cries of laughter as she and Sam chased each other, taking turns diving off the wooden dock. A fish breached the water thirty yards out, and if she tried hard enough, she could envision the boat she and her mom once fished in every weekend.

Nothing could bring those good times back, but at least now she had the opportunity to form more memories. Mack had accepted her proposal to create a platform within The Prescott Diaries dedicated to investigative work. No more Becca Allen. Just Jacqueline Darcy, working with small-town law enforcement to seek the truth.

She was meeting with Veronica next week to see if she wanted to join with her now that Dahlia hired on at *The Beacon* as a junior reporter. She had also met Marcus for lunch, and he agreed to help with her new venture in whatever way he could. Although he never admitted it, Jaq sensed he was the one who sent her the video of Henry and Derek, but she wasn't upset by this revelation. Without the video, they might never have known about Nate's involvement.

It was also nice to see the people of Prescott finally come to their senses. Not only had Ethan been run out of town—not a single business would hire him after his scandal filled the home page of The Prescott Diaries—but Henry's practice was booming. No one held him accountable for his father's misdeeds.

As time passed, Lawrence undoubtedly sensed his reign was over. His initial efforts to reach Henry failed, and he finally stopped trying. Last weekend, Henry and Jaq traveled to New York to lay Cara to rest alongside Denise. The ceremony was bittersweet but offered a sense of closure. Even Ben's mom could find peace now, knowing those responsible for taking her son's life were in jail.

Jaq held up her left hand. The diamond Henry had given her was bright against the greenish-blue backdrop. A glimmer of sunlight bounced off the stone and flashed across Henry's closed eyelids.

It was if her mother were speaking to her from above, letting her know she approved.

Henry stirred, and Jaq joined him on the blanket. He nuzzled her neck, and she leaned into his embrace.

Across the water, a bird called out and its partner responded.

The sun warmed her as she took in the beauty of the familiar surroundings. Nothing could be more perfect than this.

ABOUT THE AUTHOR

Diona L. Reeves is a full-time author with a background
in psychology and business. Along with her fiction-writing
efforts, she creates resources for others interested in
pursuing their creative dreams.

Read more of Diona's work or preview upcoming
releases at www.dionalreeves.com. For information
about this book, or to submit a media inquiry,
please visit www.justwritepress.com.

www.ingramcontent.com/pod-product-compliance
Lightning Source LLC
Chambersburg PA
CBHW021143310726
48971CB00002B/461